D1433168

BATTLE DRAGON

BATTLE DRAGON

A FANTASY NOVEL

EDO VAN BELKOM

FIVE STAR
A part of Gale, Cengage Learning

GALE
CENGAGE Learning™

Detroit • New York • San Francisco • New Haven, Conn • Waterville, Maine • London

GALE
CENGAGE Learning

LIBRARY OF CONGRESS CATALOGING-IN-PUBLICATION DATA

Van Belkom, Edo.
   Battle dragon : a fantasy novel / by Edo van Belkom. — 1st ed.
     p. cm.
   ISBN-13: 978-1-59414-671-8 (hardcover : alk. paper)
   ISBN-10: 1-59414-671-3 (hardcover : alk. paper)
   1. Dragons—Fiction. 2. World War, 1939–1945—Great Britian—Fiction. I. Title.
   PR9199.3.V362B38 2008
   813'.54—dc22
                                             2007050873

First Edition. First Printing: March 2008.

Published in 2008 in conjunction with Tekno Books and Ed Gorman.

Printed in the United States of America

1 2 3 4 5 6 7 12 11 10 09 08

To the few.

ACKNOWLEDGMENTS

I'd like to express my thanks and gratitude to the following people who helped me get this book into shape. They are: fellow writers Robert J. Sawyer and Keith Scott; poets Carolyn Clink and David Livingstone Clink; my agent, Joshua Bilmes; and my wife, Roberta van Belkom.

PROLOGUE

1

The voice was faint, but there was still a recognizable tone of urgency to it.

"Warrick returns!" cried the young boy as he appeared upon the crest of the hill that ringed the northern edge of Dervon.

Several villagers who had been laboring in the fields turned their heads northward to see what all the commotion was about.

The boy must have realized that he had drawn the villagers' attention for he cupped his hands around his mouth and shouted at the top of his voice. "Warrick returns!" There was a pause long enough for the boy to take a breath, then, "War-rick re-turns!"

The villagers had all been poised with their hands firmly upon their tools and their backs slightly bent in preparation for another attack on the soil. But upon hearing the name, *Warrick*, their stances suddenly changed. Men straightened up and stood with their hands at rest upon the ends of their spades. Women tucked their baskets under their arms or else placed their fisted hands expectantly upon their hips.

The name Warrick was a familiar one.

The boy named Warrick had first left Dervon to become a squire, returning several years later as Knight Warrick—the first knight ever to hail from the humble farming village that had, up until then, been best-known for its pale red potatoes.

Upon his return Warrick immediately became the village's

favorite son and was lavished with gifts and praise by people who could hardly believe that their little Warrie—the mischief maker of Dervon—had grown to become such a gallant knight and striking figure of a man.

But the celebrations in honor of his triumphant homecoming were cut short just a few days later when a childhood friend of Warrick's named Manfred—a bushel-maker by trade—was found dead on the road leading into town. The lower half of Manfred's body had been severely burned, the upper half made almost unrecognizable by wounds that could only have been inflicted by the sharp teeth and daggerlike talons of a dragon.

Warrick was devastated by the discovery and vowed not to rest until the death of his friend had been avenged. That night, despite the protestations of family, friends and loved ones, he left the village in search of the dragon.

Most villagers had felt it was the last they would ever see of the young knight and soon his name was rarely mentioned in Dervon without there being a hint of sorrow in the speaker's voice.

But now the name rang out with joy.

"Warrick returns!" the boy cried out once more as he started down the hill, his body seemingly moving too fast for his legs to keep up. At the bottom, he continued running, past the villagers working in the fields and on toward the village of Dervon itself.

As the young boy's voice faded, the hot summer air slowly became filled by another sound—the snort of a draft horse and the rattle and clink of the cart it was pulling.

Then, a few seconds later, the horse and cart appeared atop the crest in the hill. Holding the reins in his gloved hands, and sitting on the cart looking every inch the conquering hero, was none other than Dervon's favorite son himself.

Warrick!

At the sight of the young knight, the tired eyes of the villagers widened in surprise, and strong square jaws dropped in utter amazement.

"Hello," said Warrick, smiling broadly and waving as he drove past the villagers. "Good day!"

Several of the villagers tried to speak or raise a cheer, but most made no sound at all.

They were too much in awe.

Not so much of Warrick's return—although that in itself would have been enough to dumbfound most—but of the contents of his cart. For gently rocking from side to side in the back of the old wooden cart was the large head of a yellow-green dragon, its black-and-red eyes open, its forked tongue hanging limply from the corner of its mouth, and its neck roughly severed—as if it had been chopped off by several hard blows with a rather dull sword.

Somehow, Warrick had done it.

He had killed the dragon and avenged Manfred's death.

Spade handles toppled like wheat stalk under the scythe and baskets fell to the ground like autumn leaves as the villagers ran from the fields and hurried down the road to catch up with Warrick and his Dervon-bound cart.

The boy had done well to alert the people of Dervon.

By the time Warrick arrived at the edge of the village, almost everyone was out in the streets waiting to greet him.

"Hail! Hail!" they cried in unison. "Hail the hero's return!"

Warrick brought the cart to a halt in Dervon's central square and stood, towering several feet above the crowd. He gazed at the throng for several moments, nodding his head in appreciation. Then, he raised his arms in triumph and the assembled crowd responded to the gesture with a rousing cheer.

When the noise began to die down, he held his raised hands palms-down in order to quiet the crowd further. When there was silence, he cleared his throat and began to speak.

"Good people and good friends of Dervon," he said, placing one foot on the cart's raised bench seat and resting his hands on his bended knee. "I give you . . ." His voice trailed off and he smiled. "One less dragon to worry about!"

People laughed and cheered.

Music began to play.

Behind Warrick, several of Dervon's strongest men grabbed hold of the dragon's head and lifted it out of the cart. Together they carried it into the middle of the square and set it upon the tapered end of a thick wooden pole. The pole was then raised until its base slid into a deep hole dug into the ground. When the pole was firmly set, the dragon's head stood some ten feet high, roughly the height it had enjoyed during its lifetime.

Almost immediately after the pole was in place, young children began dancing around it, singing a traditional song.

> Dragon's dead,
> The ground is red,
> Won't be back
> 'cause it lost its head.

As the children continued to sing and dance, Warrick searched the crowd for a familiar face.

He had thought that she would have been first to greet him, but instead he found her standing alone at the outer edge of the gathering. Her hands were clasped together as if in prayer and her eyes cast upon the ground as if she were afraid to look up.

"Lavena!" Warrick shouted.

At last, his love raised her head.

She was just as beautiful as he remembered, even more so. Her long red hair flowed over her shoulders in a cascade that caught the light at every turn. Her skin was pale and unblemished, her lips full and red, and her eyes an enchanting shade of green more brilliant than valley grass in springtime.

He waved and all at once her body seemed to let out a heavy sigh, as if in relief. Her face brightened with a wide, joyful smile.

"Warrick!" Lavena cried, on the verge of tears. "It's you . . . It really is you."

"Of course it's me," said Warrick, making his way toward her with a smile on his face as big as a breastplate. "You were expecting some other knight perhaps?"

She laughed at that and opened her arms to him.

They came together in a warm embrace, Warrick wrapping his thick, muscular arms tightly around his love and lifting her off the ground.

"It's so . . . good . . . to see you," she said, struggling to get the words out.

"Good to see you too, my dear sweet Lavena."

He let her down then and for a moment they looked deeply into each other's eyes.

But before another word could be spoken Warrick was gone, pulled away by the crowd and hoisted up onto the shoulders of two men so that he could be properly paraded through the town and heralded a hero.

As Lavena watched him being carried away, she was struck by how much he'd aged since she last saw him. His coal-black hair had been streaked with wisps of white and grey, and the lines across his forehead and around his eyes had deepened into furrows. His boyish good looks had been diminished by age-lines and wrinkles, his youthful features blunted by the dull chisel of time.

He's only been away a few months, Lavena thought, but he looks as if he's aged a dozen years or more. He looks more like my father than my future husband.

And for what?

Revenge?

The head of a dragon?

She hoped that for Warrick's sake it had all been worth it.

Later that afternoon, once the initial celebration had died down and most of the village was settling back into its daily routine, Lavena finally had the chance to spend some time with her beloved. But since Warrick wanted to see and visit more of Dervon than just its central square, they decided to take a walk together, arm-in-arm through the village streets.

They began by heading north along Square Road, so named not because of its shape, but because it led directly to the square. Setting out at a leisurely pace, they walked in silence as a dozen young children eagerly trailed behind them like seagulls following a schooner. And each time they passed a home or place of business, doors and shutters would pop open and greetings and gifts would be offered to Dervon's magnificent hero.

It wasn't exactly what Lavena had had in mind when she said she wanted to spend some time with Warrick, but he seemed to be enjoying himself, and the smile on his face did wonders for his appearance, making him look years younger and more like the Warrick she knew and loved.

"Hey Warrie," said a woman from her front door as she prepared to throw out some bath water. "Dead or alive, I knew you'd be coming back to Dervon." She gave him a wink and laughed hoarsely, showing him a gapped-tooth smile.

"Thank you," replied Warrick with a polite laugh and gracious nod. "I think."

The woman laughed harder.

Lavena didn't think it was anything to joke about. "When I first heard your name being called out in the streets," she said,

"I must admit that I thought it was to report the news of your death."

Warrick turned sharply to face her, a look of surprise on his face.

"Why do you look at me so?" asked Lavena. "Why else would you return to Dervon riding in a cart?"

"I might have lost my horse," offered Warrick, his tone suggesting it was only one of many possible reasons.

"You went off in search of a dragon, wanting to kill it," said Lavena. "What else was I to think? What else was any of us to think?"

Warrick paused a moment, then said, "You could have had some faith in me, believed as I did that I would destroy the dragon and return to Dervon with nary a scratch upon me."

Lavena didn't know how to respond. Even though he had returned unharmed, she was still of the opinion that he had been lucky not to have died at the hands of the dragon. What other fate could there be for a single knight in pursuit of a fire-breathing dragon? Somehow, he had defeated the dragon—and she was glad for it—but his return still seemed unnatural, as if he'd returned not from a conquest, but from the dead.

And what of the dragon's death? Would that be the end of it? Lavena desperately wanted to believe it would be, but something deep inside her told her that it was more of a beginning than an end.

"Well?" asked Warrick after Lavena's silence had gone on for a little too long.

She opened her mouth to speak, but fortunately did not have a chance to answer.

"Warrick, you old scoundrel," said Gibbon, the village smith. "Please tell me you killed that foul beast with one of *my* swords."

Warrick slapped a hand on one of Gibbon's broad, hard shoulders. "Didn't you see how rough the cut was?" he said with a grin. "The blade was so dull I had to hack its head off with a dozen or more blows."

Gibbon looked at Warrick angrily for a moment, before the smile on the knight's face caused the smith to break into laughter. "Well if that's the case, bring the weapon on by and I'll hone it for you. That is, of course, if you don't mind telling me the story of how you killed the dragon." Gibbon punched Warrick lightly in the arm, to which Warrick feigned that he'd been injured by the blow.

"I'll come by in the morning," said Warrick, rubbing his arm dramatically.

"The fire'll be stoked and the spirits uncorked," Gibbon said, rolling up his sleeves. "Plan to stay a while."

"I'll do that," said Warrick.

"Excellent," said Gibbon, nodding to Lavena almost as an afterthought as he turned for his shop.

When Gibbon had gone they resumed their walk, turning right and heading southwest down the winding street called Crooked Lane. As they followed the twisted path of the road, Lavena waited expectantly for Warrick to prod her once more for an explanation about her lack of faith in his knightly abilities, but he had either forgotten the question or no longer wanted to hear what she had to say.

She decided it was as good a time as any to ask him a question of her own.

"Did you really have to kill it?" she said.

Warrick stopped in his tracks and looked at her strangely.

"What?" He looked as if the question had confused him.

"Did you have to kill it?" she repeated. "Was there no other way?"

"I don't understand."

"Dragons are magnificent, intelligent creatures," Lavena said, realizing her words were almost sacrilege but unable to stop herself from saying them. "We used to lie in the fields all day watching them wheel and turn in the sky . . ." Her voice trailed off at the memory. "Couldn't the matter have been settled without you having to kill it?"

Warrick was absolutely dumbfounded. "I can't believe what you're saying."

Lavena opened her mouth to speak, but was interrupted by Dempster, the village's baker.

"Warrick," said Dempster, wiping his hand on his apron as he approached. "I can't tell you how good it is to see you again. Your return has made us all proud."

Warrick looked at Lavena to make sure she'd heard what the baker had said, but she refused to give him the satisfaction and started walking away without him. Behind her she heard Warrick thank the baker for a loaf of bread and his words of kindness, then the soft padding of his feet as he hurried to catch up.

"Does it bother you so much to see how much some people appreciate what I've done?"

She stopped suddenly and turned to face him. "But is that why you became a knight? To kill dragons, or to help protect the good people of this village and others like it?"

"By my actions I have done both," Warrick said, holding his head high.

"Really? You've risked your life to kill a dragon, a dragon that may or may not have killed your friend Manfred, a man who some in the village say made his living by stealing eggs from creches and selling them to the caravans." She spun back around and continued walking.

Warrick quickly passed the loaf of bread Dempster had given him to the children following them, then quickly rejoined Lavena.

Upon receiving the bread the children began to eat, leaving Lavena and Warrick alone at the corner of Crooked Lane and

Merchant's Row.

"First of all, I might have risked my life but I am still very much *alive*," Warrick said as he stood before Lavena, looking her straight in the eye. "And second, I know that dragon killed Manfred because I found one of Manfred's boot buckles inside the dragon's lair. And as for Manfred stealing eggs, he was a bushel-maker like his father before him, and his father's father before that."

Lavena's eyes narrowed. "And what do you think he made those baskets for?"

Warrick paused, as if stunned by the connection. Finally, he shook his head dismissively. "The dragon killed my friend, so it had to die." There was a tone of finality to his voice, as if the matter was no longer open to discussion.

Lavena's hands clenched into two tight fists. "The dragon kills, so we kill it. But another will come and take its place and the killing will start all over again." She pounded her fists against her hips in frustration. "When will it end? When we are *all* dead?"

Warrick slowly shook his head from side to side. "It was a *dragon*." He said the word as if the point had somehow been missed up until now. "It killed my friend. So I killed it before it could do the same to more good people of Dervon."

Lavena opened her mouth to speak, but Warrick had already turned his back on her, walking away before she could say a word.

She did not run after him. Instead, she remained where she stood and watched him travel westward along Merchant's Row. At every stall he passed, the merchants joyfully greeted him, loading his arms with all manner of goods.

Watching the merchants' display of goodwill suddenly made Lavena feel ashamed of how she'd acted. Perhaps it really was a good thing that the dragon had been killed. Perhaps its destruction would not bring another dragon's wrath upon the village in retribution, but give them peace instead.

So many people.

So happy.

It *must* be a good thing.

She started walking again, following Warrick's footsteps, hurrying along Merchant's Row in the hopes of catching up to him and telling him that she was sorry.

2

The dragon's wings sliced through the clouds with barely a whisper. The great beast had been riding the winds most of the day, circling the skies between Dervon and Leister in search of something that was lost.

Now the sun was beginning to wane in the west, but there was still enough daylight left for one more pass.

And then something caught the dragon's eye—something that wasn't right.

The field itself was green, but in one corner there was a spot of much lighter green that was tinged by a bit of yellow. The area was surrounded by a larger, darker spot whose blackness streaked off in one direction before suddenly coming to an end.

The dragon shifted its weight, altered the shape of its wings, and abruptly descended, slowly at first, then faster as it came to recognize the thing on the ground for what it was.

Like a bird of prey, the dragon streaked over the field, wheeled around on its right wing, then pulled up vertically before landing on the ground as softly as a feather.

Without even bothering to furl its wings, the dragon took a few hesitant steps toward the green-yellow mass on the ground—each step more cautious than the one before.

And as it neared the thing, the dragon began to let out a

series of anguished cries from somewhere deep within its massive form.

Two final steps and the dragon was close enough to touch it—the headless body of its younger sibling, born two creches after him and still quite green.

The dragon crouched down and carefully gathered up the cold, stiff carcass in its arms. Then, as it slowly rocked the lifeless body from side to side, the dragon's tortured cries grew longer, louder and more shrill until they were a single, angry wail that was tinged by grief, and powered by rage, wrath, and revenge.

3

The next morning Lavena set out onto the village streets alone. Although she traveled north along Square Street, heading out of the village, she was on her way to nowhere in particular. The morning sky had looked so blue, the sun so bright and warm, that it seemed the perfect time for a long and thoughtful walk.

As she passed Gibbon's smith shop at the northern edge of town, she could hear Warrick and the smith laughing raucously. No doubt the spirits were flowing and Warrick was recounting his battle with the dragon, and no doubt embellishing his part at every turn.

The previous night he had tried to tell her several times how he'd slayed the dragon, but she'd wanted no part of it. After his third attempt he gave up on her and spent the rest of the evening recounting his conquest of the dragon to anyone who'd listen. He never seemed to tire of telling people how he'd ridden the dragon's back, pierced its scales with his sword, and finally hacked the head from its cold, lifeless body.

The thought of it made her shudder.

Such an ignoble end for a dragon. As a child she'd watched them soar the skies so high above it all. Oh, how she wished she could ride with them, flying whichever way the wind might take her, free of all her earthly cares.

Lavena let out a long sigh. How could Warrick have done such an indignity to such a regal creature? Even worse, how could he revel in the recollection of the act?

Lavena suddenly stopped and listened to the wind. It was picking up, as if a tiny pocket of air had begun to gust in advance of a rapidly approaching storm.

Just then the sun winked out, and she found herself standing in the shade in the middle of an open field.

Strange, she thought, as she looked up—

"Oh my God."

—and saw the silhouette of an enormous dragon approaching like the fall of night itself.

She turned and ran.

After just a few steps, she felt a rush of wind behind her growing stronger and stronger until it pushed her face-first onto the ground. Then she heard the roar of the dragon's wings as it swooped over her prone body. She covered her head and closed her eyes, expecting the worst, but in seconds the roar had diminished to barely a whisper.

She rolled onto her side and looked up. It was indeed a dragon, a great green-and-blue beast two or more times as big as the one Warrick had slain. It had pulled up over the field, wheeling beneath the clouds as if preparing for another pass.

Lavena pulled herself to her feet and began to run once more, this time in the direction of a jumble of rocks at one end of the field. It wasn't much, but it was her only chance for shelter.

As before, she felt the wind pick up and heard the rising sound of the beast's wings as it gained speed in its dive toward her. She turned her head to check on the oncoming dragon, then changed direction, veering off at a sharp angle in an attempt to thwart the dragon's straight-line attack.

This time she felt heat on her back, no doubt from the blast of fire bursting from the creature's angry maw. As she ran, a line of flame streaked across the field to her right, its heat blistering her heels and the skin across the back of her legs.

With a burst of speed, she reached the rocky outcrop at the edge of the field and frantically searched for some cover.

There were many caves in the area surrounding Dervon, some quite deep, but they all lay further north. Here, the best she could do was a small overhang that touched an adjacent rock wall, forming a small tunnel-like archway. It wouldn't offer much in the way of protection, but it was all she had.

By the time the dragon was ready for another pass, Lavena had positioned herself directly in the opening beneath the overhang. She knew she had left the dragon no other option but to attempt to incinerate her with its fiery breath.

She watched the dragon approach, each second passing like an hour while its head grew larger and larger.

And then at last it opened its mouth, signaling to Lavena that it was time for her to move.

Without a moment's hesitation, she crawled out of the passageway and moved to a ledge behind it and to the right. There she hugged a slab of rock while still trying to put some distance between herself and the archway.

Suddenly, a tremendous gout of flame erupted from the opening.

And then as fast as the flames had come, they were gone, leaving behind a trail of smoking, steaming rocks.

The dragon streaked past, its head moving left and right as it searched the ground for its prey.

Lavena moved back into the opening beneath the overhang and prepared for the dragon's next attack. The rocks were still quite hot and she had to be careful not to burn herself.

Again the dragon approached.

Lavena waited and waited, and again it seemed to take forever for the dragon to draw near.

Then it opened its maw.

And Lavena quickly moved out of the way and crouched behind a formation of smoking rocks, waiting for the inevitable flames.

But they never came.

Instead, a voice.

"It's me you want," cried Warrick. "Over here!"

"No," whispered Lavena, looking over her shoulder.

Warrick stood in the middle of the field, his shield in one hand, his sword in the other. He was wearing just a simple brown tunic and tan leggings, his head bare of any helm. Either he had rushed out onto the field upon the first reports of the dragon, or he knew from experience that his armor would be useless.

"No," she cried. "Warrick, no!" But the roar of the dragon's wings as it passed overhead drowned out her voice.

What kind of fool would taunt a dragon so? she thought. The answer was so obvious it pained her to think about it.

A fool who loves you.

The dragon swooped down over the field, blasting Warrick with its flame. The lone warrior held firm, crouched behind his shield as it deflected the brunt of the flames away from his body.

After making its pass, the dragon pulled up and wheeled around, landing several yards from where Warrick stood, smoldering shield in one hand, newly honed sword in the other.

Lavena was amazed that Warrick was still alive. Perhaps she *had* doubted his ability to confront the beast. Maybe it was possible to survive a battle with a dragon, perhaps even fight it as an equal.

With renewed hope, she watched as the dragon moved closer

to her love. It seemed to be stepping lightly and cautiously as it approached, as if made wary by Warrick's brazen challenge.

If such close contact were possible, thought Lavena, then perhaps there might be a chance for peace between them. If it could be made known to the dragon that the people of Dervon meant it no harm, then perhaps they might be able to live together in harmony.

She climbed down from the rocks and began running out onto the field toward Warrick.

"Come on, you filthy beast!" shouted Warrick. "If it's human flesh you want, give me a try . . . And I'll run you through, just like I did the yellow."

Lavena slowed to a stop, horrified by what she had heard.

There would be no reconciliation. There was no chance for peace.

The dragon must have understood Warrick's words, for it appeared to become enraged by them. It reared up on its hind legs and opened its maw, sending a river of flame over Warrick's head. The flames splashed onto the ground behind Warrick, putting a line of fire between himself and the village, neatly cutting off his only route of escape.

The dragon moved forward, the fire in its eyes equal to any that might escape its mouth.

"No, Warrick," cried Lavena. "Run!"

But if Warrick heard her pleas, he chose to ignore them. Instead, he raised his sword anew and stepped forward to meet the dragon head on.

The dragon remained where it was, allowing Warrick to come closer and appearing to admire the young knight's courage.

Warrick took full advantage of the moment, feigning right then darting left, then leaping upon the dragon's tail.

The dragon rose up on its hind legs, twisting and turning in an attempt to shake Warrick from its back.

In the distance, at the opposite end of the field, the villagers of Dervon let out a cheer. More and more of them were appearing, each encouraging Warrick as if he were engaged in some sort of friendly joust.

And then Lavena was struck by a thought, a sickening, horrifying thought. Perhaps Warrick hadn't ventured out on the field to save her, but had done so simply in order to save face with the villagers. How could he have spoken so boastfully about his conquest and then cower upon the appearance of this second, bigger dragon? He had no choice in the matter. He had to face the dragon, even if it meant his life.

Lavena began to cry, even as Warrick had gained a position of strength on the dragon's back at the base of its long, curved neck.

Warrick raised his sword.

The villagers let out another boisterous cheer.

And the dragon seemed to laugh.

Because then, in one swift motion it folded its wings tightly against its body and rolled over onto its back.

Warrick's scream was heard only briefly before he was crushed beneath the weight of the dragon's massive form.

The villagers were suddenly silent.

Lavena let out an anguished cry.

Triumphant, the dragon rose to its feet, its eyes fixed on the rapidly thinning crowd of villagers fleeing in every direction.

In moments the dragon was back in the air, swooping down over the village, raining liquid fire upon it.

Lavena ran to where Warrick's bent and broken body lay upon the ground.

"No!" she cried, tears now running freely down her cheeks. She lifted Warrick's limp body and cradled it in her arms, rocking it gently back and forth as she wept.

Across the field, the village of Dervon burned.

4

Eventually, Lavena had to admit that there was nothing she could do for Warrick now and that no amount of tears would ever bring him back. But she also saw that the village was already aflame and well on its way to being razed. Nothing could stop the fires that were already burning. What was needed was to prevent new fires from starting, and that meant eliminating the dragon.

But how?

This dragon was too big and powerful to be beaten by a single man—Warrick had proven that—and it was also doubtful that an army of villagers, even an army of knights, would be able to defeat it. It was just too strong.

That left . . .

Lavena considered the thought for a moment, then decided it might be Dervon's only hope.

To the south and east of the village, nestled in the pocket of a lush green valley known as the Vale of Trent, there was said to live a wizard named Asvald. Lavena had never met the man, but she had heard his name often enough and also knew of those who swore that he was as powerful as any mage in the land.

With a sigh of deep regret, Lavena gently laid Warrick's body upon the ground. Then she placed the hilt of his sword in his hand and folded his arms over his chest.

Finally, she leaned forward and kissed his now-cold lips. "Goodbye, dear Warrick," she said, placing a hand over his eyes and drawing the lids closed.

She lingered over his body a moment, struggling to hold back fresh tears, then rose to her feet and turned east in search of the wizard named Asvald.

As she stood on a hillside overlooking the Vale of Trent, Lavena wondered if she had been wise to come here. The idea that had felt so right back in Dervon seemed like a young girl's folly now that the sun was set and she felt the first cold bite of darkness upon her flesh.

She considered turning back. Although the sun was fading, she could probably make it back to Dervon by the pale light of the moon.

But what then?

How much of Dervon would there be left to return to?

And if she returned without the wizard, how long would it take the dragon to destroy what remained of the village?

No, she had come this far, she had to look for the wizard's cottage. Even if she didn't find it, then at least she could be content in the knowledge that she had done her best to try and save the village.

She looked down at the ever-darkening valley, and something caught her eye—a dim yellow light, partially obscured by the trees.

Lavena decided to head toward it, stepping lightly—and carefully—down the side of the hill toward the valley floor.

It was a small structure covered in earth, grass and leaves. Even in the darkness the cottage looked as if it had grown up out of the ground rather than been built by the hands of men. As she approached it, she detected the smell of burnt wood in the air, and just a hint of an herbal scent—perhaps from the brewing of some special tea.

She knocked on the door and as she did, the light that had guided her so well suddenly winked out. For a moment Lavena feared that whoever lived here was fearful of strangers, especially those who knocked on their door after dark, but just as she was about to call out, "Hello," the front door silently swung open.

A man stood several feet back from the doorway, his face and body illuminated by the flame of a single white candle held delicately in his hand. Although the light from the candle was faint, Lavena guessed the man to be about fifteen or twenty years older than herself.

Was this Asvald?

As he stepped forward, his movements suggested he was still rather spry. Yet, when she got a closer look at the grey-white color of his hair and short, tangled beard, she got the impression that he was old enough to be her grandfather—maybe even older.

She opened her mouth to speak, but he cut her off with a wave of his hand.

"Come in," he said, a touch of warmth to his smile.

Lavena remained where she was, astounded by what she saw. One of the man's teeth shone as if it were made of metal.

"If you're wondering," he said. "A very talented metalsmith made it for me once upon a time." He stepped back from the door. "Come in. Come in."

Lavena ducked her head and stepped through the doorway. At first the inside of the cottage was quite dark, but the old man moved quickly about the room, lighting several additional candles until the cottage was filled with a warm glow.

Lavena remained standing, not wanting to risk taking the old man's favorite chair. As she stood there, she looked around for the source of the light that had guided her. There were no lanterns or torches in evidence, only candles and hardly enough of them to produce a light that had been strong enough to be seen from a distance through the woods.

"Sit," he said, indicating a solid chair made of birch with a cloth pad covering its seat.

She sat down.

Then the old man eased himself into a larger chair by the hearth. The embers glowed orange, providing warmth but not much light. No matter, the numerous candles provided enough light to see that the man's face was marked by lines that seemed to have been etched by time's sharpest knife.

Again she wondered about his age, but was no closer to guessing it now than when she'd first entered the cottage. He could be thirty years old, he could be three hundred.

"Are you Asvald?" she asked, trying to keep her voice as calm and even as she could.

"I am."

"I've come—"

Again he cut her off with a wave of his hand.

"I know why you've come."

Lavena smiled and let out a sigh of relief.

"And the answer," he said, "is no."

"But I haven't even asked you yet," she said, both surprised and disappointed by his words.

"There's a dragon terrorizing the village of Dervon," Asvald said matter-of-factly. "You've come to ask me to fight it for you."

Lavena was unable to speak.

"Am I right?"

She opened her mouth, but no words escaped her lips.

"Eh, speak up!"

"Yes," she said at last.

"And so, the answer is no."

"But the village is being destroyed."

"Yes it is," Asvald nodded. "And that dragon probably has a very good reason for destroying it." He paused a moment. "Hmm? What do you think could make it angry enough to do such a thing?"

Lavena was silent, her eyes falling to the floor. Did everyone in the world save Warrick understand that killing a dragon would only bring the wrath of another onto the good people of Dervon?

"My betrothed," she said at last. "A young knight named

Warrick . . . He killed a yellow-green dragon outside of Dervon several days ago. Perhaps that dragon and this one are related."

"Do you think so?" Asvald said sarcastically. "Or maybe this dragon belongs to that *other* family of dragons two valleys over."

Lavena was hurt by the comment, but resisted the temptation to answer in kind. She needed the wizard's help and knew she would never receive it by arguing with him.

"I never condoned Warrick's actions," she said in an almost apologetic tone. "Even when he first set out in search of the dragon I tried to dissuade him. But he wouldn't listen—" She paused a moment as the mention of Warrick brought a sharp stab of pain to her heart. "—and now he's dead. Nothing can change that. But, there are people dying as we speak and something *can* be done about that. *You* can do something about it. And if you can, then you should."

Asvald said nothing for the longest time, then simply shrugged his shoulders. "Do I look like a dragonslayer to you?" He leaned forward in his chair so more of his face could be caught by the light from the candles.

Lavena had to admit that judging by his looks alone, Asvald would be lucky if he were able to slay an old hen.

"I am a peaceful being," he said, leaning back and fading into the shadows once more.

"But you are also a wizard," said Lavena. "And from what I've heard a very powerful one." There was a pleading tone to her voice now. "You could use your magic against the dragon."

Asvald sighed. "Even if it were within my power to kill this dragon, it would only bring the village a temporary peace. Killing this dragon would surely bring the wrath of another down upon the village, or maybe even more than one. The cycle has been set into motion, and will only stop when there is either no more Dervon, or no more dragons." He paused a moment and turned to look Lavena in the eye. "Dervon's fate is sealed, your gallant young Warrick has seen to that."

Lavena was forced to look away.

"The village," he said in a whisper, "is doomed."

Lavena shook her head, unwilling to believe it. "But what if you didn't kill the dragon," she said, unsure of what she were saying but desperate enough to try anything. "What if you did something else to it?"

"Like what?"

"I don't know, like send it away . . . to somewhere else."

She looked at him hopefully, but Asvald did not respond.

When the moment's silence had stretched into several minutes, Lavena got up to see if he might have fallen asleep. To her surprise, he was awake and staring intently at a spot on the far wall of the cottage.

He appeared to be deep in thought.

So Lavena did not bother him. Instead, she returned to her chair, made herself comfortable, and waited patiently until he was done.

5

The dawn shed new light upon the village of Dervon.

The fires had raged through the night, leaving half the village razed to the ground. There were parts of several buildings still standing—a wall here, a doorway there—but even those remnants were so badly charred they would have to be destroyed and rebuilt. Some other homes, even a few isolated sections of the village, had been spared by the flames, but instead of rejoicing in their good fortune, their owners spent most of the night and early hours of the morning emptying them of their belongings.

And with good reason.

For not only did the sun bring the light of day to the village, it also brought back the dragon.

It appeared in the sky over Dervon an hour after sunrise, then perched itself upon the summit of a small mountain to the east. It remained there for some time, either admiring the testament to its own destructive power, or making plans for another attack.

The villagers guessed it was the latter, for they all stopped their reclamation efforts and ran for the relative safety of the rocky outcropping that ringed the northwest end of the village.

The dragon soared down the side of the mountain, always keeping the ground within range of its deadly breath. Then, as it approached the village, it appeared to inhale in preparation for a fiery blast of flame.

But then it wavered slightly.

Its head rose up, as if looking past the village and at the open field beyond it.

There, standing in the middle of the wide open space, were two figures, one standing firm with a walking stick in its hand, the other with its arms waving frantically in an obvious attempt to get the dragon's attention.

The dragon pulled up and overshot the village.

Apparently, they had succeeded in catching the dragon's eye.

"Do you think it's seen us?" asked Lavena, continuing to wave her arms over her head.

"Yes," said Asvald. "You can stop that now."

Lavena's arms came to rest at her sides.

The dragon was upon them in seconds, but instead of blasting them with fire on its first pass, it swooped down low over the field as if to take a closer look.

The wind picked up as the dragon zoomed overhead, and Lavena was awed by its long neck, magnificent wingspan and the shiny green scales that covered its underbelly and tail.

Such a magnificent creature, she thought, as she watched it

make a wide and graceful turn at the far edge of the field, its scales catching and reflecting the sunlight like a suit of highly polished armor. Why must it be an enemy of the people?

"Stand back," said Asvald, extending his left arm protectively. "I think it's going to land."

Lavena did not move.

The dragon glided to a stop, gently touching down with its hind legs just a few yards in front of them. As it tucked its wings back into its body, it looked at them curiously, its head tilting first to one side, then the other. Obviously, after last having confronted a knight, it didn't know what to make of an old man and a young woman.

Lavena had never been this close to a dragon before and was captivated by the bright orange color of its eyes, the long flaring horns that crowned its head and the mass of rippling muscles that undulated below the shimmering surface of its scales. Clearly, this was a beast one would want to count as a friend, not as an enemy.

Asvald stepped forward, planted the sharp end of his walking stick firmly into the ground and placed his free hand on his hip, giving him a stance that exuded both confidence and power.

"My name is Asvald," he said in a voice that was stronger than Lavena thought possible for someone so old. "Do no further damage to the village and you will not be harmed."

The dragon continued to look at them curiously, as if surprised that such brazen words had come from such an old man. Then it suddenly began to laugh. "*I* will not be harmed?"

"It can speak!" Lavena said in a whisper.

"Yes," said Asvald under his breath. "They're not much for conversation, but telling a dragon your name can empower it to speak to you."

"That's wonderful. Then all we have to do is tell it we're sorry about the other dragon, tell it that it's already killed the one who slayed it, and ask it to leave the village alone."

"I'm afraid it's not that easy," said Asvald, shaking his head slightly. "Dragons are very intelligent creatures, but they're incredibly stubborn and supremely arrogant. You can't just reason with them—they have to be taught a lesson."

Asvald's words made Lavena think of Warrick.

"My younger sibling was butchered by a knight from this village," said the dragon in a deep and powerful voice. "Therefore, *all* who live here must pay!"

Asvald took several steps closer to the dragon.

"I do not wish to kill you," he said. "End your attack on the village and your life will be spared."

Again the dragon laughed. It was a throaty sound and seemed to reverberate up from somewhere deep within its belly.

Asvald remained where he was, standing firm.

Lavena felt her mouth go dry.

The dragon suddenly stopped laughing and leaned forward, its long neck bringing its head to within a few feet of Asvald's face.

"I am Tibalt!" it said, saying the name as if it were another word for God. "*I* am the one who decides who lives and who dies. And I fear no mortal man . . . especially one so old."

The dragon's breath seemed to grow hotter. Beads of sweat began to bubble up on Lavena's brow.

"If not me," said Asvald, seemingly unaffected by the close proximity of the dragon, "then perhaps you should fear *them*." He pointed in the general direction of Dervon. "For those mortals will not always fear you." A pause. "The knight Warrick did not fear you."

Lavena looked to that part of the field where Warrick had died fighting the dragon. Although the villagers had moved his body during the night, there was still a large bloodstain marking the spot. She wondered how long it would remain there before the sun and rain finally erased it from view.

"Perhaps not," the dragon said. "But he brutally killed one of my kind! He had to die. He *deserved* to die."

"And you killed him," said Asvald. "Well done."

Lavena was shocked by Asvald's words and couldn't be sure if he were serious or mocking the dragon.

"Now listen carefully," he continued, "and heed what I say . . . Men grow stronger and more deadly each day. They are constantly developing better and more efficient weapons of destruction. Men will conquer the earth, then set their sights on the skies. Eventually, they will learn to fly and take full control of the air."

The dragon seemed to seethe in response to Asvald's words. But instead of shooting forth a blast of flame, it chuffed, sending a thin line of fire arcing over their heads as a sort of warning.

Asvald did not flinch, but Lavena ducked and turned to watch the fire hit the ground behind her in a splash of brightly colored flame.

"Dragons will soar the skies as long as there is a sun to shine upon their wings."

Asvald shook his head. "Only if you live in peace with men and form an alliance with mankind. If you wish to continue ruling the skies, you must fight *with* them, not *against* them."

The dragon pulled its head back slightly, and stared at Asvald with an incredulous look upon its face. It remained in that position for the longest time before the doubtful expression was replaced by a smile, then finally laughter. "For a brief moment I believed you a prophet, old fool." More laughter. "But now I must simply ask, what herb fuels your madness?"

Asvald did not answer the question. Instead, he shook his head in obvious disappointment. "Very well, then," he said. "Just remember, that you have been warned."

The dragon continued to laugh.

Asvald's face darkened as he took two steps forward, pointed the thick end of his walking stick at the dragon and began to wave it in a circular motion.

The dragon saw this, but only laughed harder as if to mock the wizard's actions.

Asvald paid no attention to the slight. He was in his own world now, uttering long strings of unintelligible words and syllables under his breath, as if speaking in tongues.

And then a curious thing happened.

The end of Asvald's walking stick began to glow with a bright, otherworldly sort of light.

And slowly, the clouds and part of the horizon began to churn like water flowing into a funnel.

The dragon suddenly stopped laughing and turned to look behind itself. After several moments, its great head swung back around, an angry look on its face and a fire alight in its bright orange eyes.

Asvald continued casting his spell.

The dragon reared back and began to draw a deep breath.

Lavena threw up her arms and covered her eyes.

The beast opened its maw . . .

Asvald lunged forward, striking the dragon in the chest with the glowing end of his walking stick. Although the blow was a mild one, it was enough to start the dragon toward the funnel.

The dragon's arms began to flail through the air in search of something—anything—to hold onto.

Asvald quickly jumped back, just out of the dragon's reach.

But Lavena remained motionless, still standing with her hands in front of her face.

"Get back!" Asvald shouted.

Too late.

One of the dragon's hands caught hold of Lavena and pulled

her up into its body just as it was sucked up into the swirling mouth of the whirlpool.

The dragon, with Lavena in its arms, lingered there a moment . . .

Then vanished in a spectacular flash of blue-white light.

Asvald fell to one knee, his body heaving.

Several of the villagers ran onto the field and rushed to Asvald's side. "Are you all right?" asked one of them, a man Asvald recognized as Gibbon, the village smith.

Asvald said nothing. Instead, he gazed at the spot where the dragon had been just a moment before.

The dragon and Lavena.

Not a trace of either remained, save for a few of the dragon's diamond-shaped scales scattered across the ground.

"Where did they go?" Gibbon asked.

Asvald took a deep breath. "Not where," he said. "But *when.*"

CHAPTER ONE
Friday, August 2, 1940

1

Flying Officer Kenneth Newell leveled off his Hurricane at twenty thousand feet and searched the sky above and below for enemy raiders. The RDF stations along the coast had detected about twenty 109s on their way over the Channel which made it a good bet that there would be bombers coming in behind them, maybe even a few more fighters.

Newell glanced over his left shoulder at his first wingman, Pilot Officer Dick Simon, a veteran of the Battle of France and as good a pilot as any in the RAF. Simon's head swiveled around under the greenhouse of his Hurricane's canopy as he searched the sky for incoming German fighters.

Confident that Simon would spot anything approaching from the east, Newell looked over his right shoulder at his second wingman, a nineteen-year-old sprog named James Sawyer. A pilot officer barely a week with the squadron, Sawyer was so busy trying to maintain the tight formation that he had no time to keep an eye out for bandits.

He'll be lucky if he lasts the week, thought Newell.

"Blowtorch Leader," came an excited voice over his radio. "Bandits below, at ten o'clock!"

Newell recognized Simon's voice and looked down past the leading edge of his left wing.

About a mile to the northeast and a thousand feet below he saw a swarm of 109s coming out of some light cloud cover.

Instinctively he turned his Hurricane to the left and dove with the sun at his back, hoping he could squeeze off a burst before the Germans spotted their approach and broke formation.

As the Hurricane screamed toward the Germans, Newell quickly checked to see if his wingmen were still with him. As usual, Simon was tight to his left, but Sawyer was lagging behind after turning too widely on the crossover. He was trying to catch up but there was nothing he could do to get back into formation until they pulled out of the dive, and by that time the entire squadron would be broken up and it would be a free-for-all.

"Best of luck, chaps!" Newell said over the radio.

The 109s grew larger in Newell's gunsight as they streaked down on the enemy fighter formation at nearly four hundred miles per hour. But just before they came into range of the yellow-nosed Messerschmitts, the swarm began to break up, each 109 peeling off in a different direction.

Newell picked one of the bandits and stuck on its tail, patiently holding off firing his guns until he had it well within his sights.

Suddenly, the clouds behind the German planes seemed to light up from within.

Newell saw the flash of light out of the corner of his eye and thought that two German bombers had collided within the cloud. Either that, or one of them had been struck by lightning, detonating its bomb load.

But whatever the reason for the flash, he would worry about it later. Right now, he had a 109 dead ahead.

He squeezed off a short burst from his machine guns, fully expecting the Messerschmitt to break into a right turn. But when the 109 remained in his sights, he pushed the firing button again, this time holding his thumb firmly down on it and firing at the fighter with a long burst from all eight of his Brownings.

Just then, a mass of blue and green came hurtling out of the clouds. It flashed through Newell's line of fire, was struck by several rounds from his guns, and was gone.

But the 109 remained.

And Newell continued to fire.

Black smoke began to billow from the Messerschmitt's engine cowling, increasing in volume until it was replaced by a gout of bright orange flame. Then the aeroplane turned sharply to the right and began to spin out of control.

Satisfied he'd scored a kill, Newell peeled off and began searching the sky for more of the enemy.

There were aeroplanes all around him—Hurricanes, Spitfires and 109s—and sweeping vapor trails decorated the sky like swirls on a wedding cake.

The radio was alive with all sorts of frantic chatter.

"Look out! Blue Two."

"He's on your tail, Blowtorch Leader!"

"Thanks mate!"

"I think I've—"

Newell made a quick check of his tail, then continued to search the sky for enemy fighters, or a friendly one in trouble.

And then he saw it . . .

Looming in the sky before him was the hulking blue-green mass that had passed through his line of fire just moments before. He could discern it more clearly now and saw that it had wings and a long curved neck, and was attacking every aeroplane in sight, German and British alike.

"What in God's name . . . ," he whispered under his breath.

Then, as Newell closed in on the "dragon"—and that was the best word for the thing, because dear God that's what it resembled—it attacked a 109 at close range with a blast of flame that seemed to come from its mouth.

The 109 exploded as its fuel tank caught fire.

Newell's Hurricane shook violently as it flew through what was left of the German fighter.

Then suddenly he was clear with an excellent view of the dragon as it shredded the elliptical wing of a Spitfire with a single swipe from one of its talon-tipped hands.

And then, Newell watched in horror as the dragon turned hard to the left and pounced onto the tail of a Hurricane.

The Hurricane flown by his number-two wingman, Pilot Officer James Sawyer.

Oberleutnant Stefan Wieck felt the shock waves of an explosion rock his Messerschmitt. He instinctively checked his wing surfaces for damage, then glanced over his left shoulder.

Instead of finding the 109 of his wingman, Leutnant Kessler, by his side, there was only a ball of black smoke and the trails left behind by falling pieces of aeroplane.

"Franz!" he shouted over the radio, but heard nothing but static in reply.

Wieck was about to kick the rudder hard to the left in order to return to the fray and avenge his friend's death, when he saw something that changed his mind.

He couldn't be sure exactly what it was, but it looked to be a new type of British aircraft, as big as a bomber, yet nimble as a fighter. But as incredible as that seemed, the nightmare weapon was also armed with a high-velocity flamethrower as well as a battering ram which it used to shear the wings off passing fighters.

It was an abomination.

A flying terror.

And with such an effective new weapon, the British would surely rule the skies over England in a matter of weeks.

And then, the skies over Europe.

Wieck looked away, shook his head in dismay, then pushed the nose of his Messerschmitt forward, heading for the Channel as fast as his aeroplane could take him.

"You've got one on your tail, James!" Newell said to his wingman.

"I'm losing power . . . ," replied a frantic Sawyer. "Can't seem to shake him."

"On my way."

Newell put his Hurricane into a shallow dive that would bring him up behind the dragon in seconds. It had already fired two blasts of flame at Sawyer, but had missed each time. If the young man from Brighton Beach could hold on just a few more seconds, he'd be able to—

The dragon let go another burst of flame. This time the thing had found the range, and the fire slowly walked up the fuselage from the Hurricane's tail, engulfing the cockpit in flame.

Sawyer screamed from inside the inferno.

Newell blanked out the sound, clenched his teeth and opened fire.

His first burst of tracers overshot the dragon, but then a slight push on the stick helped him find the target. Round after round began slamming into it, but seemed to be doing little or no damage to the thick geodesic armor covering the thing's body.

All Newell seemed to have succeeded in doing was getting the dragon's attention.

Suddenly it turned onto its back, raised its head and opened its maw.

Newell was stunned by what he saw. The dragon appeared to be holding something—a person, it looked like—tightly in one of its arms. It was a woman. Yes, a woman with long, red hair.

Newell closed his eyes a moment in an effort to erase the impossible image from sight. And when he opened them again, he found himself flying through a solid wall of flame.

The controls suddenly felt sluggish as the Hurricane's engine sputtered and died from lack of airflow into its carburetor.

But the loss of power proved fortuitous for Newell as he began to fall from the sky and out of the dragon's stream of fire.

With his front cockpit glass charred and the paint on the wings still smoking, Newell pushed the stick down and to the right in an attempt to guide the aeroplane into a dive.

He was just about to try and restart the engine when one of the dragon's claws connected with the tip of his left wing. The blow wasn't hard enough to break the wing, but it did send Newell spinning violently out of control.

There was suddenly no sense of direction. Newell was thrown hard against one side of the cockpit as the sky and the horizon flashed across the top of the canopy over and over until he was no longer sure which way was up.

But instinctively he went into spin control until the aeroplane's rate of rotation slowed. Finally the horizon came back into view and then was replaced by the pale blue of the summer sky. He restarted the engine, and in seconds the powerful Rolls Royce Merlin roared into life. Then he pulled back on the stick, leveled out and made a quick check of his gauges. He'd lost over ten thousand feet while in the spin, but was otherwise unscathed.

Newell looked above him and could see nothing other than blue sky and patches of clouds. He slid back the canopy for a better look, but there was still no sign of a plane—or a dragon— anywhere to be seen.

The battle over and his fighter low on fuel, he checked his compass, put the Hurricane into a sweeping right turn, and headed back to base.

As he once again searched the sky for aeroplanes, he went over the dogfight in his mind, and began to wonder if he'd really seen what he thought he saw.

He decided that he had seen it, had shot at it, and had nearly been killed by it.

Of course he had seen it. The thing had clobbered Sawyer, sent the poor bastard down in flames!

But . . .

Would anyone believe it?

2

Blood dripped from the holes in the dragon's wings and its back was a mass of cuts and bruises.

The steel dragons had hurt him.

Where they had come from, or where they had gone, it couldn't be sure. All it could be sure of was that they were dangerous, somehow able to spit hot pieces of steel from their noses and wings.

They flew the skies as if they ruled them.

And that made them an enemy of the dragon.

It had killed three of the steel dragons so far.

And it would kill more.

Later . . .

Right now, it needed to find a place to rest where it could revive the girl and make her use her magic to heal its wounds.

And so, with a gentle flap of its wings, the beast turned west toward the setting sun, searching the ground for a familiar or otherwise safe place to land.

3

Oberleutnant Wieck eased his 109 down onto the bumpy airfield being used by the *Jagdgeschwader* just north and west of the French city of Calais.

Even though he'd landed his fighter hundreds of times before, he remained cautious all the way down since the splayed landing gear of the Messerschmitt was notoriously fragile and prone to ground loops.

After two gentle bumps, the wheels touched down and he quickly brought the craft to a stop. Then he popped open the canopy and sat there, his eyes open wide and his body shaking violently as the full terror of what he'd witnessed in the skies over England finally overcame him.

A few seconds later, a mechanic climbed up onto the wing and looked inside the cockpit. "Oberleutnant," he said. "Are you all right?"

Wieck said nothing. His eyes remained open wide.

"Are you hurt?" There was a worried tone to the young mechanic's voice. "Have you been hit?"

Wieck shook his head.

"Then what is it, Oberleutnant?"

Again Wieck said nothing.

Other members of the ground crew were beginning to converge on the fighter, checking for damage and starting to refuel and rearm it.

By this time, Oberleutnant Wieck should have been standing on the wing of his aeroplane lighting up his customary post-sortie cigar. But he was just sitting there inside the tiny cockpit of the fighter, his eyes open, his body shaking.

The mechanic looked down at the others working on the plane.

"What is it?" asked one of them. "What's wrong?"

The mechanic looked at the oberleutnant one last time, then

said, "Get the major! Hurry!"

4

Flying Officer Newell climbed out of the cockpit of his Hurricane and headed toward the Ops building to make his report. He'd had plenty of time to think about his report and had decided to tell the officer exactly what he'd seen, no matter what the consequences.

The Ops building, a wooden shack just off the southwest end of the airfield, was filled with cigarette smoke and the smell of freshly brewed tea. Newell poured himself a cup and took a seat across from the senior intelligence officer who happened to be on duty. Newell thought it was strange that the senior intelligence officer was taking his report, but it had been a morning full of strange occurrences, so why not the senior IO?

After a long moment of silence the intelligence officer nodded once, then said, "Whenever you're ready."

Newell took a sip of tea, cleared his throat and began. "We'd just reached twenty thousand feet when Simon spotted the bandits below and to our left. I led my formation into a dive and—"

"Was Sawyer with you then?"

Obviously others in the squadron had already made their reports and the intelligence officer was trying to piece together what happened to Pilot Officer Sawyer. Well, thought Newell, he won't have to worry for much longer.

"No," Newell said, shaking his head. "He'd turned late and was lagging behind."

The intelligence officer nodded, then offered Newell a cigarette.

Newell took it.

"What then?"

"I picked out one of the 109s and decided to stay on him

after he broke formation."

"And Sawyer?"

"I don't know where he was then, I was too busy with the 109. I squeezed off a burst and when he didn't turn I fired again, pugging away at him. And then . . ." Newell's voice trailed off.

"Yes?"

"Something crossed my line of fire, something blue and green."

"Was it an aeroplane?"

Newell shook his head. "At the time I couldn't be sure. I didn't get a good enough look at it then."

The intelligence officer nodded, leaned in closer. "Go on."

"Well, the 109 started to burn. I watched it fall and when I was sure the Hun had bought it, I pulled around to get back into the fight." He paused a moment to take a long drag on his cigarette. "That's when I saw him."

"Sawyer?"

"Yes."

"What happened to him?"

"There was this . . . dragon on his tail, sir."

"A dragon?" the officer said, his voice even and unchanged.

Newell realized then that he probably wasn't the first to make such a report. Yet for some reason, he didn't get the impression that the intelligence officer believed his story. "Yes, a dragon," he said with conviction. "It was blue and green, as big as a Heinkel and as quick as a . . . No, it was quicker than any fighter."

"As big *as* a Heinkel, you say, not *a* Heinkel?"

"No, as big as a Heinkel," continued Newell. "And it was armed with a flamethrower. That's how it got Sawyer. Burned him right up with it."

The officer nodded.

"It could also knock aeroplanes out of the air with its hands.

In fact, I think it got a 109 that way."

The intelligence officer looked up and studied Newell for a long time. "Anything else?" he said at last.

"Yes," said Newell. "There was a woman in one of the dragon's arms, cradled like a rugger ball. She had long red hair . . ."

The room was silent then, all except for the scratch of the officer's pen as he continued to make notes in his book.

Newell didn't envy the intelligence officer's job. It was such a fantastic story that Newell himself never would have believed it if he hadn't been right there in the middle of it. And even at that, he was still finding it pretty hard to accept.

Dragons over England.

Film from his gun-camera would have been nice, but with the way his wings had been charred, the film had likely been damaged.

At last the intelligence officer finished writing, looked across the table at Newell and snapped his book shut with an extraordinarily loud pop.

"Flying Officer Newell," he said. "I am recommending you be grounded until further notice."

CHAPTER TWO
Saturday, August 3, 1940

1

Lavena felt the cold press of hard rock against her back long before she opened her eyes. Her body ached from head to foot and her entire right side was chilled to the bone. She wrapped her arms around herself, pulled her legs up tight against her chest and rested for a little while longer.

That's when she heard the low rumble of the dragon. Tibalt was somewhere nearby and from the sounds of it he was in a bit of pain.

Her sleep-shrouded mind began to think about where she might be and how it was that she came to be here. She remembered being on the plain outside Dervon, standing at Asvald's side as the old wizard battled the stubborn dragon. No, it wasn't quite a battle. Asvald hadn't been fighting it, he had been trying to send it away—send it somewhere else.

Whatever his intentions, his spell had worked, or at least it had started to when the dragon began thrashing about.

And then . . .

And then the beast had lunged at Lavena, snatching her up and carrying her away. After that it had all been a blur. They had passed through a long, long tunnel that had been ringed with lights and people and armies and villages and *everything*. That was it. The tunnel had everything. It was all there, everything that ever was and ever would be, spinning past at greater and greater speeds until they were suddenly through it and falling through the air like stones flung from a cliff.

She had been awake for some of it after that, and had been conscious enough to hear the wind thunder against her ears, and hear the roar of the noisy, stiff-winged birds that had buzzed and zoomed about them in an attempt to chase them from their domain.

And then it had all gone black.

Black and cold.

And now, this place.

Somewhere else.

Lavena slowly opened her eyes and at first the change made little difference as there was blackness all around her. She closed her eyes again and stretched the muscles of her limbs in an attempt to get her blood moving. Every muscle was sore and she dared not stretch again. She opened her eyes once more and this time could make out different shades in the darkness. At last she moved, lifting her head slightly to peer further into the shadows.

Tibalt was there, sitting with his back against what was obviously one wall of a cave.

Lavena rose up onto her arms, trying to do so without making a sound or otherwise letting the dragon know she was awake. She rolled onto her feet, but remained crouched to take advantage of the cover of some nearby rocks. She held her breath and cautiously rose.

The next instant the dragon's hands were on her, lifting her up off the ground and bringing her to within a few feet of its fiery maw.

"Heal me!" said Tibalt, angrily.

"What?"

"Are you not the apprentice of that crazed fool of a wizard? Heal me!"

Each time the dragon opened its maw, the fire deep within it cast some light into the darkness. With each flicker Lavena saw more clearly that the dragon was wounded and needed help.

"I am no wizard's apprentice," she said.

"Then why were you on the plain with him?"

"I asked Asvald for his help in saving Dervon . . ." Her voice trailed off. "I was a friend of Warrick. He was my betrothed . . . Or at least he had been until you killed him."

"He deserved to die," said Tibalt. "He killed my younger sibling."

"And your sibling killed his friend, Manfred."

"With good reason, no doubt."

Lavena said nothing. There was obviously no reasoning with the beast.

Tibalt chuffed a slight laugh as if he had won the little argument, then said, "Heal me!"

"I told you, I don't know anything about healing, especially healing dragons. My only training has been in the creation of gowns and tunics."

"A seamstress?"

"I prefer the word *costumier.*"

The dragon laughed. "Then you can heal me."

She shook her head. "I don't know how." And besides, she wasn't even sure she wanted to help.

The dragon put her down, then raised one of its smaller talons to its mouth. In the faint light that emanated from its maw, she watched as it bit down and broke one off from the end of its clawed hand. Then it carefully placed the thick end of the talon between the teeth at the rear of its mouth and slowly bit down on it.

"There," said Tibalt, tossing the talon at Lavena's feet. "There's your needle." The beast motioned in her direction with its great head. "Tear some strips from your clothing and use them as thread to repair the holes in my wings."

She hesitated.

"I must warn you," said Tibalt, "that if you don't help me, I will have little other use for you . . ."

He didn't say it, but Lavena knew he would kill her if she refused. She reached down, picked up the talon and examined it. Its pointed tip was as sharp as a pin, the other end as thick as a candle. There was a hole punched neatly through the thick end and Lavena was shocked by the dragon's ingenuity. Such an intelligent creature, yet so devoid of the ability to reason.

"I can't see well enough to do the job properly," she said, resigning herself to helping the dragon. "I need more light."

The dragon opened its maw, leaned over to one side and breathed a steady stream of flame onto the rocks that were gathered there. He repeated the process several times until the rocks were red hot and illuminating the cave like a fire in the hearth. "Can you see now?"

"Yes," said Lavena. She was also feeling less of a chill, but wasn't about to thank the dragon for anything.

"Now," said Tibalt. "Heal me!"

She tore several strips of fabric from her clothing where small amounts wouldn't be missed, then threaded the talon with the longest piece.

"Where should I begin?"

Tibalt sat up on his hind legs and unfurled his wings so that they spanned the width of the cave. "Wherever I need your help the most."

The dragon had been hurt badly. There was blood all over its wings, most of it dripping from the holes punched through its flesh. There were countless tiny holes and several larger ones. The biggest of them all was a bloody mess of a hole that was big enough for Lavena to poke her head through. There was a large flap of skin hanging limply from the lower edge of the hole and blood dripped from the wound like water from a cracked jar. She would start with that one.

She stepped forward, made herself comfortable under the dragon's wing and went to work.

2

The sky over the field at Digby was filled with clouds. There had been intervals of sunshine and drizzle all day, and ground crews were using the downtime to make sure the squadron's aeroplanes were in top-flight condition.

Corporal Tandy and Leading Aircraftman Rankin were busy patching holes in the fuselage of one of the squadron's Hurricanes. The fabric covering of the aeroplane's metal-tube framework was easily repaired with the same doped fabric the armorers used to seal off its gunports prior to each flight. The red patches might have been a bit unnerving to the pilots, but they'd be painted over as soon as the fabric was dry.

"Know anything about this new Dragon aeroplane the Germans have?" asked Rankin as he smoothed a patch of fabric over a hole in the plane's tail.

"Not a thing," said Tandy. "You probably know as much about it as I do."

"They say it's big as a Heinkel and as nimble as a 109."

"That's what they say."

"Supposed to be heavily armored too . . . Armor plates everywhere."

Tandy shook his head. "Sounds incredible, doesn't it?"

"Yes, but what's really incredible is that it's supposed to be armed with a flamethrower instead of guns."

"I heard that too, and that's the part I don't believe."

Rankin trimmed away a bit of excess fabric with his knife, then looked at Corporal Tandy. "No? Why not?"

"Deflection shooting with machine guns is difficult enough. Can you imagine the power, velocity and size of the stream of fire required to make a flamethrower an effective weapon against a Spitfire?"

Aircraftman Rankin thought about it. "It would have to be massive."

"And how much fuel capacity would it require to suitably arm such a weapon?" Tandy shook his head. "The Germans are having enough trouble just getting petrol to their airfields."

"So you don't believe it?"

"No. The way I figure, it was probably an Me-110 on fire, streaming flames across the sky on its way into the drink."

Rankin nodded. "Yeah, that sounds more likely."

They finished the last of the bullet holes and stepped back to admire their work. It wasn't a very tidy job, but it would get the aeroplane back into the air.

"Right," said Tandy. "Next one."

3

The largest hole took some time to close. The flesh of the dragon's wings was very leathery and Lavena found it difficult to hold the loose flap of skin in place while she stitched it. After several unsuccessful attempts she was able to make a stitch that held the flap into place. After that it was easier to work and in time she had the hole entirely sewn shut. It wasn't pretty, but Lavena was still proud of the work she'd done under the circumstances.

With the biggest hole closed, she moved onto the smaller ones. These were much easier to close because they simply required that she put a stitch across the opening and pull it closed. To his credit, Tibalt never complained or cried out in pain, despite some of Lavena's more forceful attempts to pierce the flesh of his wings with the threaded talon.

As she began working on the smallest of the holes, those requiring just a single stitch, Tibalt spoke.

"What do you know about the steel dragons?"

"You mean the stiff-winged birds?"

"Birds do not grow to be so large."

"They look like birds to me."

"What do you know of them?"

"Nothing," she said, "other than they can hurt you."

"They spit steel from their wings and noses."

Lavena looked at the dragon's body. In spots there were bits of steel wedged between its scales, and in other places entire scales had been smashed or else torn away from its body. "Then steel dragons is a good name for them."

The dragon was silent for a time, then breathed new fire into the rocks to his right. When he was done, he turned to Lavena. "Where are we?"

That was a good question. "This cave seems familiar to me," said Lavena. "But I know of no place that has . . . steel dragons in its skies."

"No," said Tibalt. "I know of no place either."

"Asvald tried to warn you," Lavena said, pulling hard on a stitch.

Tibalt laughed through clenched teeth.

"What was it he said?" Lavena muttered trying to remember the wizard's words. She stopped her repair work a moment and searched her memory.

The dragon was silent.

"He said that men grow stronger every day . . . They will conquer the earth . . . and eventually control the air."

"Hah!" Tibalt scoffed.

"Laugh all you like, but maybe the steel dragons belong to the men of this place."

A look of concern crossed the dragon's face, but was quickly swept away by a stern confidence, perhaps even arrogance. "Are you done with my wings?"

Obviously the dragon was either too proud or stubborn to even consider the possibility that it could be bested by anything that had ties to mortal men. She shook her head, stepped back and looked them over. "Yes, I'm done."

"Good," he said. "Now pick the steel spits from my scales."

Lavena was tired and in desperate need of both food and rest, neither of which seemed to be near at hand. She moved in front of the belly of the beast and examined the scales there. There were several places where she could pry the steel from between the scales. There were also several bare patches where she might be able to pierce the skin with the talon needle. She considered it a moment, but knew that the talon was hardly long enough to do any sort of damage.

Reluctantly she began preening the belly of the beast.

4

Corporal Tandy and Leading Aircraftman Rankin finished patching up the last of the Hurricanes on the flight line and headed across the airfield toward the squadron workshop.

While they had worked they'd used up most topics of discussion regarding the war, everything from the merits of the German's Me-109 to an up-and-coming young singer named Vera Lynn. But as much as they would have liked talking about other things, the topic that was first and foremost in both their minds was this new German superplane—the Dragon.

Outside the workshop they circled a Hurricane in search of holes to patch and were joined by Aircraftman Robertson, an armorer in the squadron who had been, up until yesterday, assigned to Flying Officer Newell's aeroplane.

"Have you seen him?" said Tandy, obviously referring to Flying Officer Newell.

"Aye," said the Scottish erk, the tone of his voice suggesting that his spirits were quite low. "I've seen him."

"Did you speak to him, then?"

"Aye, I did."

"And what did he say of this dragon?"

"He said it was just that, a dragon."

Tandy and Rankin were silent.

"He says it was a fire-breathing dragon, and that it was holding a girl in its arms."

"How many sorties has he flown?" asked Tandy.

Robertson ran a hand over the stubble on his chin. "He was in France so it would have to be up over a hundred, I suppose."

"Poor bastard," said Tandy.

And then the three men were silent, each realizing that Flying Officer Newell had reached his limit and had finally been broken by months of continuous combat.

They resumed their inspection of the Hurricane, none of them saying another word.

5

"I think that was the last," said Lavena. She had saved each of the steel spits she had dug out from between the dragon's scales and had collected several pounds of them. It was a wonder the dragon had been able to fly after being hit so many times, but except for the few larger holes in its wings the beast looked none the worse for wear.

Tibalt stretched his wings, moving them outward to the sides of the cave, then over his head.

At one point he grunted in pain, but then continued moving his wings up and down, and finally in great circles. The movement stirred up dirt and dust from the floor of the cave and Lavena had to shield her eyes and turn away.

The dragon continued for a few more seconds and then it was over. "You've done well."

Lavena looked up. The dragon looked pleased. Perhaps, with

an agreeable disposition, it might reward her with some food or drink. She could probably finish a pitcher of water in a single gulp and as for food . . . Her stomach grumbled at the thought.

She cleared her throat. "Perhaps you could reward me for my work by bringing me some water and fruits from the surrounding lands?"

Tibalt laughed as if her suggestion was preposterous. "A dragon, forage for food for a . . . a human? Never?"

"But I'm hungry, and thirsty."

"So am I," Tibalt said, his voice booming like thunder. "But even if I wanted to bring you food, I couldn't. It has grown dark outside. Now it is time to rest."

Lavena said nothing, realizing that she might be able to escape while the dragon slept. "Very well," she said, making herself comfortable on a flat patch of rock.

She'd just closed her eyes when she felt the dragon's hands around her, lifting her up off the rock.

"You must think me a fool," said Tibalt, eying her with contempt. "You provide a valuable service to me, one that I'm not about to do without."

And with that, he placed her inside a hollow in the wall of the cave, then moved a large rock in front of the hollow, sealing it shut.

Lavena was returned to darkness.

She desperately pushed at the rock, trying to roll it out of the way, but it was too large and would not budge. She tried a few more times, but eventually gave up. She was too tired and too hungry to pursue the matter any further.

On the other side of the rock, she could hear Tibalt's low, rumbling breath ease into a regular rhythm as he quickly drifted off to sleep.

She gave one last half-hearted attempt to move the rock, then eased herself down onto the floor of the hollow.

She was exhausted.
She closed her eyes.
And moments later, was fast asleep.

CHAPTER THREE
Sunday, August 4, 1940

1

At dawn, light from outside the cave shimmered down into it like water down a waterfall. The rough, jagged surface of the rock walls cast eerie shadows, making it seem as if monsters lurked in the darkness.

Tibalt's eyes slowly slid open, first one then the other. He stretched his neck, rolling it away from his belly until his head was pointing straight up and his long neck was extended to its full height.

He remained in that position a moment, then chuffed a burst of flame against the roof of the cave. That done, he nestled back into a sitting position and began stretching his wings. He pushed them back behind him as far as they would go, then drew them in front so that the outer edges touched. Finally, he reached up, lifting his wings until they nearly touched the top of the cave. The movements had all been done without any pain, and with just a slight amount of sting still lingering in some of the larger wounds. He could feel it only when he stretched his wings to their very limits.

All of which meant he was well enough to return to the air.

More importantly, he was well enough to resume the fight against the strange steel dragons.

Tibalt moved toward the light where the cave opened up onto a wide, open stretch of farmland.

As he began crawling toward the hole, he heard the faint

cries of the girl, muted by the heavy rock he had placed in front of the hollow. He turned and listened to her wail for a moment. She was strong and persistent for one of her kind, but she could cry and scream and yell all she wanted—no one would ever hear her. She would just have to wait to be let out, and only then in order to tend to his needs.

She obviously didn't enjoy being in his service, but it was really a small price for her to pay in exchange for her life. Eventually, she would be grateful to him for sparing her.

He turned away from the hollow and once again headed toward the light. It wasn't the only opening to the cave system, but it was the largest and most easily accessible. Tibalt would use it to exit the cave, but upon his return he would use another entrance, making sure never to use the same entrance twice in succession while he remained in the cave.

It was an unnecessary precaution perhaps—he was a *dragon*, after all—but with the steel dragons about, it would be wise to be careful.

As Tibalt neared the opening, he poked his head up through the hole and took a look around. The surrounding fields were empty, the morning dew rising up from the land like mist from a boiling cauldron. Tibalt raised his head and saw that the skies above were clear.

Not a steel dragon in sight.

It was time to soar.

In a single swift motion, Tibalt surged out of the hole and bounded into the air, climbing higher and higher with each long and powerful stroke of his massive wings.

He circled the sky above the cave for a short time, rising ever higher over the countryside. Things on the ground grew smaller, and the landmarks and villages built by men appeared less and less significant.

When he'd reached a comfortable height and could soar the

wind with ease, Tibalt turned eastward for a flight over the Channel.

The hunting grounds.

2

Aubrey Newcastle scanned the eastern skies with his binoculars then let them hang from his neck while he took his customary sip of scotch.

He had a nip every hour on the hour as a way of relieving himself of boredom. When the war broke out he had joined the Observer Corps out of a sense of duty and patriotism. After serving in the Great War, he was damn glad he was too old to be on the front lines of this one. Still, the British Isles were on the brink of being overrun by the Jerries, and manning an observation post at Skegness on the Channel coast seemed like the least he could do for old Mother England.

It was just that nothing much ever happened out here.

Skegness was located on the northern rim of the bay they called The Wash. Being a hundred miles north of London, there wasn't much flying overhead. Sure there was the odd Spit or Hurricane that lost its way, but he'd yet to see a formation of German bombers, like what they had flying over Folkestone or Bexhill.

What a sight that must be, Aubrey thought. Dozens of Heinkels and Dorniers, even Stukas, all flying in formation toward England. And then the RAF boys zooming up to knock them out of the sky . . .

Aubrey sighed and returned to his routine.

He lifted the binoculars to his eyes and panned them across the landscape to the west.

He was about to turn around and scan the Channel when something struck him as odd. He raised the binoculars to his eyes again and searched the sky.

It took him several seconds to find it, but when he did he realized it had become larger in his sights. It didn't look much like an aeroplane and its wings moved up and down—almost like a bird's—but it was big and fast and somehow, he knew, deadly.

Aubrey held the binoculars with a single hand and used his free left one to lift the receiver that linked the post at Stegness directly to Observer Corps Headquarters and ultimately to Fighter Command Headquarters at Bentley Priory.

"This is Stegness calling," said Aubrey.

"Go ahead Stegness," said the monotone female voice on the other end of the line.

"I've got a large aircraft approaching from the west, at an altitude of approximately five-hundred feet."

"Is it a bomber?"

"It's big enough to be one," said Aubrey.

"Heinkel, Dornier or Junkers?"

Aubrey took another look, and felt his jaw drop against his chest. Whatever it was, it was closer now. Painted blue and green, its bendable fuselage was covered with all sorts of armor plating and spikes. It didn't look like an aeroplane at all. In fact, it looked a lot like a, like a . . .

"Stegness, are you there?" said the voice, calm and even. "Please make your report."

"It's as big as a bomber," said Aubrey. "But it's not."

"Is it a flock of birds, then?"

Aubrey shook his head. It was closer now, so close he didn't need his binoculars to see it.

"I repeat, is it a flock of birds?"

"No, no, it's not that."

"What is it, then?"

"A . . . a dragon. It's a dragon."

"Are you referring to the DeHavilland biplane?" A few of the old twin-engine DeHavilland Dragons were being used as transports, but there were none operating in that part of England at the moment.

"No, I mean it's a dragon," Aubrey said, shouting now as the wind kicked up as the beast approached. "It's a big, blue-green, fire-breathing dragon."

Just then, the dragon roared overhead, drowning out the reply from the woman at HQ and knocking the telephone receiver out of his hand. Aubrey grabbed hold of his helmet, turned around and watched the dragon continue eastward over the Channel. When it was almost out of sight, he picked up the receiver again, but by now there was no one on the other end of the line.

He hung up the telephone, took another nip to settle his nerves and resumed his watch of the skies.

3

The dragon was gone.

When she'd first heard him stir she had cried out in desperation, yelling at the top of her voice in the faint hope that the dragon would hear, remember she was there, and let her out of her stone-walled prison.

But he had done nothing.

After she had yelled and screamed for what seemed like ages, her throat became rough and her voice hoarse. She stopped to catch her breath and listened to the sound of utter silence. The dragon was gone and she'd been left alone.

To starve to death.

To whither away to flesh and bones, and then just bones as the spindly-legged creatures of the cave came to dine on her remains.

The thought of it gave her determination, if not strength.

With renewed vigor she attacked the rock placed in front of

the hollow. She placed her back against it, planted her feet firmly against the walls of the cave . . .

And pushed.

Nothing happened. The rock did not move.

Undaunted, she adjusted her back, placing it in a more comfortable position, and moved her feet to give her legs more room to stretch out.

She inhaled and exhaled deeply several times, then held her breath, and pushed again.

The rock budged. It wasn't a very discernible movement, but she felt that it had moved. She continued pushing as hard as she could and perceived the rock to be moving away from the mouth of the hollow.

She stopped pushing, and as she did the rock rolled back into place. The strange thing was that it had moved back further than she had pushed it. That meant that the rock had shifted somehow and was now in a different position than it had been previously.

Perhaps it gave her a chance.

She braced herself to push the rock again, but the strength was now gone from her back and legs. Her efforts were feeble and ineffective.

Lavena fell to the floor of the hollow, breathing hard. She would lie there for a few moments to catch her breath and restore her strength.

Then she would try the rock again.

And again . . .

As many times as needed in order to be free.

4

"I've got something on the screen, sir," the young blond-haired WAAF said into the microphone hanging from her neck.

"How many?" came the reply from the group captain through

her headphones.

She leaned in closer to the small radar screen in front of her and her face took on a greenish hue. She studied the screen for a few seconds, then shook her head. "I can't really tell, sir. It could be one aeroplane or as many as five."

"Why wasn't it picked up by the Chain Home radar stations?" the group captain said softly, as if thinking aloud.

The Chain Home radar stations operated on a ten-meter waveband and had a much longer range than the one-and-a-half-meter waveband of their Chain Home Low transmitters. If there were incoming German aeroplanes, the Chain Home Stations should have picked them up ten to fifteen minutes ago when they were halfway across the Channel.

"It's not an incoming flight, sir," said the WAAF. "It's heading out over the Channel."

"We haven't had any reports of RAF flights in that area," said the group captain, now standing over the WAAF's shoulder and looking at the screen himself.

"Whatever it is, sir, it's stopped heading east and is holding over the coast."

The group captain leaned in for a closer look. From his expression, it was obvious that he'd never seen such a blip before. It was more like a shadow than a blip, as if whatever was in the sky was absorbing or deflecting part of the energy released by their transmitters. If the Germans had developed a new paint or reflective covering for their aircraft, it would nullify Britain's early-warning advantage and have a drastic effect on the battle being waged in the skies over England.

"Sir!" said another WAAF, standing slightly behind him and to the left.

"What is it?" The group captain took his eyes off the screen for a moment and turned to face the young dark-haired WAAF.

"There was a report made by an observer in Stegness not five minutes ago . . ." Her voice trailed off, somewhat uncertain.

"Yes, yes. Go on!"

"The observer reported a large object heading east toward the Channel."

"An object?" said the group captain. "A large object? Did the observer say what this large object was?"

"He did, sir."

"And, what was it?"

"He said it was a, uh . . . dragon, sir."

"A dragon?" He said the word slowly, considering it.

The young woman held up a slip of paper and read from it. ". . . 'a big blue-green fire-breathing dragon,' to be precise."

If the Germans had indeed developed a new skin for their aeroplanes, who knew what it might look like. In fact, an aeroplane with special reflective paint, done up in a tightly mottled camouflage pattern might even look like a dragon from the ground.

"Is it still on your screen?" he asked the WAAF seated in front of him.

"It seems to be circling, sir."

"Good." The group captain turned to the WAAF on his left. "Call the filter room at Bentley Priory."

The WAAF seemed to hesitate. "And what shall I tell them, sir?"

The group captain considered the question. There was no time to go into details now. He would put all his thoughts on the matter into his report at the end of the day. "Tell them a couple of Heinkels are straggling."

That should get them up in the air, he thought. At least for a closer look.

5

Several pilots sat around the card table inside the dispersal hut playing euchre while others lay back in their chairs catching a few winks of sleep.

As a rousing cheer rose up from the card table over a deftly played hand, the dispersal telephone rang its shrill warning.

The dispersal hut went silent as all eyes turned onto Squadron Leader Lane who picked up the phone in the absence of the orderly. He nodded a few times, then calmly hung up.

"Relax lads," he said.

The pilots in the room breathed a collective sigh of relief.

"Hillary," he barked.

Pilot Officer Hillary leaped to his feet. "Sir!"

"How about you and I have a go?"

"Yes, sir!" Hillary beamed, eager for the chance to accompany the squadron leader on a sortie.

The two men ran from the dispersal hut to their waiting Spitfires.

"What will we be looking for, sir?" asked Hillary.

"Fighter Command seems to think they're some stragglers over the Channel, but if they are circling over the coast then my guess is it's a Heinkel floatplane looking for a downed pilot."

The floatplanes had rescued many downed German pilots in the Channel, prompting Air Chief Marshal Sir Hugh Dowding to give the order to shoot the planes down. The rationale was that a rescued pilot could be back in the air the very next day.

"I've never seen one of those up close," said Hillary, wondering if this might be his chance for his first kill.

"Neither have I," said the squadron leader.

The ground crew was already waiting for them and quickly strapped the two pilots into their cockpits. They were rolling down the grass runway seconds later, and, scant minutes after the call came in, they were in the air.

"That was a good takeoff this time around, Blue Two," said Lane over the radio.

"Thank you, Blue Leader," said Hillary with pride. His last few takeoffs had been rather bumpy and on one of them he'd almost clipped the tops of the trees at the end of the airfield with his propeller. The others had kidded him about it when he landed, but it was clear that he would be allowed to make a mistake like that only once.

The compliment from Squadron Leader Lane, a pilot with five months on ops and four kills to his credit, made Hillary feel as if he'd cleared another hurdle on his way into the club. All that remained was his first kill. Perhaps today would be the day.

They flew east at full power for two minutes before the Channel coast became visible on the horizon. There were no aeroplanes visible, but at this distance spotting a single plane would be difficult, if not impossible.

"Eyes sharp," Squadron Leader Lane reminded him.

Hillary's eyes looked to the left and right of the nose of the Spitfire, and every once in a while he'd swing the aircraft left and right to get a good look straight ahead.

Nothing.

"And don't forget to keep an eye out above and behind you."

Hillary felt like he'd been caught with his pants down. He'd been so intent on searching the coast, he'd neglected to check his rear. No wonder young pilots didn't last long in battle. He immediately began to crane his neck looking for enemy aircraft above and behind him.

"There's something," barked Squadron Leader Lane. "About angels two below. Eleven o'clock."

Hillary looked out over the leading edge of his left wing and saw it. "Got it."

It was too big to be a floatplane. Perhaps it was a bomber with its controls stuck, or a pilot looking out for a downed crewman in the water. Whatever the reason the aeroplane was there, it was an easy target. They had the crucial height advantage, and the sun was behind them, giving them the all-important element of surprise.

"Tally ho," said Lane as his aircraft went into a shallow dive.

Hillary hesitated a moment before he pushed his stick forward. The nose of his Spitfire dropped slightly and he followed the squadron leader in. His moment of hesitation had put some hundred yards between. The plane began picking up speed as he tried to catch up to Squadron Leader Lane. They'd be on top of the German in seconds.

"What the . . ."

Hillary didn't have a good view of the German plane because the squadron leader's Spitfire was directly between it and him. At best he'd have a few seconds to squeeze off a burst after the squardron leader peeled away. He tightened his grip on the ring at the top of the stick and rubbed his thumb over the firing button.

"It's not an aeroplane . . ."

Hillary tried to look past the squadron leader's plane. At first he couldn't see a thing, but as they closed on the target parts of it began to appear.

And he saw something.

A wing.

Moving.

The squadron leader started firing. Tracers arced out from the wings and shell casings rained down from under the wings.

And then the squadron leader's Spitfire was suddenly engulfed in flame. It wasn't on fire as much as flying through a blast of flame. The flames passed over the streamlined shape of the Spitfire, hugging the wings and fuselage like air itself. The squadron leader must have accidentally toggled his RT because

Hillary heard Lane screaming inside the burning coffin that was his cockpit.

The plane exploded in a fireball.

The screaming stopped.

Hillary flew through a cloud of flame, smoke and debris, then was suddenly clear.

And there it was in front of him . . .

A winged monster.

Hillary gasped, then instinctively let off a burst before pushing the stick hard forward to avoid a collision.

Under the shock of the negative G-forces, Hillary's stomach leapt up into his mouth. Dust and dirt flew up from the floor of the cockpit into his eyes and his head cracked heavily against the canopy. The engine cut out for a second as the negative G's starved the engine of fuel, but then it cut back in and Hillary pushed the throttle forward to get away.

Each second seemed to pass an hour as the ground slowly rose up to meet him. He dove four-thousand feet in just a few seconds before he dared pull the aeroplane level. The Spitfire shuddered slightly as he pulled back on the stick and he was forced down into his seat. A second later he was flying straight and level, and breathing hard to catch his breath.

He could hardly believe what had happened. One second Squadron Leader Lane had been in front of him, firing his guns. The next second he was enveloped in flames. It didn't make sense. No German plane could do that.

He took a moment to calm himself down. His breathing slowed and he began to search the sky.

All clear.

He checked his rearview mirror bolted to the top of his armored windscreen. But instead of blue sky, he saw a flash of yellow and green.

Hillary turned and looked behind him.

"Oh, God," he cried.

The beast was on his tail.

He was caught without enough altitude for another dive and there were no clouds around to hide in. There were some to the north, but it would take minutes for him to reach them—and a minute was a lifetime in a dogfight.

He had only one chance for survival. If he was lucky, the turning radius of this monster of an aeroplane wasn't as tight as that of the Spitfire. If he could out-turn it long enough he might be able to get away.

He slapped the stick and kicked the rudder to the right. As he'd hoped the pursuing craft shot past him. But that didn't stop it from blasting him with a shot of flame. It was bright yellow and hot, licking at the tip of his left wing and warping the metal. The Spitfire suddenly became more difficult to fly. He turned toward the bank of clouds in the distance and prepared for another tight turn, this time to the left.

On the next pass, Hillary saw the enemy approaching. He thought he had enough time to prepare, but it was on him in seconds. He snapped the plane to the left and everything suddenly went dark as flames streamed around and into the cockpit, then down the fuselage. He kept on the stick and in a moment he was free, everything hot to the touch and smelling of smoke.

He turned again and again, fire lapping at the aeroplane's tail, elevators, and wings.

The clouds were closer now.

He dove for them and in an instant the plane was shrouded in glorious white mist. Once inside the cloud, he turned left and climbed. When he came out of the cloud there was nothing but empty sky around him.

The Hun was gone.

Thank God.

He looked around the cockpit for damage. The flames had

burnt a hole in the cockpit wall on his left and fire had burned away his gloves and part of his left pant leg.

He glanced over the gauges, the glass on them had been darkened by smoke. To his horror the fuel gauge was stuck on *E*, but a quick check of the other gauges showed that none of them were working, all likely short-circuited by the fire.

Hopefully he'd have enough petrol to reach base.

He turned west, pulled back on the throttle to save fuel, and began searching the ground for a familiar landmark.

6

Lavena couldn't be sure how much time had passed since her last attempt at moving the rock. It could have been minutes, it could have been hours. All she knew was that she was ready to try again, and felt stronger than ever before.

On her last attempt she had managed to move the rock so that almost a foot-wide gap opened up between the top of the rock and the upper mouth of the hollow.

The possibility of escaping had given her hope, which had made her forget all about her thirst and hunger. And now she had a plan, and this above all else gave her the inner strength to continue her efforts.

She had gathered up several stones from the floor of the hollow and held them firmly in her hands. She placed her back against the rock and her feet against the wall. Then she pushed the rock so that the gap opened up above her and to the sides. When the gap was at its widest, she wedged a stone into it and eased the large rock back into place.

The stone prevented the larger rock from falling back into place in front of the hollow. Now she took a larger stone from the pile she had collected and repeated the process, each time placing a larger and larger stone into the gap.

After doing this four times there was a gap between the top

of the rock and the hollow wide enough for her to climb through. However, since the gap was so high off the ground it would be difficult to reach. She could crawl through it, but the struggle might jar the stone holding the larger rock in place. If it moved while she was in the gap, she would be crushed to death.

After a few moments' thought, she inserted a series of smaller stones into the gap in the hopes that they might prevent it from closing up completely if the stone at the top of the rock gave way.

When she was sure it was as secure as she could make it, she climbed up on the rock and began squeezing through the opening.

Her head and shoulders slipped through easily, but her midsection was too tight to pass through. It felt as if she could push the rock further open, but if she did so, the gap would grow larger and she would probably lose the security offered by the stones she'd placed in the gap.

She lay there thinking about it, then decided to push with all her might. The large rock rolled forward slightly, opening up the gap. Inside the hollow she could hear the smaller stones falling from the expanding gap onto the floor.

She was holding the rock open now, nothing else.

With one swift motion, she swung her legs out from behind her and out of the way of the rock as it closed tight against the mouth of the hollow.

She'd made it.

After a few deep breaths to calm herself, Lavena tried to climb down from the top of the rock, but she couldn't move.

She tried again. Nothing.

She felt down the length of her legs. They were in one piece and unharmed, but one side of her dress was stuck between the rock and the hollow, pinning her to the side of the cave.

Lavena began to laugh. After all she'd been through, she wasn't about to let something like this hold her back. She reached down with her right hand and began clawing it at her dress, shredding the material with her bare fingers. In seconds she had torn herself free.

She stood up on top of the large rock, a sense of accomplishment washing over her.

"Now," she said. "How do I get out of this cave?"

7

Sergeant Hillary reached the airfield at Beachy Head, his engine sputtering and trailing a long plume of thick black smoke. The landing itself was a bit of a wreck with one wheel burnt flat and the tailwheel bent to one side. But despite the condition of his Spitfire, he was able to walk away from it when it finally came to a stop, only to collapse a few yards away.

He was rushed to the airfield hospital where his burned clothing was peeled from his skin and his wounds cleaned and dressed. He'd suffered burns to his legs, hands and face, although none were severe enough to cause any permanent disfiguration. Still, he was heavily sedated, and would likely stay that way for the next few days, perhaps even a week.

It was mid-afternoon when Flying Officer Johnstone entered the ward and was directed to Sergeant Hillary's bedside by a young dark-haired nurse.

"Thank you," said Johnstone. He waited for the nurse to reach her desk at the entrance to the ward before sitting down on the wooden chair next to Hillary's bed.

Although the young flier's head and hands were wrapped in bandages, Johnstone could see that his eyes were open. There was something unsettling about the young man's eyes. They were filled with terror, as if he'd looked down into the mouth of hell itself. Judging by the condition his Spit was in, thought

Johnstone, he just might have.

"Cigarette," said Johnstone, taking one for himself, then shaking another free for Hillary. "They're American."

Hillary didn't move. His eyes shifted to glance at the cigarette a moment, then quickly returned his gaze to a spot on the far wall. Johnstone took the cigarette from between his lips and placed it back into the package. "Want to tell me what happened, then?" he said.

Hillary's eyes remained fixed and unblinking. He was silent for several moments, then finally began to talk.

"Squadron Leader Lane saw it first. We were about a thousand feet above it and a mile away. The squadron leader went into a dive. He fired off a burst, and then . . ."

Johnstone said nothing. He'd learned long ago when to prod a pilot with questions and when to keep his mouth shut.

Hillary sighed. "And then his aeroplane just burst into flames."

"Was he shot at by the German bomber?"

Hillary shook his head ever so slightly. "The thing fired at him, but not with any guns. It didn't have any guns. It hit him with a blast of flame . . . Burned me up too."

"I saw your plane," said Johnstone. "There was quite a lot of damage to it considering there wasn't a bullet hole to be found anywhere on it."

"I told you, the thing didn't have a gun."

"Then what did it have?"

"Giant wings . . . that moved. They flapped up and down like a bird. A big bird."

Johnstone felt his heart fall. Obviously Hillary was too heavily sedated to make a proper report. "And weapons?" he asked, more a formality now than anything else.

"The nose of it was like a giant, horned turret. But it didn't move in circles like regular turrets do. It moved any which way it pleased. It didn't have to be in position to fire, it could shoot at you from anywhere."

Johnstone sat there thinking. Something about Hillary's description sounded familiar. He'd heard a similar story recently from one of the chaps down the coast . . . A Hurricane pilot in 262 Squadron had reported seeing something like what Hillary was describing. If Johnstone wasn't mistaken, the pilot had even gone as far as to call the thing a dragon.

"Sergeant Hillary," said Johnstone. "If you had to describe this aircraft in layman's terms, you know, give it a name. What would you call it?"

The sergeant closed his eyes a moment and ran his tongue over his blistered lips. "It was like a bird, but birds don't get that big."

Flying Officer Johnstone was tempted to suggest the word "dragon" but that would diminish the significance of his report. "Much bigger than a bird, then?"

"Yes, it was a monster, a beast . . ."

"Yes."

"It was a . . . a dragon. That's what it was. It looked like a dragon, and it breathed fire like one too."

"Thank you, Sergeant Hillary," Johnstone said, getting up from his chair. "You be sure to get some rest now."

The young sergeant did not move or otherwise acknowledge Johnstone's departure. His eyes remained focused on a spot on the wall.

Staring.

8

There was a faint glow at one end of the cave, which could only mean one thing—light.

Light from the sun.

She headed toward it.

When she'd first realized she was in a cave, Lavena had thought she'd been taken to one of the many caves around Dervon that she'd played in so often as a child. But while the inside of this cave was similar to those she'd known in her youth, the arrangement and structure of it was quite different. For one thing, it was far larger and the rocks much smoother than she remembered. It was as if the caves had been widened and their walls worn smooth by the passage of time.

Something suddenly struck Lavena's head.

She stopped in her tracks and another drop of water splashed against the top of her head. She looked up but couldn't make out the cave roof because the walls simply seemed to converge overhead in a mass of darkness. While she was looking up another drop hit the tip of her nose.

She immediately opened her mouth and waited for the next drop to come. It seemed to take forever, but when it finally splashed against her tongue it was as if a river had streamed into her open mouth.

She made herself comfortable and waited for the next drop to fall. And the next. And the next.

It took a long time, but eventually she began to notice the bitter metallic taste of the water. Her thirst sated for the moment, she decided it was time to move on.

The tiny amount of water had helped. She felt rejuvenated. There was a bit of a spring to her step now and she was able to move more quickly and easily toward the light.

In moments the faint glow had grown into a disk of light. Then the disk of light transformed into a jagged circular opening.

There were clouds in the sky.

Lavena rose up through the opening and breathed in the sweet smell of rain and grass . . .

And freedom.

CHAPTER FOUR

1

Wing Commander Ian Jones pulled up in front of 12 Group Headquarters in Wattnall and turned off the engine of his staff car. He'd not been looking forward to this meeting with Group Captain Parks. He had tried to handle the matter over the telephone, but the group captain would have none of it. He wanted the wing commander to look him in the eye and tell him again about the incredible occurrences in the skies over England.

Probably wants to gauge whether or not I've gone mad, thought the wing commander.

It was an incredible story, but at least he wasn't the one who'd seen the dragon and swore to its existence. His pilots had done that, and it was his job to relay their reports to his superiors.

Nothing more.

He stepped out of the car, adjusted his uniform, then slipped his portfolio under his arm. It was a short walk to headquarters. Inside, he was greeted by a WAAF manning the reception desk. She acknowledged the wing commander with a salute and before he could say a word, she said, "The group captain has been expecting you. This way please."

He followed her down a long hallway, past several closed doors and a few that were open. The closed doors led into communications rooms, while the open ones were designated as lounges and waiting areas.

At the end of the hall, she stopped and knocked sharply three times on a door to her right. A second later she opened the door a crack and said, "Wing Commander Jones to see you, sir."

"Good, send him in."

She pushed the door open further, and stepped back to allow him past. He nodded politely in her direction and stepped into the room. The group captain was a large man, well into his forties and sporting touches of grey around his temples. He'd been an ace in the Great War and earned a DSO by shooting down a German Gotha bomber over London in 1917.

As the wing commander entered, the door closed behind him. He saluted and the group captain returned it. "Sit down."

Wing Commander Jones made himself comfortable.

"Now tell me about this dragon."

The wing commander repeated the accounts of his pilots, checking a few of the details along the way with the written reports he'd brought along in his portfolio. To his surprise the group captain said nothing the whole time, never even raising an eyebrow when he used the words *fire-breathing dragon*.

When he was done, the group captain silently filled the bowl of his pipe with tobacco and lit it. Finally, he said, "What do you make of it?"

"Well, sir, each of the pilots who reported seeing the dragon have been logging incredible amounts of hours in the air. Flying Officer Newell spent over twenty hours over Dunkirk and has been in the air every day since then."

"When is he due to be rotated north to 13 Group?"

"At the end of the month."

"Do it immediately."

"Yes, sir," said the wing commander. Then, after a moment, he asked, "So you think all this is related to fatigue?"

The group captain sucked on his pipe. "No, I don't."

Wing Commander Jones leaned forward in his chair.

"In addition to the reports made by your pilots," the group captain continued. "There have also been reports of dragons from members of the Observer Corps, from Home Guardsmen, even a few civilians—none of whom are suffering from fatigue."

"Surely you don't believe—"

"No, of course not. But I also can't ignore the fact that there have been some strange images showing up on our radar screens and two fighter planes that have burnt up without suffering a single bullet hole or mechanical malfunction."

"So what do you think it is, sir?"

The group captain's voice suddenly lowered. "The Germans have been doing a lot of tests with rockets. My guess is that they've either got a rocket-powered aeroplane or they've developed a way to use the blast of a rocket as an offensive weapon."

"But that's not possible."

"I wouldn't underestimate the Germans. They wouldn't have started this war if they weren't confident they had the weapons to win it."

Wing Commander Jones felt his heart sink into the pit of his stomach. He'd always been confident of a British victory, but suddenly wasn't so sure anymore. "What can we do about it?"

"Well, first thing is to keep your aeroplanes on the ground until scrambled by Fighter Command. No flight tests or training flights allowed."

Wing Commander Jones wanted to protest the order, but knew it would be pointless to do so.

"In the meantime I'll be asking RAF Intelligence to conduct an investigation into the matter. Who knows, maybe they even know what it is."

"Can I do anything to help?"

"Yes, you can," said the group captain. "Carry on day-to-day operations as you normally would and try to get the pilots' minds off of this dragon business. I don't want them any more afraid of stepping into the cockpit than they already are. It's bad enough they have to face the 109s, let alone a dragon."

"Yes, sir."

"Right, that's all."

The wing commander rose from his chair and saluted. After the group captain returned the salute, Jones spun around on his heels and left the office.

He felt somewhat relieved as he headed down the hallway. At least now responsibility for the dragon would be handled by another branch of the RAF. Maybe he and his men could get back to the job of beating back the Hun.

2

The steel dragons had come and gone.

There had been two, brown and green in color. The first had attacked with its steel spits, hitting Tibalt several times in the belly and wing, but he had suffered no serious injuries.

And then, after the first steel dragon had made its attack, Tibalt had turned on it, blasting it with his fiery breath and sending it falling to the ground in flames.

He had killed it.

The best the steel dragons could do was hurt him with tiny steel spits—little more than cuts and scrapes—but he on the other hand could kill the steel dragons with ease.

And, the steel dragons were afraid of him.

When he had turned on the second one, it had flown away, fearing for its life.

Tibalt felt surges of pride and power course through his body. The fool wizard's warning had been nothing more than words.

An empty threat.

Men grow stronger every day . . . They will conquer the earth . . . and eventually control the air . . .

Ridiculous!

Even if mortal men had anything to do with the steel dragons, they had no more control of the skies here than they'd had over the skies over Dervon.

He, Tibalt, ruled the sky.

All skies.

Always.

If he did not, then why had he not seen any other steel dragons approach after the first two?

Surely the wind, the drizzle falling from the dark cloudy skies, and the rough seas below were not enough to keep them out of the air. It had to be because they were afraid of him and his power to destroy them all.

Tibalt soared higher and higher, then dove straight down toward the water, sweeping over the waves before zooming straight up into the air. He finished with a slow roll so that anyone watching from the ground could see him in all his glory.

That will show them who rules the sky!

Still heady with power, but growing tired, Tibalt turned for land. He was hungry, as no doubt was the mortal girl back in the cave.

He adjusted his wings slightly and put himself into a long, shallow dive that would allow him to search the countryside for a suitable meal.

After a short time he was gliding over the treetops. Farmyards were scattered across the countryside and he was presented with several different possibilities in regards to food. He decided he was in the mood for beef.

With a slight movement of his wings, Tibalt turned right and swooped down over a pasture where several cattle were innocently chewing on their cud.

Without hesitation, he selected a target, brought his hind legs forward and opened his claws wide. In a single, swift motion, his claws clamped onto the body of the cow and it was lifted off the ground.

The cow let out a surprised *mooo.*

Some of the others in the herd also let out a *mooo* as they watched one of their kind being carried away, but they were soon back to chewing their cud as if nothing out of the ordinary had happened.

Tibalt flapped his great wings with long powerful strokes, easily clearing the stand of trees at the edge of the pasture. The cow tried to shake itself free of Tibalt's grasp, and let out another *mooo.* Tibalt squeezed his left claw, crushing the animal's windpipe and choking it to death.

It was a good-sized beast, thought Tibalt.

It would make a good meal.

3

Reichsmarshall Hermann Goering, Air Minister and Commander-in-Chief of the Luftwaffe, sat at one end of the table in the dining car of his personal train, *Asia.* The train was parked at the mouth of a tunnel, for protection against air attack, several kilometers east of the Pas de Calais.

Today's lunch consisted of a pheasant he had shot that morning in the French countryside. Normally, the Reichsmarshall gave specific instructions that he not be disturbed while dining, but recently a matter of some urgency had come to his attention and he was awaiting word from one of his SS generalmajors.

The Reichsmarshall had just begun eating when Generalmajor Erich Goetz entered the dining hall.

"Heil Hitler," said Goetz, saluting with a crack of his boot heels.

"Heil Hitler," said Reichsmarshall Goering, not bothering to salute or look up from his plate.

Goetz approached the table and stood at attention.

"Hungry?"

"No, Herr Riechsmarshall."

"Well, what is it?"

"The pilots who reported seeing it have all called it a dragon."

"A dragon?"

"Yes, Reichsmarshall. They said it was green and yellow and breathed fire."

Goering continued to eat. The bird was getting cold and if he stopped now it would soon become dry. "Could the British be testing an aircraft similar to the prototype 262s?"

"As far as we know, Reichsmarshall, a British engineer named Frank Whittle patented a turbojet engine in 1930, but he hasn't built an aircraft yet."

Goering quaffed a gulp of dark French wine, then finally looked up at Generalmajor Goetz. "Tell me, Eri," he said, using the generalmajor's nickname. "What do you think?"

Generalmajor Goetz straightened up and thrust out his chin. "I think the British are developing a new weapon that might change the course of the battle."

Goering's eyes narrowed on the young, blond-haired general-major who had flown with the Condor Legion in Spain and had become an ace over France. Surely he wouldn't make such a pronouncement lightly. Maybe the British did have a new weapon. "How many of these dragons have been seen so far?" asked Goering.

"Only one, Reichsmarshall."

Goering nodded. "Get rid of it, then."

The generalmajor stood in silence as if wondering what the Reichsmarshall had meant by that. Should it be shot out of the sky? Bombed on the ground?

"Dismissed," said Goering, resuming his meal.

Generalmajor Goetz hesitated a moment, then clicked his heels and saluted.

Goering continued eating.

Goetz turned on his heels and exited the dining car.

4

"You sent for me, sir?" said Flight Lieutenant Sheridan Ballard.

"Yes," said Air Commodore Trask. "Come in."

Ballard pushed the door in front of him fully open, then limped into the air commodore's office.

"How's your leg, then?" asked the commodore.

Ballard had bailed out of his Spitfire over the Channel eight weeks ago. When he exited his burning craft, he'd thought he'd jumped far enough to the side to clear the tailplane, but he hadn't. The Spitfire's rudder had struck his left leg, breaking it in three places and making his parachute landing excruciatingly painful. He'd worn a cast for six weeks and was now hobbling about with a slight limp. Currently, he was assigned to the Intelligence Office at Fighter Command Headquarters at Bentley Priory, an old Gothic house northwest of London, while he completed his recovery.

Ballard knew his services were desperately needed by Fighter Command and he himself was eager to get back into the air. If Douglas Bader could lead a squadron with two artificial legs, then he sure as hell could fly a Spitfire with one leg still on the mend. But despite his willingness to return to active duty, Fighter Command had given him more and more time to heal. Rumor had it that the order had come down from Air Chief Marshal Sir Hugh Dowding himself, all part of his plan of pacing the commitment of his forces and maintaining the ability to be able to continue the fight tomorrow and next week.

"I'm able to use it more every day," said Ballard, standing

straighter and surer to show the air commodore that his wounds had fully healed. "I'll be leading the squadron scramble in no time."

"Don't be so sure," muttered the air commodore.

"Am I being re-assigned?"

"Not exactly."

"Then what is it?"

Trask adjusted himself in his seat. "Have you heard the rumors about a dragon?"

Ballard laughed slightly. "Who hasn't? I've even heard that a few of the chaps at Biggin Hill have written a song about it."

Trask frowned.

The dragon story had become a bit of a joke among the pilots and ground crew. And the more the frontline men of the RAF found it a source of amusement, the more seriously it seemed to be taken by high command.

"Well, not everyone finds it so amusing."

"Oh, really."

"Yes, whatever this thing is, it's knocked two of our fighters out of the sky, killing both pilots. Not only that, it's also terrified every pilot who's seen it, to the point where they don't want to or can't get back into their aeroplanes."

Ballard was silent. Obviously this was a more serious problem than he'd been led to believe.

"What is it, then, sir?"

"We're not sure," said Trask. "The pilots and people on the ground who have seen it say it's a fire-breathing dragon—"

"You mean like the beast of legend?"

Trask was silent, obviously not wanting to answer the question. "From what we know of the German's research into rocketry, we believe it some sort of new weapon."

Ballard nodded. It was all quite fascinating, but he still wasn't quite sure why he was being told all this. "And what does this have to do with me, sir?"

"The dragon seems to be concentrating its activity around the area of Derbyshire. It's been spotted several times between there and the Channel coast. We need somebody to go up there and find out what the devil is going on."

Ballard was flattered that he'd been considered for what was obviously a very important job, but he really didn't like working for RAF Intelligence and taking on this assignment would likely keep him out of a fighter for several more weeks. The battle in the skies over England might be over by then.

"While I appreciate the fact that the RAF thinks I'm capable of conducting such a vital investigation, I really don't think I'm the right person for the job."

Trask said nothing. Instead, he opened a folder on his desk and looked over the few sheets of paper contained within it. "You attended Oxford, didn't you?"

"Yes sir."

"Studied paleontology while flying in the university's reserve squadron."

"That's right."

"Then you're the perfect man for the job."

Ballard sat there, thinking. The only way his schooling in paleontology would be of use would be if . . . "You think it's really a dragon, don't you?"

"We have to consider the possibility."

Ballard laughed. "I'm not sure I want to leave the fight for England to go looking through the countryside for a dragon, sir."

Air Commodore Trask's eyes narrowed and his lips pressed together into a thin white line. He looked at the flight lieutenant for a moment, then bellowed, "I don't care what you want," he said. "You are an officer in the RAF and you'll do as you're told."

Ballard sat up straight in his chair. "Yes, sir!"

CHAPTER FIVE

1

Tibalt circled the entrance to the cave twice, making sure there were no steel dragons in the surrounding skies. Although he had proven his mastery over them, they were still quite dangerous, especially since he now carried a full cow in his claws, making him more vulnerable to attack than ever. Also, landing at the mouth of the cave required that he fly in a slow, straight line which would make him defenseless for an extended period of time.

Sure that the skies were clear, Tibalt glided in for a landing, setting down at the mouth of the cave. The moment he'd stopped moving, he pushed the dead cow into the mouth of the cave until it rolled halfway into the entranceway. That done, he followed it inside, pushing it along until they were both deep inside the cave and comfortable in the lair he had called home overnight.

"I've brought you something to eat," said Tibalt, rending the cow's limbs from its body with powerful jerks of his hands. He swallowed a hindquarter whole, snapping his jaw at the air to work it down into his gullet.

"You must be hungry," he said with a devilish grin.

He sliced open the cow's belly with a single pass of one of its talons. Blood and entrails flowed out, which Tibalt lapped at hungrily before lifting the cow and biting off a chunk of its body. He chewed the bones a few times, crunching and snapping them in his mighty jaws, then swallowed the mass in a single gulp.

"Of course, humans don't eat raw meat, do they?" He was enjoying teasing Lavena. She must be ravenous to the point where the mere mention of food would be enough to make her mouth water.

"What would we need to cook the meat, then?" he said in the direction of the rock-covered hollow. "What's that you say? A fire? Where would we find fire in a dark, damp cave such as this?"

Tibalt paused a moment, laughing quietly to himself while listening for Lavena pleading to get out.

But the cave was silent.

"Oh, I know," he said, mockingly. "Dragons breathe fire, don't they. I could breathe fire onto this hind leg here and cook this meat for you." He picked up the remaining hind leg and blew a gentle stream of fire onto it. In seconds the meat began to cook, filling the cave with a delicious aroma.

"Hungry now?" he said, leaning an ear in the direction of the hollow.

The cave remained silent.

Suddenly it occurred to Tibalt that the girl might have died inside the hollow, from thirst or hunger, from the cold, or by suffocation. He tossed aside the hindquarter and rushed to the hollow. With a single swift motion he pulled the large rock from the entrance and looked with astonishment at the open hole before him.

Empty.

Somehow the girl had escaped.

And not only did she escape, but she managed to get away without moving the rock. Surely she was the wizard's apprentice.

Anger roiled up from within Tibalt's belly. He'd been

thoroughly deceived by a mortal, and if that wasn't bad enough he'd been left alone in this mysterious place to mend and fend for himself.

He raised his head and let out an angry roar. Fire spewed out from his maw and splashed against the cave's ceiling like water.

He vowed that when he found the girl again, he would kill her . . . slowly.

2

Lavena was weary. She'd had nothing to eat and only a few drops of water to drink since she'd left the cave. But in that entire time she'd been on the move.

It wouldn't have been so bad if she'd had a sense that she knew where she was going. If she were walking to get to someplace she would be spurred on and able to push herself farther than she already had. But instead, she seemed to be walking in circles. She'd come across the same landmarks several times, each encounter more disappointing than the last.

The countryside was tremendously frustrating here. There were places that she swore she recognized as being just outside of Dervon, but as she approached the rock formations the lay of the land seemed to change slightly until she was utterly lost.

This last formation had been just like the others. From a distance it looked very much like the rocks she had hidden within to escape Tibalt's first attack on her. But as she neared the rocks they appeared much different than she remembered. Some were gone, others added and the largest of them looked as if it had broken in two, the top falling to the ground and disappearing as it crumbled into countless little pieces.

She approached the rocks slowly, her feet dragging behind her. Where in the world was she? A place that looked so much like Dervon, and yet was not Dervon? She sat down on one of the larger rocks and rested her head in her hands.

It had been bad enough to lose Warrick to the dragon, but now she had lost everything—her family, her village . . . everything—all because she tried to stop the dragon from destroying the village.

Perhaps the village had been saved, she thought. Wherever it might be.

She looked out over the empty countryside and resisted the urge to cry.

Her situation seemed hopeless. But then again, all had seemed lost in the cave and she had escaped from there. Whatever had happened on the plain was not yet finished. She knew that, somehow. And somehow, she knew that she would have to find the strength to carry on and see this to an end—good or bad.

She rose up from the rock and began walking in a direction she hadn't yet tried.

After a time she came upon what looked to be a settlement of some kind. There was a large grey building at the top of a slight hill. As she neared the building she realized it was made of wood and surrounded by a long line of wooden fence. She climbed over the fence and ran toward the building.

It was a farmyard with rabbits and chickens running freely around the yard. She stepped quietly between the animals and found an entrance to the building. It creaked open and in the cool darkness inside she smelled the unmistakable scent of animals and straw.

She entered and padded about. There was a cow inside one of the stalls, her udders full and heavy. Quickly, Lavena took a pail from where it hung on the wall and began drawing milk.

The cow let out a *moo* of protest at Lavena's initial and somewhat clumsy efforts to milk it.

"Sorry, milady," she said, nodding gracefully, then trying a more gentle approach.

Soon, the animal settled down and Lavena slipped into an easy rhythm. When she was done, Lavena drank the milk in a hurried series of gulps, spilling much of it down her front. When she was done, she still felt hungry, but the worst of the pangs were gone. She looked down, drew her foot across the dirt floor to hide the milk she had spilled, then looked up to the loft.

It was full of fresh straw and looked soft, warm and inviting. She decided to take a closer look. After all, she could do with some rest before setting out again.

She hung up the pail back on its spot on the wall and climbed the wooden ladder that led to the loft. Once there, she stretched out over the straw, something she couldn't do inside the hollow, and closed her eyes.

3

Pilot Officers Donovan and Hall stood at the edge of the airfield at Hawkinge and looked out at the dark clouds forming over the Channel.

The two fliers, as well as the rest of the squadron, had been on stand-by most of the day, but as the weather got worse and no activity had been reported on the French side of the Channel, the call came prohibiting flights the rest of the day.

Good news for Donovan and Hall who had seen three of their closest friends die in the last week—two to the Germans and the other to a landing accident. Being ordered to remain on the ground was like being granted another day of life.

They celebrated by opening the bottle of brandy Donovan had been keeping under wraps since his days in France. Originally, the bottle had been intended for his victory celebration at the end of the war, but after seeing so many pilots being killed—many of them better fliers than himself—he decided he might not live long enough to sample the brandy. It was better, he reasoned, to enjoy the bottle while he could and today seemed to be as good a day as any.

"Sure glad I'm not flying today," said Hall, motioning to the darkening sky.

Donovan took a sip, one of many he'd had in the last few minutes, and reveled as it burned its way down his throat and into his belly, making him feel warm all over. "I know what you mean. I have enough trouble setting my Spit down on a clear day, I can just see me sliding across the airfield in this cross-wind."

"That's not what I meant," said Hall, taking the bottle from Donovan and taking a gulp.

"You telling me you want to fly in that!"

"I don't want to fly today, clear weather or foul."

"What are you talking about?" said Donovan, snatching the bottle from his friend.

"The dragon the others've been talking about. Sounds like a horrible thing."

"The dragon—" Donovan looked at Hall quizzically, wondering how he could say such a thing when the bottle was still more than half full. "You mean to tell me you believe that nonsense."

"It's not nonsense," said Hall.

Donovan took a swig. "Look, there it is there. The dragon!"

Hall sat upright and craned his neck to search the sky. "Where? Where is it?"

"Here it is!" laughed Donovan, holding out the bottle. "Have some more of this and you'll be seeing flying elephants too."

Hall refused the bottle.

"Suit yourself," said Donovan, taking another sip. "More for myself, that's all."

Hall said nothing.

"My guess is that in another hour I'll spot a whole squadron of dragons. Maybe I should gather up a few buckets of water so's I can beat them back, ha!" Donovan laughed long and hard at that, rolling back onto the grass and clutching his stomach.

Hall got up and headed back to the readiness-room.

Donovan watched Hall leave, then took another sip of brandy. For some reason, it didn't taste as good as it had a few minutes before.

4

When his anger subsided, Tibalt finished the cow and ventured to the mouth of the cave with the intention of taking to the skies in search of more to eat.

But when he poked his head out of the mouth of the cave, his head was dappled by rain that, from the looks of the clouds overhead, was only going to grow stronger. So rather than risk flying through a storm, Tibalt decided to go back down to the bottom of the cave for a rest.

Now that he was settled in his lair, he found he couldn't get comfortable. His wings seemed to ache and there were parts of his body that felt cold, as if his insides had been laid bare to the elements.

At first Tibalt thought that he might have ingested a diseased cow and its poison was now working its evil on him. But after checking his limbs and body he realized that his aches and pains were too localized to be caused by bad food.

No, although he wished not to admit it, the steel dragons had hurt him before he'd been able to destroy them. He'd been hit by a few steel spits and now they were festering inside his body.

And what was worse was that now he didn't even have the girl to help him. Tibalt would have to heal himself. He raised his left wing, stretched it out as far as it would go, then lifted it up—stopping abruptly as he let out a sharp cry of pain. After a moment, he brought the wing forward so he could take a closer look at its underside.

Most of the old wounds had stopped bleeding, but there were several new spots on his body that ached, including one at the joint of his left wing and body. Tibalt looked for the exact spot, but couldn't see well enough in the darkness to find it. Although some light filtered down through the opening to the cave, there was hardly enough of it to see something as small as a wound made by a steel spit.

He took a deep, deep breath, then slowly exhaled, allowing a small but constant flame to escape the narrow opening at the end of his maw.

Now, with the added light from the flame to aid his sight, Tibalt was able to find the trouble spot. A steel spit had wedged between two of the scales near the root of his left wing causing one of the scales to dig into his flesh whenever he moved the wing.

He brought his right hand up to the wound and scratched at the scales. To his surprise, one of them peeled away from his body and fluttered to the floor of the cave like a snowflake. He picked up the scale and looked at it under the light from the flame. Its color was off. Instead of a rich blue or vibrant green, it was a pale greyish blue. Obviously the steel dragons were taking their toll on him.

He let the scale fall to the cave floor, then used one of his talons like a knife to gouge the steel spit from where it lay within his flesh. As he did so, a second scale was torn away. Finally, the steel spit came out. It fell to the floor and tinked and clinked its way to the bottom of the cave.

He took another deep breath and picked up the second scale from where it lay at his feet. For a moment, as he looked over the scale, he was touched by fear.

Who was here to help him?

There wasn't another dragon in sight.

And the girl had run away.

What bothered him most about that was that it had been his own fault. The girl had tried to help him from the start, first by contacting the wizard, then by helping to heal him the first time he'd been wounded.

Tibalt sat in silence for a moment, contemplating his situation. While it was true that the girl had helped him, she had also brought him to this cursed place. That meant that it had been her doing, all of it, and whatever hardships she'd had to endure because of her own foolishness were totally deserved.

Tibalt shook his head and chuffed a tiny ball of fire at the mound of hot rocks to his right. If it hadn't been for the meddling girl and the old fool of a wizard he'd have razed the village of Dervon and been on his way.

Anger roiled within him once more, gathering more strength than ever before.

He would make them pay for what they had done to him.

All of them.

5

Flight Lieutenant Ballard was briefed on the weather conditions by the forecasters at Bentley Priory and decided he might as well risk the flight since delaying his investigation by a single day, especially one in which no one was flying and all aircrews were safely on the ground, would be a wasted day that could end up costing lives.

He could have driven to Derbyshire, but with all the stops by Home Guardsmen along the way, he'd be lucky to reach his destination before nightfall. And then with the blackouts in effect he'd be lucky to find the steering wheel in the dark.

The forecasters had told him he'd be all right if he left within the hour, but if he waited any longer, he'd be denied permission to take off. And so he'd packed what he thought he might need over the next few days and hurried to the airfield at Northolt

where an army co-operative unit kept several Westland Lysanders ready for use as command staff transports.

As he rode out to the plane, Ballard wondered if there might
be anything to this dragon. So far, the people he'd spoken to
about it had been split into thirds, one third believing it to be a
beast, one third believing it to be a German secret weapon, and
another third thinking it was nothing but fatigue on the part of
the pilots.

Ballard almost wished there were another explanation for the
dragon. After all, it didn't bode well for England if its pilots
were so strained that they'd begun to see things in the air.
Likewise, if it were a new German weapon, then England's days
were numbered. And finally, if it were just a silly story, a hoax,
it reflected poorly on the state of the population and the effect
that the war was having on them.

He was hoping it was nothing more than a large bird, or
natural weather phenomenon, or maybe a barrage balloon that
had gone untethered and floated into a squadron's flight path—
anything that could be easily explained.

As they neared the line of Lysanders at one end of the field,
Ballard saw that the ground crew had already prepared one of
the planes and were patiently awaiting his arrival. Seeing the
men standing there, Ballard began to get a better sense of the
urgency of his mission. He'd flown co-operative aircraft before,
but he'd never been sent off in such a rush.

The driver pulled to a stop next to the aeroplane and said,
"Good luck."

Ballard looked at him a moment, wondering if the man knew
anything about his mission.

The driver must have noticed a bewildered look on Ballard's
face because he was compelled to explain himself. "Nasty
weather for a flight," he said, pointing his thumb skyward.

"Oh, yes," said Ballard. "But I'll be all right."

"Good luck, just the same, sir."

Ballard closed the door and the driver sped away. He turned to face the aeroplane and examined it. The Lysander was a far cry from the Spitfire and had been given the nickname "The Flying Carrot" by the men who'd flown it. It had a high parasol-type wing, spatted fixed landing gear and a round, stubby nose. But while it was no match for an Me-109 or even an Me-110, it performed its job of ferrying passengers quite adequately. Just the same, it was a good thing he didn't expect to run into any enemy aircraft on this flight. If he did, he'd likely have to bail out before they'd even fired a shot.

"Sure you want to take her up in this?" said one of the ground crew as he began stowing his gear in the canopied section behind the cockpit.

"I've my orders," said Ballard, remembering the stern words of Air Commodore Trask.

"Going to join the squadron at Digby, then," said the crewman. "I heard they've been hit bad."

"No, I . . . ," said Ballard, stopping a moment to wonder if he should say anything more to the man or not. The longer he thought about it the more he realized that half the RAF had heard some rumor or another about a dragon, so he might as well find out what the men on the ground in Northolt had heard. "Actually, I'm flying up to Digby to find a dragon."

"You mean that new German superplane they've been talking about?"

Ballard looked at the crewman in surprise. "What do you know about it?"

"Only that it flies without an engine, has armor plating everywhere and it can knock our boys out of the sky with a stream of fire from the cannon in its nose."

Ballard was impressed. Word of the dragon had reached London with most of the details still fairly accurate. "That's what I've heard too," he said as he slipped into the pilot's seat.

The crewman helped Ballard with his belts.

When he was securely strapped in, Ballard nodded to the crewman, who then moved out of the way and prepared to close Ballard into the plane. But just before he sealed him in, the crewman looked at Ballard and said, "Hope you find it before it finds you."

The groundcrew closed the cabin door.

And a chill ran down Ballard's spine.

CHAPTER SIX
Monday, August 5, 1940

1

Flight Lieutenant Ballard had arrived at Digby just before nightfall and just after the storm front that had been threatening the eastern part of England for much of the day.

He'd been met by a driver and staff car on the airfield and was quickly driven to the squadron's Ops Office where he was briefed on the dragon by Digby's squadron leaders and given a stack of written reports of sightings in the area—by pilots, Home Guardsmen and civilians. From there he was driven to a manor house on the outskirts of Derbyshire which was to serve as his base of operations during the course of his investigation. The driver had been instructed to leave the car with Ballard and managed to hop a ride back to the airfield on a troop lorry on its way to London.

The manor house had six bedrooms, modern conveniences and a housekeeper named Clary Norris who was looking after the house while its owners followed the current battle from a safe distance—New York City to be exact.

Mrs. Norris greeted Ballard with tea and biscuits, which he accepted and quite enjoyed. Later, when he was finished eating, she seemed eager to leave him alone to his work. "I'm sure you've got important business to attend to, flying up here from Bentley Priory and all."

"Thank you," he said, "but I'd just like to go to my room."

He hefted the stack of reports. "I've a lot of reading to do before morning."

Mrs. Norris nodded and said, "Follow me."

She showed him to his room, and then was gone. Ballard quickly changed into his nightclothes, slipped into bed and began working his way through the reports, falling asleep in the middle of an account by a Mrs. Edna Abernathy who chastised the dragon for trampling through her vegetable garden.

When he awoke the next morning at five (a habit he'd fallen into while on ops with his squadron) Mrs. Norris was there in the kitchen, a hot pot of tea and warm toast and jam waiting for him on the table.

"You're amazing, Mrs. Norris," said Ballard, biting into his toast.

"Listen, son," she said with a touch of humility in her voice. "There's nothing amazing about rolling out of bed in the dark and making a man's breakfast. Not when you compare it to young men like you rolling out of bed in the dark, climbing into an aeroplane, and getting yourself killed in defense of Mother England."

Ballard said nothing. What *could* he say in response to that? Instead, he decided that in future he would express his gratitude to Mrs. Norris by simply saying "thank you."

He took another bite of toast. "Thank you," he said.

"You're welcome," she answered with a smile.

2

Lavena woke along with the sun as its rays peeked through the cracks between the wooden boards on the east side of the building. After a long cat-like stretch of her limbs, she scampered down from the loft, a little refreshed and very hungry. When she was sure that no one was about, she took the bucket off the wall and had herself another drink of warm milk. As before, the milk took away some, but not all, of her hunger, which meant that finding something to eat was still a going concern.

She thanked her friend the cow, who acknowledged her with a soft *moo*, then set out across the countryside in search of . . . what, she didn't know. She needed help, that was obvious, but who would give it to her? Who could she trust?

As she came to the edge of a field, she saw that past the fence there was a wide, smooth road that stretched into the distance. She'd come across them before, but none as long and as straight as this one. She decided to walk along it, reasoning that whoever had taken the trouble to make the ground so flat and so smooth must have done it for a reason. That reason, she guessed, was to make it easier for people to travel to and from some great town or village. So she decided to follow it, hoping that her guess would turn out to be right.

Just then she heard a buzzing in the sky.

She looked up and saw two birds flying through the air, one next to the other, their wings not moving. It was hard to see, but there seemed to be something on the nose of the bird that helped it to fly. They were noisy birds, droning loudly at the effort it took to remain in the sky.

She watched them approach, growing louder and larger by the second. They were brown and green for the most part, with a whitish underbelly and a black pointed nose. On each wing were large colorful circles that looked a little like eyes.

And then all at once she realized that these must be the steel dragons Tibalt had mentioned to her in the cave.

Fear gripped her body and her heart leaped up into her throat as she watched them swoop down on her, the noise they made shaking her insides and the ground around her. She leaped off the road and ran toward a nearby growth of bushes.

The steel dragons roared overhead, then waggled their wings as they flew away.

Lavena remained crouched in the bushes, trying to catch her breath. Such large and noisy creatures, she thought, and able to spit steel too.

Tibalt was a fool not to fear such creatures.

At last her breathing returned to normal and her heart settled back down into her chest. She looked out from the bushes and up and down the road she'd been walking along.

All seemed clear.

She stepped out onto the road and began walking again, only to hear a sharp whistle blowing in the distance.

What wonders were to be found in this place? she thought. What impossible devices had been devised by man and beast?

The whistle blew again.

Across the fields to her left, a great white plume of smoke rose up from the horizon. The whistling had stopped, but had been replaced by a chuffing, chugging sound like the dragon sometimes made.

Up ahead, the road opened up slightly and was crossed by a pair of steel rails as shiny as two newly honed swords. She looked along the length of the rails and saw a huge metal monster approaching from the left. It was gliding along the rails as if it were riding on air. And behind it, there were many boxes, all joined together making the beast look like one huge serpent.

A steel serpent, she thought. Steel serpents on the ground, steel dragons in the air.

She ran toward the growth of trees that lined the right side of the road and hid behind one of the larger ones. She waited there for the steel serpent to pass. As it went by, Lavena could only watch it with wide eyes and an open mouth. It was so big, so powerful, and so loud . . .

She sat in the woods for a long time after it was gone, marveling at what she'd seen.

When all was quiet and peace had returned to the woods, she

continued on her way, wondering . . .

Will the wonders of this place never cease?

3

Just after six that morning Ballard got into the staff car and headed west to the town of Burton-Upon-Trent where an Air Raid Warden had reported seeing a dragon circle the northern part of the town, then fly off in a northeastern direction toward Derby.

The Air Raid Warden's description of the dragon wasn't very detailed, but he wanted to ask the man a few questions since, as an Air Raid Warden, he'd spent the last few months watching the sky and could no doubt tell the difference between a Dornier and a dragon.

Ballard pulled up to a small cottage by the River Trent and knocked on the door. It was a peaceful morning, with a warm sun in the sky and birds singing in the nearby trees.

The war seemed a million miles away.

"Who's there?" came a voice from inside.

"Flight Lieutenant Ballard, RAF," he said. "I need to ask you a few questions."

"About what?"

"About a dragon."

"Right."

The door opened a moment later and in the doorway stood a frail old man with a withered face and thin white hair, dressed in a jacket and tie, and wearing a steel helmet with the letters ARP painted across the front.

"Are you Sam Wheedle?" asked Ballard.

"That's right."

"Mr. Wheedle, I'm investigating the dragon sightings in the area."

"I seen it, I did."

"Yes, of course. Now I've read your report, but I was wondering if there was anything else you'd like to add to it."

"Like what?"

"Well, you described in your report that you saw a *dragonlike* aeroplane in the northeast."

"That's right."

"I thought you might want to speculate on what this dragonlike aeroplane was."

"I wanted to say what I thought it was, but the Regional Commissioner wouldn't let me. He said there was no way a 109 had the range to get this deep into England without falling out of the sky. He also thought we shouldn't try too hard to identify it in case it was a new British weapon."

"Nonsense," said Ballard, shaking his head. "What did *you* think it was, then?"

Mr. Wheedle looked left and right, as if he thought the conversation might be overheard by spies or nosy neighbors. "With that big scoop under its nose, them big bent wings, and the two front feet hanging down near the wing roots, it had to be a Stuka."

"A Stuka," repeated Ballard.

"That's right, a green-and-blue Stuka."

The Stuka was the gull-winged dive-bomber the Germans had used so effectively in the *Blitzkrieg* in Poland. The large, slow, and lightly armed plane could have made it this far inland, but not back across the Channel. The Regional Commissioner had been right on that account, but the old man's description was a good fit against the other descriptions of the dragon. Some Stukas even had shark's teeth and eyes painted on their noses. But, as plausible an explanation as it was, it still didn't explain why an already vulnerable aeroplane would be painted green and blue, or how it suddenly became such a devastating match for the faster, nimbler and more heavily armed Hurricanes and Spitfires.

"You said it flew away from here in a northeastern direction."

"That's right, toward Derby," said Mr. Wheedle, pointing into the sky.

"Thank you for your time, Mr. Wheedle," said Ballard.

"You believe me, don't you?"

Ballard sighed, realizing the sighting had probably caused the man to question his own sanity. "Of course I do sir," he said. "I wouldn't have come all this way if I didn't."

Mr. Wheedle smiled at that. "Thanks, son," he said with a wink.

Ballard got in the staff car and headed northeast, first along the Vale of Trent, then turning north toward a small farm West of Derby. There, halfway between Derby and Stoke-on-Trent, he visited the dairy farm of a Mr. and Mrs. Roy Crowell, who had reported to the local constabulary that one of their cows had been snatched away from one of their fields by a flying monster.

"What do you want?" asked an angry Roy Crowell, who greeted Ballard at the door of his farmhouse with a rifle of Great War vintage cradled in his arms.

"I'd like to speak to you about the dragon that took one of your cows."

"Is that what you call it?" Crowell said through the screen door. "A dragon?"

"Well, that's the word people have used to describe it . . . people other than yourselves, of course." The Crowells had reported that their cow had been snatched up by a large bird of prey.

"You know anything about my cow?"

"No sir, I don't."

"I told you it was gone, mum," Crowell said over his shoulder to his wife who was hovering about back in the kitchen. "I knew it was gone."

"Perhaps you could describe the, uh, bird of prey."

"Sure," said Crowell. He pointed the gun toward the ground, opened the screen door and stepped out of his house. He walked down to the rock wall bordering the north end of the grounds and then pointed to the fields that stretched out to the north. "It came out of the sky without a sound, swooping down over the field as if it were singling out one of the cows. It slowed up some as it neared a group of about six cows, and then it reached out with these huge claws and picked up one of my best Herefords like it was nothing more than some fish in a pond."

"Picked it up while it was flying?"

"That's right. Snatched it right up, then started flapping its wings. Three or four strokes and it was out of sight, cow and all."

Ballard took a moment to envision it, but was having trouble picturing such a large and powerful bird. "What color was it?"

"Black and white."

"No, not the cow. I mean the . . ." He was about to say dragon, but stopped himself in time. "The bird."

"Blue and green," said Crowell. "Strangest bird I've ever seen too."

Ballard nodded. "Indeed."

As they walked back to the house, Ballard felt compelled to ask the farmer one last question. "Why do you carry the gun around with you, Mr. Crowell. The Germans don't intend to invade England until they've won the battle in the skies."

"This was for the Germans in 1918," said Crowell. "Now it's for that bloody bird. If I see it again I'll shoot it full of holes."

"But I didn't see any cows in your fields."

"No, I've got them all inside my barns, behind the house there, and over that ridge to the north. I won't be letting them out until the beastie's dead."

"A wise move, Mr. Crowell."

"Will you be killing it if you see it?"

Ballard was caught off-guard by the question. He'd been so concerned with simply finding out if the dragon existed that he hadn't given any thought to what he might do to it if and when he'd actually crossed its path. "I don't know."

"Well, if you find it, you can be rest assured that it won't be wondering if it should kill you or not."

"Yes, sir," said Ballard.

He left Crowell to his dragon watching and continued in a northeast direction around the outskirts of Derby and toward the village of Hucknall where Mrs. Edna Abernathy had seen a dragon in her garden.

As he neared Hucknall, Ballard came upon a man driving a large green tractor toward the village. Since the address and directions to Mrs. Abernathy's cottage were a little vague, he decided to stop and ask the man on the tractor for help.

He drove past the tractor, then pulled to the side of the road ahead of it. He got out and waved his arms over his head until the driver slowed the tractor and brought it to a stop behind Ballard's staff car.

"Afternoon," Ballard said.

"Afternoon," said the man.

"I was wondering if you might help me find my way."

"Be my pleasure to help an RAF flier," said the man.

"I'm looking for . . ."

Lavena had seen two more steel dragons, but no other steel serpents. She had also come across a few farmhouses and had desperately wanted to go to them asking for food, but she couldn't bring herself to beg. She'd done her best with the pine nuts and berries she'd come across in the woods, but they were a far cry from a fresh loaf of bread and a thick piece of cheese.

As she continued on through the forest, wondering where she might sleep after dark, she heard a rattle and thrum coming down the road behind her. Considering the beasts she'd seen, she had decided to stay in the woods for the rest of the day. There didn't seem to be any steel creatures among the trees and she could move along quickly enough if she kept the roads within her sight.

As the noise grew louder, she moved to the edge of the woods to be closer to the road. She positioned herself behind a sturdy spruce and waited for the rattling noisemaker to approach.

Through the trees she could see the head of a man, moving toward her at a speed that suggested he was riding atop a horse. However, his head did not rise and fall, but stayed in place as if he were riding on a cart.

Intrigued, she stuck her head further out from behind the tree and saw that he was riding a sort of wheeled horse, a green one that snorted and puffed white smoke as it moved along the road. Obviously, this was a steel horse, comparable to the steel dragons and steel serpent she'd seen.

But then there was another steel horse coming down the road. This one was black with large eyes out front and no man riding upon its back. It passed the green horse at a high speed, then slowed in front of it until it stopped at the side of the road.

And then, to Lavena's utter astonishment, a man climbed out of the belly of the steel horse. His clothes were the color of the sky and judging by the decorations on his shoulders and chest, his dress was some sort of uniform.

A handsome man, he reminded Lavena a little of Warrick.

He began waving at the man riding the steel horse, causing him to stop at the side of the road. The green steel horse let out a puff of white smoke, then rattled its last and was silent.

"Afternoon," said the young man.

"Afternoon," said the older.

"I was wondering if you might help me find my way."

"Be my pleasure to help an RAF flier."

"I'm looking for a Mrs. Edna Abernathy. Do you know her?"

The older man laughed. "Aye, she's a spunky old maid."

"Can you tell me how to find her?"

"Now that depends."

"On what?"

"On what kind of news you've got for her. If it's bad you best tell me and I'll tell her myself."

"No, it's nothing like that. I want to ask her about the dragon she saw the other day."

Lavena gasped at the mention of the dragon.

"Are you looking for it, then?" said the older man.

"Yes. Have you seen it?"

"No, I haven't. But there's plenty around here what have."

"I intend to talk to all of them."

"All right, then. If you're looking for Edna's cottage you follow this road . . ."

The two men began walking away from Lavena and she couldn't hear what they were saying. It didn't matter, really. All that mattered was that one of them was looking for the dragon. That meant that she could help him, and in exchange he could help her.

She wanted to run out onto the road, but she was too afraid to do it.

This was such a *different* place . . .

Lavena stayed where she was, hidden by the trees and the grass of the forest, and was gripped by fear. She watched the men shake hands, then ride away *on* and *in* their steel horses, and realized the moment was lost.

She wanted to help the younger man, but what if she led him to Tibalt and the dragon killed him? Then she'd have the black marks of two young warriors' deaths on her soul. Or, she could lead him to the dragon, only to have him kill it. That wouldn't do either since all this trouble was caused by her wish to save the dragon's life. Killing it now would make it *all* so meaningless.

And yet, she couldn't roam the countryside like a lost lamb forever. If there were such things as steel dragons and steel serpents and steel horses here, she was in danger every moment she was on her own. Eventually she'd have to approach someone and ask them for help and shelter. And if that was the case, she might as well approach the man who was searching for the dragon. She had knowledge that was useful to him, and that would be reason enough for him to help her.

At last she decided.

She would help the young man . . .

She looked up and down the empty road.

. . . If she ever saw him again.

4

"Silly old country bumpkin," muttered Flight Lieutenant Ballard under his breath. "You can't miss it, he said." Ballard slapped the steering wheel with his hand. "Well, somehow I missed it. Top honors at navigation school and I missed it."

The farmer had given him what had seemed like simple directions, much of which depended on seeing a sign for the Dove River which would indicate the road he needed to turn onto. All well and good, but the Home Guardsmen in the area had taken down all the road signs in order to confuse German paratroops who would be trying to find their way. Again, all well and good, but the move wasn't going to confuse any German paratroopers who were currently stationed in Germany!

And now, with an hour lost he was driving back along the same road, hoping to find the old farmer, or anyone for that matter, who could help him find Mrs. Edna Abernathy.

He stepped harder on the accelerator, intent on making up for lost time.

"You can't miss it, he said . . ."

After walking for a time through the forest without seeing or hearing another steel creature, Lavena decided to move onto the road. It was easier to walk on for one, and if she was out on the road, there was a better chance that she would cross paths with the man in the black steel horse.

She'd been on the road only a short while when she heard a soft rumble, like that of a cat purring contentedly by a fire. She looked around her, up and down the road, but saw nothing.

And yet the noise grew louder.

She looked around one more time, and then behind her.

Suddenly the black steel horse crested a rise in the road and was bearing down upon her with great speed.

She ran, but her tired legs and aching feet could not move fast enough to avoid the oncoming beast.

It was closer now, the sound of a once-purring kitten had grown into the roar of a some great bear.

Lavena ran left and right and the beast matched her movements, intent on running her down.

And then it *honked*.

It was a silly sound, like a duck that was quite ill.

Honk! Honk! barked the beast.

It was such a funny little sound for such a large and powerful creature that Lavena found herself turning to look at the steel horse to see if it were carrying another steel creature on its back. As she twisted around, she stumbled over her own feet and fell heavily to the ground.

The steel horse grew larger, its front end looking more and more menacing with each passing moment.

Lavena closed her eyes and prepared for the worst.

But then the steel horse stopped, its wheels digging into the dirt of the road as if they were claws. A moment later the droning sound of the steel horse stopped as well and all was quiet.

Lavena did not move.

The side of the steel horse opened up then, and a young man got out of its belly. The same young man that had been looking for the dragon.

"Are you all right?" said the young man. "I'm so sorry, I was going too fast and didn't see you until I came up over the rise. I hope I didn't startle you."

Lavena slowly got to her feet.

The man helped her up.

"Can I give you a lift somewhere?"

She stared at him a moment, saying nothing. He was a very handsome young man, and up close, reminded her of Warrick even more.

"I say, you're not hurt, are you?" There was a worried look on his face.

But instead of answering his question, she opened her mouth and said, "I know where the dragon is."

CHAPTER SEVEN

1

They climbed into the steel horse and to Lavena's surprise, the inside was made of soft cloth and had comfortable chairs to sit on.

The young man moved his feet against some levers, pushed a small button on the board in front of them and the steel horse suddenly came to life. It shook as if it trembled with fear, and yet each time the young man pushed one of the levers with his foot, it roared with a sort of power.

"I'm Flight Lieutenant Sheridan Ballard," he said. "Who are you?"

"Lavena."

He smiled warmly at that. "That's a pretty name," he said, his eyes moving over her body as he spoke. He put his hands on the big wheel in front of him and said, "Which way is the dragon?"

She smiled at him a moment, wanting to tell him, but knowing that her need for food was stronger than his need to know where the dragon was.

"Which way?" he said again, indicating the road they were on with a sweep of his hand.

She hesitated another moment, then said, "Do you have anything to eat?"

"Of course," he said. "Where are my manners?" He reached for the seat behind him and lifted a large bag into his lap. "Mrs.

Norris prepared a lunch for me, but I haven't had the time to eat it. Help yourself."

Lavena opened the bag and marveled at what was inside—bread and biscuits, an apple and a pear, a slice of cheese, and what looked to be a container of ale. She took one of the bread buns and bit into it. She didn't wish to look unladylike, but she couldn't help herself. She was so hungry, and the bread tasted so good, that she quickly put as much of it as would fit into her mouth.

"Easy now," said the man. "There's no rush. Take your time and have as much as you like."

She took him up on his offer, scooping another piece of bread from the bag as well as the piece of cheese. She also ate these quickly, but with a little less urgency than before. When she at last bit into the apple, she did so slowly, enjoying the fruit's sweetness on her tongue.

"Now, Lavena," said the man, still smiling but obviously wanting to get moving. "Which way?"

She pointed forward.

"All right, then," said the man. "We're on our way."

He moved a lever with his hand, then pumped the pedals at his feet and miraculously the steel horse began moving.

Lavena's last pangs of hunger were taken over by sheer excitement. She stopped eating the apple and watched the countryside pass her by.

They traveled for a short while before coming upon another road crossing the one they were on. The young man, Ballard, brought the steel horse to a stop and said, "Which way is it now?"

Lavena looked left and right along the intersecting road, but didn't recognize it as one she had crossed before. Everything looked so different from inside the steel horse.

"Well?"

Lavena took another look around, this time studying the countryside more closely. But it was no use, the longer she looked the less certain she was about her location.

She glanced over at the young man and could tell that he was growing impatient with her. She had to make up her mind soon or he wouldn't believe anything she had to tell him about the dragon.

Just then, something in the distance caught her eye. It was a grey-brown rock wall that was somewhat similar to the wall she had seen edging one of the farms she had crossed earlier in the day.

"That way," she said.

He placed both hands firmly on the wheel, but before he put the car into motion, he turned to her and said, "Are you sure?"

She was tempted to tell him the truth and say *no*, but she knew that would ruin what little trust he had left in her. She nodded, pointed, then said again, "That way!"

He seemed pleased by that and Lavena thought it funny that she had to lie to him in order to maintain his trust.

"That way," he said, smiling. He worked the lever and pedals of the steel horse and turned the wheel to the right.

They turned the corner and were on their way.

Lavena only hoped it was the right way.

Flight Lieutenant Ballard felt a little unsettled.

First of all, he hadn't been able to get a consistent description of the dragon from any of the eyewitnesses he'd interviewed. If their stories were to be believed, the dragon he was looking for was either a brightly colored German dive-bomber or a huge bird of prey that snatched cows out of pastures like children plucking cookies out of a jar. Maybe it was just as well he didn't interview Mrs. Edna Abernathy and the rest of them.

Now he was driving around with a young woman who

claimed to know where the dragon was. She seemed sincere and sane for the most part, but her shredded clothes and disheveled appearance looked more at home in a Charles Dickens novel than in 1940 England—war or no war. She was nervous and skittish too, looking around the inside of the staff car as if she'd never seen a motorcar before. And when she wasn't marveling over the car, she had her head out the window, enjoying the wind in her face like a dog he used to have.

The saddest thing about it all was that he had to take this woman at her word. If she said she could take him to the dragon, then he had to believe her. After all, if the other witnesses on his list were anything like the first two he'd spoken to, then she might be his only hope.

They came upon another crossroads. She seemed to have difficulty with them, always unsure about which way to go.

"Left or right," he said.

"Left," she said, pointing west.

"We've already been down that way."

"Then, right."

"You're sure."

She nodded.

"Fine," said Ballard.

He turned right, deciding that if she wasn't able to give him any surer directions in the next thirty minutes he would stop the car, let her out and resume the investigation on his own.

He drove on for twenty minutes, turning left and right when she told him to, but not getting any sense that they were any closer to the dragon than when they had begun.

"Left here," she said, "that way."

Ballard looked left. It was another road he'd driven down before, except heading in the other direction. He let out a sigh.

"Look, miss," he said. "I realize that you probably have the best of intentions but—"

"That way!" she said. There was a strength and confidence in her voice that hadn't been evident before.

Ballard decided to give her a bit more time and turned left.

A few minutes later, she was sitting up straight in her seat trying to see over the rises in the road. There was an expectant look on her face.

They crested a slight hill.

"Stop!" she said.

Ballard applied the brakes and the wheels dug into the soft dirt covering the road. The car came to a halt and the engine tickety-ticked a constant rhythm as the cloud of dust surrounding them slowly cleared.

"Over there," she said. "The dragon is over there."

Ballard looked in the direction she was pointing. "I don't see anything."

"That is because it is under the ground."

"Dead?"

"No, in a cave."

"Oh, right," said Ballard, getting out of the car.

She began walking across the field, but Ballard called out to her and asked her to wait. While she waited, he opened the rear travel compartment of the staff car and took out a few pieces of equipment, including his service revolver and a heavy flashlight, both of which he thought might come in handy if there really was a dragon, or something, beneath the ground nearby.

When he was ready he looked over to her and said, "Lead the way."

At once she began walking across the field with long, confident strides, obviously quite sure of where she was going.

The more Ballard thought about it, the more it seemed to make sense. According to some of the briefing notes he'd read, the Peak District of Derbyshire was home to several caves and tunnels deep beneath the ground. Around Castleton especially, there were supposedly a number of shafts and sinkholes that fed water down to the resurgence system of the . . . He tried to remember the name . . . The Peak-Speedwell Caverns. The caves there were supposed to have a massive arched entrance, several large chambers, and a large main stream that ran through a long jagged tunnel. If something like that were nearby, it would make the perfect place for a dragon to call home.

Maybe this woman *does* know about the dragon.

"Listen . . . Lavena," said Ballard, hurrying along to catch up to her. "I hope I wasn't abrupt with you before. I'd been driving around the country all morning without much luck and—"

She turned and smiled at him, but said nothing.

"Are you from around here?" he asked, deciding it would be better to start off simply, rather than with some long-winded explanation that she probably didn't care to hear.

"I come from the village of Dervon," she said.

"Dervon? I've never heard of Dervon. Don't you mean Derby?"

"I come from the village of Dervon," she said again. "I have never heard of Derby."

Now that was strange. How could she know her way around the area if she wasn't from here? It was possible that Dervon was a small village somewhere nearby, but even so, how could she live nearby and not have ever heard of Derby?

Perhaps she had escaped from some institution? That would explain a lot of things, like her appearance, her clothes, her fascination with the staff car, and her self-professed knowledge of the dragon. He tried to recall if there was a facility in this part of England, but couldn't come up with a thing.

"Can I ask you a question, Lavena?"

"Of course."

"How is it that you know where the dragon is?"

Without a moment's hesitation she said, "Until yesterday, I

had been the dragon's prisoner."

Ballard's hopes were dashed. He shook his head in dismay. For a while he had actually started believing in the existence of the dragon, but obviously he was being led on some wild-goose chase—or perhaps a wild-dragon chase—by an obviously mentally unstable young woman.

"If you were the dragon's prisoner, then how is it that you are now here with me?"

She looked at him, her smile absolutely beaming with pride. "I escaped."

"Wonderful," said Ballard, shaking his head. "Just great."

2

Generalmajor Erich Goetz sat at the long oak table in a meeting room inside the Hotel Meurice, which served as the military headquarters for the German occupation of Paris. It was a magnificent old hotel, well-suited to the tastes of commanders such as Goering and a much more sedate place from which to conduct business than the Gestapo headquarters on the Avenue Foch.

"Heil Hitler!" barked a voice at the door.

"Heil Hitler," Goetz answered. "Come in."

Hauptmann Hermann Von Hesse entered the room. He possessed all the desirable features of the perfect "Aryan," and had been a favorite of Hitler's for some time. But somehow the exemplary nature of Von Hesse's fair hair, light-blue eyes and pink-white skin was overshadowed by his all-black uniform with its death's-head cap, double-lightning-bolt SS on the collar and the red swastika-emblazoned armband on his left arm. To Goetz, Von Hesse looked more like the cool embodiment of evil than the perfect German specimen.

Perhaps Goetz's opinion of Von Hesse was tainted by the knowledge that Von Hesse was a cold-blooded killer whose loyalty to the *Fuhrer* and the Nazi Party had overstepped the code of chivalry—and even morality—that so many officers in the Luftwaffe were trying to remain faithful to despite the horrors of the war. For example, it was well known that Von Hesse's questioning of twelve downed Polish fliers outside Warsaw had left every one of the men dead, either as a result of the beatings they'd endured, or from a bullet to the head after they'd told Von Hesse what he wanted to know. And if that wasn't enough to make people wary of Von Hesse, there was also the fact that the SS officer had volunteered for this assignment, one that in all likelihood he would not be returning from. If he was successful there was little chance he could make it back across the English Channel. And if he failed and was captured by the British, he would be summarily shot for being a spy. In short, it was a suicide mission and this young man had volunteered for it gladly.

"Make yourself comfortable," said Goetz.

"Thank you, Generalmajor!" said Von Hesse curtly.

"Cigar? Cigarette?"

"No thank you, Generalmajor."

Goetz lit himself a cigarette. "How much do you know about your mission?"

"The English have a new weapon."

"Yes, and . . ."

Von Hesse was silent.

Goetz nodded, then explained. "The secret weapon is some sort of new fighter. We call it a dragon because that's what it resembles, but we're not really sure yet what it is."

Von Hesse listened carefully.

"It seems to be able to knock our fighters out of the sky with ease," continued the generalmajor. "We need you to find it for us."

"Yes, Generalmajor."

"Your first priority will be to capture the aircraft and fly it back to German-occupied territory," Goetz said, pausing a moment to allow Von Hesse the opportunity to comment on the slim chance of success for such a mission. To his surprise, the young German said nothing.

"If that is not possible for whatever reason," he continued, "you must attempt to bring photos and other information back to Germany." This was slightly more of a possibility with U-boat pickups already scheduled in the north of England, but the chance of a successful return to Germany was still very small.

"And if you are unable to acquire information, or make good your return to Germany, then you must destroy the new weapon and everything to do with its development and construction."

Again Goetz paused, waiting for some comment from Von Hesse. But the young man said nothing. Instead he looked across the table at Goetz, his cold, steely eyes unnerving the battle-hardened generalmajor.

"Do you have any questions?" Goetz said at last.

"Yes, Generalmajor," said Von Hesse. "When may I leave for England?"

3

After walking across a grassy field for several minutes, they came upon a large opening in the earth.

It was at the bottom of a hollow in the middle of the field. It was situated on a bit of a slope giving it the appearance of something that was halfway between the entrance to a cave and a hole in the ground.

"So this is the cave?" said Ballard. "The dragon's lair?"

"This is the entrance," said Lavena quietly. "His lair, if he has chosen to make it so, is much deeper in the ground."

"Of course."

Ballard waited for the woman to lead the way, but instead of entering the cave, she merely stood off to the side of the entrance.

"Lead the way," said Ballard.

She shook her head.

Ballard wanted to laugh and tell her there was nothing to worry about, but the fear in her eyes was far too real to be scoffed at.

"You don't want to go in?"

"No," she said. "There's a dragon in there."

"How can you tell?"

"I can feel the warmth of his breath rising up from inside the cave."

Ballard stood at the entrance of the cave a moment and realized that she was right. There was definitely a slight warm draft coming from the entrance, which was somewhat difficult to explain considering that the only thing running through the cavern was a river of no doubt ice-cold water.

Still, in order for him to attribute the warm draft to the dragon, he would have to wholeheartedly believe in its existence, and he wasn't quite ready to do that. There had been several detailed descriptions of the creature, a plausible reason why it chose to make this area of England its home, and a reasonable explanation as to why warm air might rise up from the ground in a country devoid of hotsprings and other volcanic activity.

But all of it was circumstantial evidence. There was still no proof that the dragon existed. As far as he knew, he was still on the trail of some devastating new German secret weapon, and if that was the case, it seemed very unlikely that he would find that weapon stored underground on British soil.

However, in order to concentrate on the German-secret-weapon theory, he had to completely eliminate the possibility that it was a dragon. That meant he had to inspect the cave.

"Now . . . Lavena, I'm sure there is nothing to be afraid of," said Ballard. "I just need you to show me the dragon and then we'll be on our way."

She shook her head. "I've brought you to the dragon."

"That has yet to be determined."

"You can go inside if you like," she said. "I shall wait for you here." She sat down on a flat rock to the side of the opening.

Ballard was silent, thinking about it. He didn't really need her inside the cave with him. He wasn't exactly a spelunker, but he had trekked through a few caves while on field study trips at Oxford. He could probably find his way in and out without incident.

"All right," he said at last. "You wait for me here. I'll be right back."

She nodded appreciatively.

Ballard took a deep breath, and entered the cave.

CHAPTER EIGHT

1

Flight Lieutenant Ballard stepped into the cave, and immediately lost his footing on the jagged rocks beneath him. He righted himself and started again, this time moving more cautiously as the hard soles of his shoes weren't exactly suited to the terrain.

He was careful to keep his flashlight down in front of him, but soon realized that enough light filtered in from the opening to allow him to continue without having to hold the light. He shut it off and hung it on his belt.

The entrance to the cave was both long and deep, his footsteps taking him further along as well as down under the ground. He estimated that while he'd gone perhaps twenty yards in, he was likely five feet underground.

At several points along the way, the cave narrowed considerably, making it unlikely that a dragon, especially one as big as people have been reporting, could get out this way. But, that didn't mean there wasn't a dragon here, since there were supposedly several entrances to the cave.

Finally, the way in front of him grew too dark to continue without the aid of his light. He switched it on once more and continued on into the cave.

With each step he took, numerous thoughts crossed his mind. Had he been led into some trap by Lavena, a German agent? If there was a dragon inside, would he be burned to a cinder upon discovering it? If it was a German weapon hidden in the English countryside, would he be killed by the agents guarding it? If he fell and tumbled into the depths of the cave, who would come to rescue him? And finally, what the bloody hell am I doing creeping into a cave, anyway? I'm a RAF flier, not a dragon miner!

Just then he heard a low rumble.

Ballard stopped in his tracks, and extinguished his light.

He heard it again.

It was an animal-like sound, rising up from a large chest cavity and traveling down a thick windpipe. It was the sort of sound a large animal like a rhinoceros or hippopotamus might make awakening from a pleasant sleep.

The sound came again, this time accompanied by the scratch and scrape of rock. Something was moving in the darkness ahead of him.

Fear gripped Ballard. There wasn't supposed to be anything living underground, but there was definitely *something* nearby. He could feel its body heat and smell its breath.

For a moment he believed he had come up with the most logical explanation of what this creature might be. What if it were a cousin of the famed monster at Loch Ness? It certainly would have been possible for a reptilian creature to exist under the ground for centuries without being detected. Perhaps this one had been disturbed by the shockwaves of nearby bombing. Now there was a theory that would fit nicely with all the accounts.

Ballard steadied his footing and raised his light. He was feeling quite proud of himself for coming up with such a rational explanation. His only regret was that this discovery had to occur during wartime when it would have to be put on hold until war's end. Still, it would be quite a feather in his cap to be the one to discover such a creature.

He pointed his light in the direction the sound was coming from and switched it on.

The light twinkled and sparkled off the surface of the creature's spikes and scales, but was almost completely absorbed into the matte blue color of its wings.

Wings?

Slowly, Ballard directed the light over the creature's wings toward its body. After, seeing the scales of its body and underbelly, he brought the light up to its head. There were horns atop its head, a small pair of ears and two eyes that were open . . .

And looking directly into the light.

The thing opened its maw and down deep inside its throat Ballard could see a small flicker of flame.

"It *is* a dragon," he said softly, as if he were identifying an animal at the London Zoo.

The eyes of the dragon narrowed angrily into two thin slits. Its maw opened even further and it appeared to suck in a deep breath.

Ballard wondered if that meant it was about to expel a gout of flame, but wasn't terribly interested in sticking around to find out. He turned on his heels and began scrambling up the long tunnel toward the entrance.

There was a roar behind him. Suddenly the cave in front of him lit up as if the house lights had been turned on in some theater. He was grateful at being able to see where he was going, but there was an intense heat at his back. He imagined his uniform was being licked by flames but didn't want to take the time to confirm it. He continued moving as fast as he could, through the tighter parts of the tunnel and then finally to its mouth.

He dove out of the cave and onto the grass in front of it, rolling around to put out any fire alight on his clothing.

After a few seconds his body began to feel as if he'd stepped into a large freezer. He turned to look at the mouth of the cave. Wisps of smoke rose out of it while a low roar echoed through the caverns beneath the ground.

"There's a dragon in there!" he said.

Lavena looked on, little more than a half smile on her face. "I know."

Lavena had been drifting off to sleep as the afternoon sun felt warm on her body. The young man named Ballard had been in the cave for some time and she began to wonder if he'd be coming back out.

But just as the thought had crossed her mind she'd heard what was surely Tibalt's roar coming from inside the cave. That sound was followed by the sounds of Ballard scurrying out of the cave, most likely with a lick of flame spurring him on.

She sat up on the rock and waited.

Moments later, Ballard emerged from the mouth of the cave like a cork from a bottle. His clothes were smoking and he rolled around on the grass as if he were on fire.

Eventually he stopped moving and caught his breath. He looked up at her and said, "There's a dragon in there!"

Lavena nearly laughed at him, but remained composed. She wanted to tell him of course there was a dragon in there, why else would I have brought you here, but she checked herself and merely said, "I know."

"I've got to get more supplies," said Ballard, rising to his feet. He began running across the field in the direction of the steel horse. When she didn't move from her rock, he turned to her and said, "Well, come on."

Lavena jumped off the rock and caught up to him. He didn't seem to notice her at his side and continued muttering things as if she weren't even there.

"A pair of .303 Brownings might do the trick, but they'd be difficult to carry inside . . ."

She had to hurry to keep up with Ballard who was almost across the field.

"A single Hispano cannon might be better, easier to bring down in there . . . Maybe a rocket too. One shot to the belly."

Ballard seemed to be off in a world of his own, and Lavena wondered if he had hit his head in his rush to get out of the cave. She didn't even understand many of the words he was saying or what he was talking about.

"But if you're going to use a rocket, then why not just toss a few grenades into the cave, bring the whole thing down on top of it . . . Maybe it would be easier just to rig the entrances with explosives so the remains could be uncovered by scientists after the war."

They reached the steel horse.

Ballard hardly slowed his pace, climbing inside the horse almost without stopping.

Lavena got in too, not wanting to be left behind. She still didn't understand what Ballard was talking about, but she was beginning to get a good idea about what he was thinking. It sounded as if he were trying to decide the best way to kill the dragon.

She only hoped she was wrong.

2

"Mortal worm!" cried Tibalt, firing a long stream of flame into the tunnel after the man who had dared disturb his slumber.

The man had carried with him a strange and powerful light that pierced the darkness like nothing Tibalt had ever seen before. Looking into it, he had nearly been blinded, unable to look anywhere but directly into the bright beam. For a few awkward moments he had thought that the light had belonged to some strange cave-dwelling creature, but then he'd heard a few mumbled words, and knew . . .

The light was a mortal thing, controlled by men.

Perhaps like the steel dragons were.

If that were true, the light had to be extinguished, the man behind it destroyed.

Tibalt sent another line of fire up into the tunnel, but the man was too fast, managing to get out before the shooting flames could turn him to ash and cinder.

Tibalt roared with rage.

The next mortal who ventured into this cave, his lair, would be destroyed, and the charred body would be dropped in the center of the nearest village to serve as a fierce warning that Tibalt was a dragon not to be disturbed or trifled with.

Tibalt's blood ran hot. He seethed with anger and hatred toward all mortals. It was an all-consuming rage, a fury smoldering within him that needed to be quenched.

Now!

He hurried toward one of the larger entrances of the cave, looked up at the sky and decided it was high time he proclaimed his dominance over the troublesome mortals of this place.

He would destroy them, as many as he could until they recognized his power and left him alone to rule the skies.

The mortals would scream in agony beneath his flame.

The steel dragons would fall, burning from the sky.

And he would reign over all.

With a heady rush, Tibalt leaped from the entrance of the cave and into the blue clear sky.

3

The steel horse lurched forward like a cat pouncing on a mouse, then Ballard turned the wheel quickly to the left. They turned around the road and were soon speeding away . . .

Toward what, Lavena didn't know.

"A few grenades, maybe a few mortars if it manages to get out of the hole."

Ballard was continuing to mutter long strings of words. As before, Lavena didn't know the meaning of each of the words, but she was getting a better feel for their meaning. He sounded like a man who was determined to kill the dragon.

At that moment, the realization struck her hard.

The similarities between Ballard and Warrick went deeper than simply their appearance. Ballard was a warrior, just like Warrick had been, and they both wanted to see the dragon dead.

It seemed impossible that she would be in the same predicament so far removed from Dervon, but here she was in this strange place with another young warrior who fully intended to destroy the dragon.

Lavena was torn over what to do. On the one hand, she detested Tibalt for what he'd done to Warrick, and because of his utter arrogance when it came to humans. She also disliked him for the harsh treatment he'd shown her after she had done her best to save him from harm. But on the other hand, she had gone through so much to try and save the dragon, so perhaps she should continue the fight for its life. After all, this new place was so different from where they'd come from, maybe it was possible to reason with the dragon here.

It might be worth a try.

And if it didn't work, killing the dragon could always remain as final solution. But in the meantime, she owed it to herself—and to Asvald—to try and save the dragon's life.

The old wizard's name rekindled his memory in Lavena's mind and caused a flutter of regret to tickle at her throat. She wondered if he might be found in this place of wonders; it certainly seemed possible, considering some of the magical things she'd seen in her travels. And then, a strange feeling came over her and she knew with certainty that Asvald was somewhere nearby. She couldn't be sure how or why—she just knew.

"A squad of crack soldiers and it will all be over with."

"No!" said Lavena, speaking up at the mention of the words *soldiers*. There could no longer be any doubt in her mind that Ballard wanted to kill the dragon. "You can't kill it," she said.

"No?" Ballard slowed the steel horse and looked at her. "Maybe I should just kindly ask it to stop knocking our aeroplanes out of the sky and killing our fliers, hmmm?"

Lavena looked at him curiously. "Do you mean the steel dragons?"

"Steel dragons?"

"Yes, that's what it calls your *aer-o-planes*."

Ballard brought the car to an abrupt halt.

Lavena was forced to throw her hands out in front of her to prevent herself from hitting her head.

"Are you saying that it can speak?" asked Ballard.

"Yes," said Lavena. "His name is Tibalt. If you want him to speak to you, you must first tell him your name."

Ballard looked at Lavena for a long time, studying her as if deciding if what she was saying might be true. Finally he said, "Why don't you tell me more about this dragon. Everything . . . from the beginning."

Lavena took a deep breath, and told him.

"Warrick was a handsome young knight . . ."

Chapter Nine

1

"Ops Room, Bentley Priory," the twentyish, raven-haired WAAF said into the telephone. She listened to the voice on the other end for half a minute, then hung up.

The group captain to her left looked at her expectantly.

"Another strange signal on the Chain Home Low screens in Lincoln."

"Is it the same sort as before?" asked the group captain.

"Yes, sir. An outgoing flight in a slightly northeastern direction."

"Heading for the Channel."

"The Channel coast of the North Sea, sir." The distinction was important, since no German aeroplanes based in France had the range to fly home via a North Sea route. And the bombers stationed in Norway had only enough range to reach targets in Scotland. The image on the screen had to be something other than an aeroplane on an operational mission.

"Bigger or smaller than before?"

"As before, it could be anywhere between one and five aircraft."

The telephone rang again. The WAAF answered it. After a moment, she hung up and turned to the group captain.

"What is it?" asked the group captain.

"Chain Home radar in Grimsby reports a small formation over the North Sea."

The group captain was silent a moment, considering the information. "Right," he said at last. "Scramble the wing at Digby and put Kirton-in-Lindsay and Coltishall on alert." He paused a moment, thinking. "And alert the ground defenses and anti-aircraft sites in the area as well. *Codename Dragon.*"

"Yes, sir," the WAAF said, picking up a phone and giving the order to scramble the fighters at Digby . . .

Below her, on the floor of the Ops Room, another WAAF placed a tiny marker on the plotting table in front of her and pushed it with a long stick into position over Digby. Then she placed a second marker onto the map and pushed it into position over the North Sea to indicate the incoming flight of German aeroplanes.

And then she reached down under the plotting table, picked up one of the tiny dragon figurines stored there.

It had begun as a joke among the WAAFs staffing the Ops Room, but when Fighter Command was unable to come up with a suitable designation to represent the mysterious flying object, it was decided that all future sightings of the so-called dragon would be plotted with the dragon figurine. At the very least, everyone in the Ops Room would know what it meant.

The WAAF pushed the tiny dragon into position over the Channel, then waited patiently for her next instruction.

2

Hauptmann Gerhard Ebbighausen and his wingman, Oberleutnant Wilhelm Kriepe, had been flying over the Channel for less than ten minutes and were nearing the British Channel coast.

Their orders for the day had simply been "Free Range Over England," which meant they were free to fly over the country and shoot up anything of military significance, including anything resembling a dragon. While most in the *Jagdgeschwader* had opted for London and the white cliffs of Dover, Ebbighausen and Kriepe had decided to try further north for more vulnerable prey.

After leaving their base in St. Omer in Belgium, they had turned north in search of coastal targets in the ports that served the British industrial heartland, as well as British radar installations along the coast.

As the British coastline grew larger and more distinct below them, Ebbighausen picked out a ship sailing into the large bay the British called "The Wash." It was a merchant ship rather than a Royal Navy vessel, but it was a target, and an easy one at that.

Ebbihausen was about to inform Kriepe of his plan to attack the ship when he heard the young oberleutnant's voice over the radio.

"*Achtung,* Spitfires!" shouted Kriepe.

Ebbighausen looked westward and saw a section of Spitfires approaching in two vics, below them and to the left. Although outnumbered, Ebbighausen had several advantages over the Tommies—altitude, the sun at their backs and surprise.

"Horrido!" cried Ebbighausen, calling on the German fighter pilots' fictitious patron saint, St. Horridus. He put his Me-109 into a sharp, diving left turn that would bring his guns to bear in a head-on attack on the formation of Spitfires.

Kriepe followed him down.

With luck, they would be able to get in a single pass before the formation broke up. After that they could climb up into the clouds and make their way back across the Channel shrouded in the mist.

Tibalt watched from the clouds.

There was no shortage of steel dragons in the air today. From across the water came two yellow-nosed greyish-green dragons with white underbellies and black crosses on their square-shaped wings and sleek, thin bodies. And coming up from the land below were six green-and-brown dragons, each with a black nose, blue underbelly and round spots on its finely tapered wings and well-shaped body.

In addition to their overall shape, there were many things about the steel dragons that were the same. Both types had the whirling wing on the tips of their noses and behind that, just back of their wings, there was a sort of covered opening that exposed the inside of the dragon. It was a small opening, but perhaps big enough for a man to crawl into.

What a ridiculous notion!

An absolute impossibility!

What dragon would lower itself to allow a human to ride upon its back like some ignorant beast of burden?

But while the thought repulsed him, it also piqued his interest. And so, curious, he came down out of the clouds for a closer look.

The two groups of steel dragons were upon each other now and the yellow-nosed green dragons began attacking the green-and-brown with their steel spits.

Caught unaware by the yellow-noses, the green-and-browns scattered.

As the two groups went into long and graceful turns, Tibalt closed the gap on a single green-and-brown. He was able to come up behind it while it was still in its turn, getting close enough to it to almost catch it by the tail.

He looked down into the covered opening between the wings, and could not believe what he saw.

Not only was there a man riding on the back of the steel dragon, but the man appeared to be controlling the steel dragon with movements of his hands and feet.

Anger roiled anew inside Tibalt. Not only had mortal men dared to reach for the sky, but they had also enslaved a race of dragons to do it.

No, not dragons! No dragon would allow itself to be so humiliated by a lesser life-form. These creatures were not even remotely his kin, not even worthy of the name steel dragon.

Tibalt clenched his right hand into a fist and slammed it down onto the tail of the green-and-brown in front of him. The fragile tail of the creature shattered under the force of the blow, scales and bits of bones falling away like crumbs from a cake.

Tibalt watched with delight as the green-and-brown steel dragon fell from the sky. It arced toward the ground in a long and graceful spiral, unable to right itself without the help of its rear wings.

Tibalt felt an intoxicating form of power course through his body. He would destroy all of them as easily as he had this one—with his bare hands, with his flame, with the flick of his tail.

It all seemed too easy.

He watched the green-and-brown near the ground. Suddenly, the man inside it leaped from the back of the steel dragon, falling through the air and leaving the steel dragon to fend for itself.

And then, as if by some magic, a cloud opened up behind the falling man, slowing his descent and easing him toward the ground.

In the distance, the steel dragon hit the ground, throwing up a gout of orange flame and black smoke.

Tibalt's contempt for the men in the steel dragons grew twofold. Not only did they control them like pack mules, but when they became disabled, they left them to die like some horse with a broken leg.

Tibalt turned his wings to dive on the man floating down beneath the cloud. He would not escape death so easily!

Steel spits suddenly tore through Tibalt's wings.

He looked over his shoulder and saw two green-and-browns coming at him from out of the sun. There were pinpricks of flickering light coming from points on their wings. Steel spits buzzed like fireflies around his head and body.

Tibalt wrapped his wings tightly around his body and fell from the sky like a stone.

Ebbighausen and Kriepe zoomed through the Spitfire formation with their machine guns and cannons firing. The leader of the formation suffered a few hits, but managed to dive away before any serious damage occurred to his aircraft.

Immediately, the rest of the fighters broke away, leaving the two German pilots nothing more to shoot at and sending them home without a kill.

After making the pass, Ebbighausen used the extra speed he'd gained in his dive to streak almost straight up toward the cloud cover. Kriepe followed.

It took several long seconds before they were surrounded in white, but they had reached the clouds without incident. Now it was simply a matter of turning east, putting the plane in a shallow dive and hoping their fighters had enough fuel to make it back across the Channel to their base.

"Where did it go?"

"Dropped out of the sky!"

"I see it there, below us near the coast."

The chatter over the radio was deafening. Normally the fliers in 611 Squadron conducted themselves in an utterly professional manner. But sight of the much-storied dragon had turned the usually level-headed killers into a group of unruly schoolboys.

"I'm on it!" said Squadron Leader Patrick Marston. "And shut the bloody hell up the rest of you!"

The radio chatter faded.

Marston put his Spitfire in a steep dive and watched the speed indicator as it climbed past four hundred miles per hour. The dragon was getting larger in his sights, but was still too far out of range. He kept on the throttle, feeling the Spitfire shake and its controls growing heavy.

The dragon was five hundred yards away and closing.

A few more seconds and it was in range.

Marston pressed down on the gun button at the top of the control column and all eight of his Brownings fired, every tenth bullet a tracer arcing red-hot toward the target.

A few rounds from Marston's initial burst hit the dragon in the wing area, but instead of falling to the ground the dragon curled its body and flew straight up, climbing vertically with just a few flaps of its giant wings.

One moment the dragon was filling Marston's gunsight, another moment it was gone . . .

Leaving him hurtling toward the Earth at four-hundred-plus miles per hour and nothing to show for it.

He began to pull back on the stick, but the windspeed over the control surfaces made them stiff to operate.

There was a good five thousand feet between him and the ground. He'd be able to ease the aeroplane out of the dive and hedgehop his way back to base. One thing was certain, he was traveling too fast for anything—Me-109 or dragon—to be following him down.

His airspeed slowed somewhat and Marston felt the Spitfire begin to respond more readily to the controls. He was pushed down into his seat ever so slightly, as the nose of the aeroplane came up. Ground was replaced by sky in his windscreen.

He checked his altimeter and saw that he still had a few thousand feet to play with.

"Watch out, Paddy!" came the cry over the radio. "It's on your tail."

Marston looked over his shoulder . . .

Just in time to see the flames.

The two German fliers had been flying east for just over a minute.

"Nothing this time," said Ebbighausen over the radio after setting his course back to St. Omer.

"It must be Tommy's lucky day," replied Kriepe.

No matter, thought Ebbighausen. We shall console ourselves with a bottle of schnapps and a good cigar. Ebbighausen's thoughts were cut short by the sound of an explosion. A moment later his Me-109 was rocked by the blast and it took all his skill as a pilot to keep the tiny fighter flying straight and level.

"Willy!" Ebbighausen called. "Willy! Can you hear me? Are you all right?"

But the radio was silent.

The steel dragons were falling from the sky like autumn leaves.

Once Tibalt realized that they were only dangerous from the front and that the steel spits could easily be avoided, he began to destroy them almost at will.

Of the six green-and-browns that had first met the two yellow-noses, only three remained. The first he had destroyed by smashing its tail and making it unable to fly. The second he had burned up with a blast of flame. It had burned for a long time, and then burst into a ball of fire that was almost pretty to look at. The last one he had torn the wings off after it had hit him several times with its steel spits. He'd been hit in the wings and belly, and one lucky spit had shattered one of his horns. That one shot had infuriated Tibalt and he had exacted his revenge by pulling off one of the green-and-brown's wings and watching it spin to the ground like a maple seed.

And, in the middle of all that, there had been a yellow-nose that he'd chanced upon. He had smashed blindly into its tail as he entered a line of clouds. What surprised him most was how fragile the steel dragons were. As if they weren't made out of steel at all, but a lighter metal that crumpled like dried leaves upon impact.

Now he was being attacked by the surviving three green-and-browns. They were tenacious fighters and Tibalt respected their courage, but they could not turn as quickly as he could, and aside from their steel spits, they had no other method of attack.

The first green-and-brown managed to hit him with a few spits along his tail. The spits stung as they struck him, but it wasn't anything he couldn't handle. As the green-and-brown continued to fire its steel spits, Tibalt retaliated with a wide blast of flame that forced the green-and-brown to fly through the fire.

The steel dragon began to smoke, and then its right wing burst apart at one of the points where the steel spits had been coming from. And then, on fire, the green-and-brown turned away, trailing a long line of smoke.

Tibalt watched the man inside crawl out of the burning steel dragon. He wanted to go after him, kill him as he fell, but there were still two other steel dragons he had to destroy.

He turned to face them, but they had turned away from each other and were heading back toward the coast, one heading southwest, one northwest.

Tibalt could only destroy one.

He decided on the one heading to the south and put himself into a sharp dive that would bring him up behind the green-and-brown in moments.

3

In the Ops Room at Bentley Priory a group of RAF officers and WAAFs listened to the radio transmission of 611 Squadron as one by one their aeroplanes were knocked out of the sky by the dragon.

Apparently, the fight was moving south.

"Scramble Coltishall, and put Wittering on alert," one of the group captains said to the WAAFs operating the phone lines connecting Fighter Command with the airfield. "And tell Kirton-in-Lindsay they're released."

"Yes sir," said the WAAF, picking up the telephone.

4

This green-and-brown was a good flyer.

It was able to turn from side to side and roll away quickly whenever Tibalt shot a line of flame in its direction. Its speed was also considerable as Tibalt had to constantly flap his wings just to stay behind it. Normally, such speeds wouldn't have been a problem, but a few steel spits from the other green-and-browns had re-opened the holes in his wings. His flapping was as strong as ever, but his wings weren't moving nearly enough air to keep up with this elusive green-and-brown.

As they approached the coast, the steel dragon put its nose down and dove steeply to the ground.

Tibalt followed, grateful that such a move did not require more flapping of its shredded wings. The dragon proved faster in the dive and was getting closer to the green-and-brown. He let go with a long line of flame and managed to catch the steel dragon's tail. It smoked a little, turning black and grey, but the steel dragon flew on.

As they leveled out over land, Tibalt had closed the gap and was now close enough to see the man inside the steel dragon looking over his shoulder and frantically moving the controls to pitch the green-and-brown into a wild series of dips and turns.

At last Tibalt had the green-and-brown close enough to destroy it. He drew a deep breath and opened his maw to blast the steel dragon out of the sky.

But before he could get off a lick of flame, something big and hot tore into his right wing.

And then his left wing was hit, ripping a large hole in its center.

Suddenly it had become very difficult to fly.

Tibalt was unsure about what had happened. The steel dragons couldn't spit steel behind them and there were no other steel dragons in the sky.

He looked to the land below, and saw the source of these unexpected steel spits. There were men on the ground able to spit steel into the air. Tiny bursts of flame and points of light were sparkling all over the ground below him and the air was filled with flying steel.

He could hear the spits *zinging* and *zooming* past his head.

And then the men on the ground found the range and his body began being pelted by spits. His wings, his body, his tail, neck and head were all being pounded by bits of steel. He closed his eyes and turned away, but the spits followed him.

Aching and bleeding, Tibalt gathered his strength and flapped his wings with as much power as he could muster. He rose slowly, his wings unable to bite into the air as they usually did. But slowly, and with incredible effort, he began to gain height. Below him the points of light still flickered, but the steel spits fell short of their target.

In the distance, the green-and-brown he'd been chasing continued flying west, unfettered by the men on the ground.

Tibalt did his best to soar since flapping his wings had become too painful. Despite his best efforts he was slowly losing height. Hopefully, he would have enough height to make it back to the cave.

He slowly turned to the northwest, and headed for his lair.

Tibalt was still some distance from the safety of the caves when he heard the drone of more steel dragons growing louder.

Searching the sky in front of him, he saw a line of green-and-browns approaching from the south. He noted that these steel dragons were somewhat different in shape than the previous ones he'd encountered. These had the same round markings on the body and wings, but it had a bigger tail-end, thicker wings and overall a less attractive appearance.

But despite whatever low opinion Tibalt had of these new adversaries, they were able to spit steel as well as the others.

As the steel dragons neared, he counted eight in total. How many of them can there be?

He flapped his wings harder, trying to gain height and the advantage over his adversaries. But the harder he flapped, the more his wings ached. What had started out as small tears in his wings had now been ripped into large holes.

The green-and-browns were upon him.

Tibalt decided to turn and fight. He sent a blast of flame at the first steel dragon and watched as its tail caught fire. It streaked toward the ground, trailing flame and smoke. The man inside it jumped out before it crashed.

Tibalt felt proud that he was still able to destroy the steel dragons with ease, but the feeling was short-lived. The others in line began spitting steel at him.

There were too many of them.

As he turned away from one, he was caught by another.

On and on it went until Tibalt was forced to fold his wings into his body and fall from the sky.

He dropped a considerable distance, then opened his wings

once more. The high wind tore at the flesh, and steel spits punched new and bigger holes in his wings.

It was a nightmare.

Tibalt pointed his nose down and dove for the ground as quickly as he could.

It seemed impossible for him to be doing such a thing, but Tibalt was running from the steel dragons and the men inside them.

He only hoped he hadn't waited too long to admit defeat.

CHAPTER TEN

1

She talked all the way back to the manor house, recounting in precise detail the series of events which brought her and the dragon to "this place," as she called it.

Of course, it was an utterly fantastic tale. Flight Lieutenant Ballard didn't want to believe it, but what other explanation did he have?

If he believed her story, then all of the other details seemed to fall into place. For example, Lavena said she was from the village of Dervon. Over time it would make sense that the village name of *Dervon* might evolve into the name *Derby*. And, there was something odd about Lavena's use of language. She seemed to have no knowledge of modern words and spoke very simply. That could also be explained by a movement forward in time. If nothing else, she seemed to have been plunked down into 1940 without any knowledge of aeroplanes, cars, or any other piece of modern technology. It was as if she had literally been born yesterday.

All of it was quite incredible, but most incredible of all was the irrefutable fact that there was indeed a large, fire-breathing dragon deep inside one of the caves on the outskirts of Derby. He could choose to accept or disregard Lavena's story, but he could not ignore the existence of the dragon. Therefore he decided to accept Lavena at her word and move forward from there.

"So you see," she said. "He is a very clever creature. If you explain to him about all of the killing weapons you have, then maybe you can persuade him to stop destroying your steel dragons."

"Our fighters."

"Fighters," she said. "That's a good name for them. They are a threat to his rule over the skies. He wants to destroy every last one of them."

"Well, he's been doing a pretty good job of it so far," said Ballard. "From the accounts we received at Bentley Priory, this Tibalt of yours is already an ace."

"Well, he's very angry at Asvald . . ."

As Lavena continued talking about the dragon, Ballard thought about what he'd just said about the dragon being an ace. It was certainly a powerful creature and it had exhibited an ability to destroy aeroplanes in any number of ways. Such a creature would make a devastating addition to RAF Fighter Command.

A slight smile crossed Ballard's face at the thought of it. Why the bloody hell not? They were already taking fliers from anywhere they could find them—Poland, Belgium, Czechoslovakia fighter Command had even raided the Fleet Air Arm and Bomber Command for pilots, regardless of their lack of experience in single-engine fighters. If they could add a dragon to the ranks of the RAF—and an ace dragon at that . . .

". . . He's been hurt a few times by the steel dra—uh, aer-o-planes, but I was able to fix the damage pretty well and he was able to fly again."

Ballard drove through the gates in front of the manor house, and came to a stop at the end of the driveway.

Lavena, seeing that they had arrived somewhere, stopped talking about the dragon. She looked at Ballard expectantly.

He turned to her, looked into her eyes for a long time, still thinking. Finally, he said, "All right. Couldn't hurt to try and talk to it first."

Lavena's heart soared at the sound of the words. She'd had to struggle so hard to make Warrick understand, but here in this wonderful place, this soldier named Ballard had easily agreed to try and talk to the dragon.

She looked at Ballard, smiling. He possessed all of the qualities she'd admired in Warrick, but he also understood the value of the dragon's life. From what she had seen, she imagined that Ballard and the other soldiers in this place could easily destroy the dragon if they so desired, but instead of slaughtering it, he was willing to try and save the creature.

"Thank you," she said.

"No need to thank me," said Ballard. "It's worth a try to have a dragon on your side."

Lavena wanted to know what he meant by "having a dragon on your side," but before she could ask him, he'd gotten out of the steel horse and was walking toward the building.

"Well, come on," he said over his shoulder.

She climbed out of the steel horse. "Inside?" she said.

"Of course, inside. You might as well get cleaned up and looked after before we go back to the cave."

She closed the door to the steel horse and hurried to Ballard's side.

"Wait until Mrs. Norris gets a look at you," he said, a sly grin on his face.

Mrs. Norris, thought Lavena. That must be the lady of the house.

Ballard entered the house first, calling out the name of the lady of the house rather rudely. "Mrs. Norris!" A pause. "Mrs. Norris!"

There was no response. They stepped into the house, entering curiously by the back way through the kitchen.

"Mrs. Norris!" he called again.

"Keep your shirt on," came a voice. "I'm coming."

Ballard turned to Lavena and smiled.

A moment later a large, heavy, older woman in a rather plain dress appeared in the kitchen. When she saw Lavena she put her hand up over the "O" of her mouth.

"Mrs. Norris," said Ballard. "This is Lavena. I met her on the road and she's helping me with my investigation."

The hand came away from the woman's face and her expression changed. She seemed to be impressed.

"I was wondering if you might be able to take care of her for a bit while I go to Digby for some equipment."

"Of course I can," said Mrs. Norris.

Lavena bowed in Mrs. Norris's direction and said, "Milady."

Mrs. Norris laughed at that.

Lavena was afraid she had said something foolish, or offended the lady of the manor. "Excuse me, milady. I meant no disrespect."

"Oh," said Mrs. Norris, looking in Ballard's direction. "She is a wonder, isn't she?" She turned toward Lavena. "No, child, no offense taken. I'm just flattered that you confused me with a lady. I must say it's the first time that's ever happened."

"Mrs. Norris is the housekeeper, tending to the house while the owners are away."

"Oh," said Lavena, hoping her face wasn't turning too deep a shade of red. "I see."

"Come on," she said. "From the looks of it you could use a warm bath. And then maybe a few scones to eat."

Lavena smiled. She'd never had a warm bath before. No one in Dervon had. And scones, well, she could eat a dozen. "Yes, please, that would be wonderful."

"Well, I see that she'll be in good hands. I'll be back in a few hours."

"Take as much time as you need," said Mrs. Norris, shooing Ballard away with a motion of her hands. "I'm sure us girls will have plenty to talk about."

Ballard nodded, tipped his cap, and was gone.

Mrs. Norris put her hands on her hips and looked Lavena over from head to toe. "Now, let's get you cleaned up. I'll just bet there's a pretty young girl hiding somewhere under all that dirt."

The warm soapy water felt good against Lavena's skin. She could stay in it forever, washing away the dirt, the memory of her time imprisoned by the dragon, and perhaps a bit sadly, her memories of Warrick.

The fields of Dervon seemed so far away now, another world. She knew that she belonged there, but this place was too full of wonders still to be explored for her to want to go back. She might return there some time, but this place made Dervon so easy to forget.

"So you're helping Flight Lieutenant Ballard with his investigation, eh?" said Mrs. Norris, who had been asking a lot of questions while Lavena bathed.

"He was looking for the dragon," said Lavena. "I showed him where it is."

Mrs. Norris looked at Lavena as if she thought she was being fooled.

Lavena nodded. "It is true."

Mrs. Norris raised her eyebrows. "If you say so, luv."

"He is very handsome, is he not?" said Lavena.

Mrs. Norris, who was busy washing Lavena's back, paused. "You mean Flight Lieutenant Ballard?"

"Yes."

"Well, of course he's handsome. A young man like that, all dressed up in a uniform."

"So he is dressed in a uniform."

The washcloth fell from Mrs. Norris's hand and splashed into the water. She looked at Lavena with a slightly open mouth and wide eyes, as if Lavena had suddenly begun speaking in tongues.

"Where are you from, child?" asked Mrs. Norris.

"Dervon."

Mrs. Norris paused a moment. "Is that in Wales?"

"No, it is on land."

Mrs. Norris was silent a moment. "You really aren't from around here, are you?"

"No," Lavena shook her head. "I'm not from this place."

"And you don't know what is going on, I mean about the war?"

"What war?"

Mrs. Norris searched in the water for the washcloth. She scooped it up, wrung it out and resumed giving Lavena a bath. "I might miss some things, but I'll do my best to explain it all to you." She took a deep breath and began. "Last year, the Germans invaded Poland . . ."

2

Reichsmarshall Goering paced back and forth in front of a line of men made up of the best young fighter pilots in France.

The large-scale attacks of German bombers on Britain were set to begin in the next few days, but the air supremacy necessary to make large formation bombing possible had not yet been achieved.

"Have the young men of the Luftwaffe lost their nerve?" asked Goering, snapping the end of his riding crop against the end of his long, white coat.

"The Stuka squadrons have suffered unacceptable losses in both pilots and machines, all because the fighters have been unable to protect them from the British. A few of you have been bagging record numbers of enemy planes, but our bombers are still being knocked out of the sky by British fighters . . ."

One of the men in the line, Major Adolphus Galland, seemed at odds with Goering's assertion.

"Something to say, Dolpho," said Goering.

"The new British dragon has been—"

"Enough," said Goering harshly. "There is no proof of any new British weapon, and I won't allow you to use such a rumor as an excuse for the fighter force's loss of nerve and fighting spirit."

Galland grit his teeth at the suggestion that the fighter pilots weren't doing everything they could to best the British over England.

Goering ignored the young major and continued speaking harshly to his young knights of the air.

"Nothing is more important than our bombers reaching their targets . . ."

Goering continued speaking for several more minutes, never missing an opportunity to chide the pilots for their lack of courage and will to fight.

Eventually, as the time for Goering to leave grew near, he became more amiable.

"What do you need to better equip your squadrons, Vati?" asked Goering.

"A series of Me-109s with more powerful engines, Reichsmarshall," answered Werner Moelders, one of the top German aces of the war.

"Fine," said Goering. "You will have them."

Goering moved down the line and stopped in front of Galland. "And you?" he said.

Galland did not hesitate. "I should like a squadron of dragons for my wing."

The sheer audacity of Galland's words left Goering speech-less. Instead of reprimanding the young pilot, Goering simply turned and stomped off, growling as he went.

3

Flight Lieutenant Ballard returned several hours later with three portable lights, a half-dozen grenades, a Tommy Gun, and a first-aid kit filled with bandages and other medical supplies. While it was true that he would be trying to talk to the dragon and convince it to join the RAF in its fight against the Hun, he wasn't averse to persuading it by more forceful means.

He also had a WAAF uniform for Lavena. It was obvious that she wouldn't be able to wear her own clothes anymore and if she was to accompany him around, it would be easier for everyone if she was dressed as a WAAF and identified as his assistant.

When he'd arrived at the manor house, Mrs. Norris acted as if the past few hours had been an utter delight. She seemed almost smitten by the young girl, and every word uttered by her was a complimentary one.

"Does my heart good to see a girl with an appetite," said Mrs. Norris. "Most girls today are worried about their figure, but not Lavena. She ate every scone I had, even the burnt ones, and didn't complain once when all I had to wash it down with was well water. Imagine that!"

Ballard had no trouble at all imagining it, remembering how she absolutely gobbled up the food he'd given her in the staff car.

"Speaking of her figure," said Ballard. "I hope this fits her."

"We'll make it fit," answered Mrs. Norris, taking the uniform from Ballard. "But if you ask me, this girl would look good in a potato sack. She's got a fine body on her, hard like an athlete's."

"Indeed," said Ballard, noticing Lavena's shape before, but

not knowing what else to say.

Now he waited while Lavena got dressed.

He was anxious to get to the cave and address the dragon, although the matter seemed to be less urgent to Fighter Command now than it had just a day before. The dragon had been spotted that morning and attacked by squadrons of Spitfires and Hurricanes. Although none of the pilots saw it crash, many saw it damaged and the dragon was written off as a probable kill. That assumption seemed to be borne out by the fact that the dragon had not been seen since.

But while the rest of the RAF was getting on with the task at hand, namely beating back the Germans, Ballard was convinced that the dragon was still quite dangerous and could be a powerful ally in the skies over England.

Mrs. Norris was first to come down the stairs into the kitchen. There was a smile on her face as wide as the English Channel. "May I present to you, Aircraftswoman Lavena!" she said, stepping away from the bottom of the stairs.

A moment later Lavena appeared at the top of the stairs dressed in a pale blue shirt and black tie, blue jacket, blue skirt and blue peaked hat. She had grey stockings and black shoes. She took the steps one at a time, holding onto the stair rail tightly with both hands. The shoes, no doubt, would take a little getting used to.

"Well," said Mrs. Norris. "What do you think?"

"She's uh . . ." Ballard struggled for the words. He wanted to say she was pretty. That might have applied before, for when she was dressed in her rags, Ballard had often thought of her as being a girl. But now, in the striking blue WAAF uniform she was a full-grown woman, not just pretty anymore, but ". . . beautiful."

Lavena smiled at the compliment, but her exuberance seemed to go deeper than that. She seemed thrilled to be dressed in the clothes, as if the uniform had opened up a different side of her, or gave her an outward appearance that matched her inner fighting spirit.

Maybe it just made her feel as if she belonged.

"Of course she's beautiful," said Mrs. Norris. "She's a young British girl, isn't she?"

Ballard nodded. "You won't get any argument from me."

Mrs. Norris approached Ballard and grabbed him firmly by the arm. "Now you take good care of her, you hear me!" she said softly. "You two are too fine a couple to be torn apart by this war."

Ballard was surprised by Mrs. Norris's words. Obviously the two women had gotten to know each other better while he'd been gone. "I'll make sure she's all right."

"Good," said Mrs. Norris, letting go of his arm.

There was a long moment of silence before Ballard said, "I've got everything in the car. We best get going."

Lavena hurried past Ballard, out of the house and to the car.

"Will you be back?" asked Mrs. Norris.

"I'm planning on it," said Ballard.

"I'll leave a candle burning."

They were able to find the cave easily this time. Ballard came to a stop at the side of the road and quickly began taking things out of the back of the *car*. That was the word Mrs. Norris had used for it.

Among the things Ballard wanted to bring into the cave were metal boxes with lights on one side of them. They would help them find their way in the darkness, but might also let Tibalt know that they were in the cave.

"There's a switch," said Ballard. "On." The light came on. "Off." The light went out.

Wonderful, thought Lavena.

Ballard also brought an odd-shaped device whose purpose was not immediately obvious to her. "What's that?" she said.

"It's a gun," said Ballard, leveling it at his waist. "It shoots bullets."

"Steel spits?"

"I guess you could call them that."

"So it is a weapon?"

"Yes, it's a weapon."

The admission angered Lavena. Ballard had promised to talk to the dragon, but here he was bringing in a weapon that could hurt it badly. "You said you would talk to it."

Ballard said nothing for several moments. "I do intend to talk to it, but if it doesn't want to talk to me, I want to be prepared."

"To kill it?"

"No, to defend myself."

Lavena said nothing more. She could not be sure if Ballard was telling her the truth about the purpose of the weapon or not. She decided to take him at his word and watch him closely to make sure that he made every effort to reason with the dragon before using force against it. She knew she couldn't stop him from harming the dragon if he fully intended to do so, but if he was going to kill the dragon he would have to do it without any help from her.

"Are we ready?" he asked.

She nodded.

And they were on their way across the field toward the mouth of the cave. When they arrived, the opening felt cool.

"The dragon might not be inside," she said.

Ballard peered into the darkness, then used his light to look further into the cave. "You might be right. But if he's not here, then it will give us the chance to look around in there, maybe even find someplace comfortable and wait for him."

The thought of waiting in the dark with Ballard sent a little tingle of excitement down Lavena's spine.

Ballard entered the cave and Lavena followed. The further they went the more it seemed likely that the dragon was not there. Neither of them could hear any movement in the depths of the cave and there didn't seem to be any light coming from within.

All of a sudden Lavena stopped in her tracks.

Ballard continued on for a few steps before realizing she had come to a halt. He turned around, "What is it?"

"Listen," she said.

Ballard was motionless and together they listened to the cave. Mixed in with the odd drip of water was a soft, hissing, wheezing sort of sound. Lavena had a difficult time placing it, but it sounded almost like a blacksmith's bellows, slowly drawing in air and blowing it out again.

"Do you hear that?" she asked.

Ballard nodded. "Yes, what is it?"

And then all at once Lavena knew. "It's the dragon," she said. "It's been hurt."

She switched on her light, passed Ballard and led them the rest of the way into the cave.

When they reached the bottom, they both flashed their lights at the floor of the cave, catching the dragon within their beams.

The usually magnificent wash of green and yellow was stained with angry scarlet slashes and crimson holes. Its neck had been riddled with perforations. Each time the dragon let out a wheezy breath, tiny gouts of flame would leak out of its neck, casting a dim glow over the rest of the cave.

"He's been clobbered," said Ballard.

Seeing the dragon that way caused Lavena's heart to sink into the pit of her stomach. She'd started out trying to save both Warrick and the dragon, and now it looked as if she had failed both of them.

They continued to shine their lights on the dragon. It must have noticed the flash of their beams because it lifted its head—a slow and arduous-looking task—and looked directly into the lights.

"Help me . . . ," said Tibalt in a raspy voice. "Help me . . . please."

CHAPTER ELEVEN

1

"What did it say?" asked Ballard. It had sounded as if the dragon had said *something,* but it had been little more than gibberish to his ears.

"He's asking for our help," said Lavena.

"I didn't catch a word of it."

She looked at him and said, "Tell him your name."

Ballard looked at her strangely.

"If you tell him your name, he'll be able to speak to you."

Ballard hesitated a moment, then thought, why not? "My name is Flight Lieutenant Sheridan Ballard, RAF."

The dragon groaned, then opened its maw. "I am Tibalt," he said. "Help me, please . . ." His voice trailed away.

Ballard could only stare at the dragon, overwhelmed by the creature's size, strength, and obvious intelligence.

"You said you had a box of medicine," said Lavena.

The words brought Ballard out of his daze. "Yes," he said. "It's in the car."

"Perhaps you should get it," she said, taking off her jacket and rolling up her sleeves.

"Maybe I should," said Ballard.

Lavena approached the dragon. "It looks like you have finally met your match . . ."

The dragon, Tibalt, groaned.

Ballard turned and headed back out of the cave to retrieve

the first-aid kit. Along the way, he couldn't help thinking how much of a turn his plans had taken.

When he'd first put it in the car, he'd intended that the first-aid kit would be for his and Lavena's use.

Tibalt had made Lavena another sewing needle out of one of his talons, but she didn't dare ruin her new uniform by tearing away strips of fabric to close the holes on Tibalt's wings.

So she began by pulling steel spits—bullets, Flight Lieutenant Ballard had called them—from Tibalt's back and belly.

"There were too many of them," said Tibalt. "Swarms of them, buzzing around me like bees."

"Of course there are," said Ballard, returning with the medicine box. "What did you expect with a war going on?"

Lavena said nothing, allowing Ballard the chance to talk to Tibalt himself.

"War?" said Tibalt.

"The Germans have overrun Western Europe, and we Brits are all that's left to fight them." He handed the medicine box to Lavena and took over the task of removing the bullets from Tibalt's body. "Every day they send Stukas and Heinkels over, dozens of them, escorted by even more Me-109s and 110s—"

Tibalt looked confused.

"The steel dragons," said Lavena.

"Yes, German steel dragons," continued Ballard, "all trying to destroy our ability to fight. But they haven't licked us yet."

Lavena opened the medicine box and took out a roll of white cloth. She tore it in half down its middle and threaded the strips that remained through the talon.

"Tell me more . . ." said Tibalt. "About the steel dragons."

"All right," said Ballard. He dug a bullet from between two of Tibalt's scales. "See that," he said, holding the bullet up between his thumb and forefinger. "That's a bullet from a .303

163

Browning machine gun."

Again, Tibalt looked confused.

"Steel spit," reminded Lavena.

Ballard looked at her strangely, then continued. "Each of our fighters have eight of these guns, and each gun carries three-hundred bullets, uh, steel spits, and can fire them at a rate of twenty per second."

"Which are your fighters," asked Tibalt, "the yellow noses, or the green-and-browns."

Ballard paused a moment to think. "The green-and-browns are ours," he said. "Hurricanes and Spitfires."

"Spit-fires?" said Tibalt. "That's a good name for them. When their steel spits hit me, they burn like fire."

"The Germans prefer to number their aeroplanes, although they do call the Me-110 the 'Destroyer' . . ."

Ballard pried more bullets from Tibalt's scales while he talked about the war and Lavena continued working on Tibalt's wings. As Ballard talked about the war, Lavena couldn't help but feel sorry for the British people.

First of all, she could identify with the British. As the people of Dervon had had to deal with a winged terror in the skies over their village, so too did the British. Instead of that terror being a fire-breathing dragon, it was German fighter and bomber aeroplanes.

And, Lavena was also beginning to think of herself as having been moved from one time to another rather than from one place to another. If that were true then the British people were really her people. For if she and Tibalt had been brought forward in time, then some of the British might actually be her descendants. The more she thought about that, the more she wondered why there were no dragons in this place. No dragons meant that none of Tibalt's descendants had survived.

Asvald's plan suddenly seemed to have more reason to it

than she could have ever imagined, and her struggle to save the dragon became all the more important.

"The Americans have been helping us out as much as they can," Ballard said. "We even have a few of their chaps flying in our squadrons. As a country they aren't in the fight yet. But it's only a matter of time if you ask me."

Ballard took a step back, raised his light and looked over Tibalt's scales. "I think that's pretty much it. There are a few others, but I'd probably do more damage taking them out than if I just left them where they are."

Lavena had a few more holes to close up, and continued working.

Ballard helped her by preparing strips of the white fabric to use as thread. They worked well together, and soon, the last of the large wounds on Tibalt's wings were closed.

But while the dragon had been patched together as best they could manage, he was still a long way from being well. He had lost a lot of blood, some of his wounds had become infected, and he was generally very weak. He needed the attention of a healer, someone who could heal him from the inside out.

Just then, as if the dragon had been reading Lavena's mind, Tibalt said, "Asvald."

"Who?" asked Ballard.

"Asvald," said Lavena. "He's the wizard I told you about."

"Oh, yes. I remember now." Ballard looked up at Tibalt's face. "Sorry to disappoint you, Tibalt, but just as there are no dragons in England in 1940, neither are there any wizards."

"Asvald," said Tibalt. "Bring him here . . . Maybe he can send me back . . . to where I came from. To where I belong."

Lavena looked expectantly at Ballard. She had wanted to look for Asvald herself but knew she'd be lost without Ballard's help. She had even intended to ask him to help her search for the wizard at some point, but knew he had to deal with Tibalt first before doing anything else.

"That's easier said than done, Tibalt," said Ballard. "From what Lavena has told me, and what I can piece together myself, the two of you have been sent forward in time somehow. How far forward I can't say, but a conservative guess would put it at something like one thousand years. Now, even if this Asvald chap led an extremely long life, he still would have died some nine hundred years ago. So you see—"

"Find Asvald," said Tibalt as if he hadn't even heard what Ballard had said. "He will know what to do."

"I just finished explaining to you that your wizard is dead."

Tibalt shook his head slowly, refusing to believe.

"You'll never get him to believe that so many years have passed. The trip took no longer than a few seconds. One moment we were there, the next we were here in this place. I find it hard to understand it myself, although I'm slowly beginning to believe."

Ballard looked frustrated. "Regardless of whether he believes it or not, there are no wizards in England in 1940."

"Find Asvald," repeated Tibalt. "He can help."

"No, no, no," said Ballard. "It's not possible."

For a moment, neither Tibalt nor Ballard said a word. Finally Lavena spoke up. "I think Asvald is in this place too," she said.

"What?" said Ballard.

"I don't know why, but I believe that Asvald is here in this place too."

"But it's impossible."

"As impossible as a dragon?" she asked.

Ballard said nothing.

"When I first met Asvald, I could not guess his age. He could have been thirty years old, he could have been three hundred and thirty years old."

"Yes," hissed Tibalt.

"He is alive in this place," said Lavena, more convinced than ever. "We must find him."

Ballard looked at her for a long time without saying a word. "All right," he said at last. "You haven't steered me wrong yet and there's no reason why you should start doing so now. We'll look for this Asvald character . . . on one condition." He raised his light and shined its beam directly into Tibalt's face. "You must remain in this cave until we get back. If you venture outside, you'll be killed as easily on the ground as in the sky. Do you understand?"

Tibalt moaned, and shifted his weight slightly. "You need not worry. I'm in no condition to leave the cave, nor do I want to go outside."

"Fine, then Lavena and I will head to London to find some record of this Asvald. We'll be back as soon as we can."

Tibalt nodded.

As they were preparing to leave, Tibalt tore a fresh scale from his body and gave it to Lavena. "Here," he said.

"What is that for?" said Ballard.

"A dragon's scale is said to bring good luck," she said.

"Well, we'll be needing all the luck we can get trying to find this man."

They said good-bye to the dragon and headed off. When they neared the entrance to the cave, the words came up behind them from the depths of the cave in a warm rush of air.

"Good luck!"

2

In a large building on the grounds of Bentley Priory, several scientists and engineers in the Air Ministry's Accident Investigation Branch were busy examining some of the wreckage from the aeroplanes that had been brought down by the dragon.

Sydney Shires, a civilian chemical engineer, had been

performing tests on the charred wings and fuselage of a Hawker Hurricane brought down by the dragon on the previous day just east of Derby.

He was bent over the gnarled piece of wreckage, a section of wing about the size of a piece of luggage. The metal was black for the most part, but along one side were many neatly arrayed circles where he had dabbled chemicals to test their reaction with the residue left on the metal.

The number of circles, more than two dozen, was indicative of the extent of his tests. The only other time he'd had to test a charred wreckage of a Hurricane, he'd reached a conclusion after just his second circle.

Air Commodore Trask, who had been in the building trying to get some answers to the dragon problem, came up beside Shires and watched him work.

After a while, Shires became aware of the air commodore's presence. He turned to the commodore and nodded, "Sir."

"What do you make of it?"

Shires stepped back from his workbench, wiped his hands off on a rag and placed his hands on the lapels of his grey knee-length lab coat. "Well . . . The traces of residue I've found are inconsistent with any known fuels or otherwise flammable substances."

"We've had reports that the Germans have been doing all sorts of tests with rockets. Is there a chance that it could be a new type of rocket fuel?"

Shires shook his head. "It's possible, but there are just so many different types of flammable liquids and gases. Even if it were some new type of fuel, it would still leave a recognizable chemical residue on the metal. But what is there is like nothing I've ever seen before."

"I see." The commodore's expression turned pensive. "What's your best guess, then?"

"Well, I hate to say this, but I think the Germans have developed a very secret and very deadly new weapon."

The commodore let out a long sigh. "Thank you, Shires."

"Sir."

3

It was late in the afternoon when Ballard and Lavena drove up to the lone Lysander waiting for them at one end of the Digby airfield.

"Will we be riding in that steel . . . aeroplane?"

"It's only a Lysander, but it's still the quickest way to get to Bentley Priory," said Ballard, bringing the staff car to a stop next to the aeroplane.

"You are going to take me flying?"

"That's the idea."

Lavena felt a thrill run down her spine, just as she did the time Warrick had taken her for a ride on his steed.

They got out of the car and walked over to the Lysander. There were two men working on the aeroplane and each of them were looking at her with curious smiles on their faces. One of them even whistled, but stopped when Ballard gave him a harsh look.

"See you're taking a passenger with you back to HQ, eh Flight Lieutenant?"

"My assistant," said Ballard. "Aircraftswoman Lavena."

One of the men smiled. "Always pleased to meet a fellow erk," he said.

Lavena was at a loss as to what he meant, but he held out his hand so she took it in hers and he shook it.

"Is it ready to go?" asked Ballard quickly.

"The tanks have been topped up and the engine's already warm," said the other man. He was older than the first, and appeared to be in charge.

"Right," said Ballard. He turned to face her. "Lavena, you'll be in the back."

She was disappointed by that. "Can't I ride up front with you?" she said.

"There's only one seat in front," said Ballard, his face suddenly turned a light shade of red as he quickly looked at the other two men.

Lavena got the feeling that she had said something wrong, but knew it was not the time to ask what. "Of course," she said, climbing up into the back of the aeroplane.

Ballard continued talking with the two men for a few minutes, then put on a leather hat and climbed into the front seat. A few more minutes passed and then the aeroplane roared into life and began to shake.

Lavena's heart leaped up into her throat and she grabbed onto whatever she could find to steady herself.

"Are you all right?" asked Ballard.

Lavena was both excited and terrified. The noise and power of the aeroplane was thrilling, and the mere thought that something so big and heavy could actually fly was wondrous. Part of her wanted to jump out and run for her life, but another part of her would not miss this experience for anything in the world. "Fine," she said, nodding emphatically. "Good."

Ballard balled his right hand into a fist and raised his thumb. The men outside the aeroplane did the same.

The noise grew louder and they began moving forward, so slowly that Lavena wondered how they would ever get off the ground. After rolling along for a little bit, the aeroplane stopped and the noise grew louder still, so loud that Lavena could barely hear herself think.

And then suddenly they were moving forward, faster and faster, bumping over the ground, once, twice . . . and then all was smooth. Lavena could feel herself being picked up, lifted from the ground as if she weighed no more than a feather.

She looked out the window and saw the men had shrunk into small points on the ground. Everything was smaller, as if the land below were nothing more than a map drawn in the sand.

The loud noise lessened slightly. The aeroplane's nose dropped, and for a moment, Lavena felt as if she were floating weightless in the air.

She let out a shriek of fear.

Ballard looked over his shoulder and smiled. "How do you like flying?"

She put a hand over her stomach, trying to keep its contents where they were. "Wonderful," she said.

Ballard laughed.

She looked out the window once more. The land below stretched out into the distance for what seemed like forever. On the other side the land met with the water, and the water continued the journey toward the horizon.

She forgot all about her upset stomach, and drank in the view. "Wonderful," she whispered to herself. "Absolutely wonderful."

It was well after dark by the time a driver dropped them off at Bentley Priory. Lavena recognized that her uniform matched those of the women stationed at Fighter Command and she seemed to enjoy fitting in with the crowd. Once when Ballard was busy signing them in, he caught a glimpse of Lavena watching a group of WAAFs walk past. She followed them closely with her eyes, studying every movement, and then when they were gone, she got up from her bench, adjusted her hat and tried walking the way the other women had walked. She also practiced a few of their hand gestures, but when she noticed Ballard looking, she pretended to be adjusting her hair.

Ballard had wanted to meet with Air Commodore Trask, but

he was in a meeting with Air Chief Marshal Dowding and would not want to be disturbed. So he made an appointment to see the commodore in the morning and decided to get some rest for what would likely be a very long and tiring day.

"We best get some sleep," said Ballard.

"We can sleep here?" asked Lavena, indicating the hallway.

"No, not here," Ballard smiled. "There are rest rooms off the Ops Rooms. You can sleep on a cot in one of them tonight so we can start bright and early in the morning."

"Will you be with me?"

At that moment a major walked by, looking at him and Lavena rather strangely. "Sir," said Ballard, saluting and lifting Lavena's sleeve by the shoulder of her jacket so she would do the same.

The major nodded, then slowly continued on.

"No, I won't be with you," said Ballard. "You'll be in the dorm with other WAAFs. Try not to say too much to them, because the dragon is still a secret."

"I understand," Lavena nodded.

"Good, good," said Ballard. "Now, let's find you a room."

4

Just before midnight, a German Fieseler Stork took off from IX Fliegerdivision Headquarters in Soesterberg and headed out over the black waters of the North Sea.

The small, high-wing co-operational aeroplane kept low over the water to avoid British radar, the wheels at the end of its fixed, stilt-like landing gear sometimes getting wet from the spray of the churning waves beneath it.

After a few minutes in the air the pilot, Sergeant Josef Zurngibl, relaxed somewhat knowing that for the next hour or so he would be in little danger. It would be at the end of that time when the slow-flying Stork came in sight of the British coast that things would get dangerous. Although he'd dropped agents behind enemy lines before, this was the first time he'd be landing in England.

The Stork was slow, small and quiet and could usually fly undetected into enemy airspace, but *landing* in England was an entirely different matter. All it would take to end the mission would be a single aeroplane on patrol, or even one separated from its squadron. Ground forces could shoot it down just as easily since it would be in range of even the smallest of small-arms fire. And when he landed he would be totally vulnerable for several minutes and could even be incapacitated by a farmer with a shotgun.

Zurngibl glanced over his shoulder at the black-clad hauptmann behind him. The man had said nothing to him while he'd loaded up the aeroplane, and only said, "Let's go," when he was done. Now he was still in his seat, eyes wide and body motionless. Must be an important mission to take such a risk, thought Zurngibl. He was glad not to know anything about the mission since it was dangerous enough as it was.

The white line of water breaking against the coast came into view, and Zurngibl throttled back the Stork's tiny engine until he was almost gliding through the air. He crossed the coast and began looking for a place to land. He'd been instructed to drop the hauptmann in a field several miles inland.

Not such an easy task, especially in the dark.

In preparation for a German invasion from the air, British farmers had placed obstructions throughout their fields, mounding dirt, digging trenches, or placing old cars in the middle of roads—all of which were very difficult to see at night.

Luckily, most of the obstructions were designed to foil large transports like the Ju-52, and troop-carrying gliders. Those craft needed some three hundred yards to land and take off, but the Stork could do it in much less. Some in the Luftwaffe had jokingly said that the plane could land on a bedsheet. That was an exaggeration, of course, but not much of one.

In addition, reconnaissance photos taken earlier in the day had identified several fields that were clear enough for the Stork to take off and land.

At last the first of the fields came into view. It was lined by high trees at one end—which would provide some cover—and a hedgerow at the other.

Zurngibl looked over his shoulder and said, "I'm putting it down."

The hauptmann turned to look at him and Zurngibl felt a chill run down his spine. Even in the dark the man's eyes seemed to have an icy chill to them. For a moment Zurngibl was glad he'd be leaving the hauptmann behind.

The field was a grassy meadow, somewhat hilly and dotted by rocks, but it would be enough. Zurngibl pulled the engine throttle all the way back, and descended on the field in silence.

The landing wheels hit the ground hard and for a moment the aeroplane was airborne again, but the second time the wheels touched down the Stork seemed to stick and Zurngibl was able to stop it in just a few yards. As the aeroplane came to a stop, Zurngibl adjusted the throttle to keep the engine running while the hauptmann unloaded his supplies.

Most of what he had was stored in black bags, but Zurngibl had been able to make out several cases of grenades, explosives and timing devices. He also carried a Luger and one of the largest knives Zurngibl had ever seen. In fact, it was almost a sword.

Zurngibl shuddered to think what the group captain intended to do with such weapons.

It seemed to take forever, Zurngibl's head constantly swiveling around on his neck in search of the British, but eventually the hauptmann had unloaded all of his supplies. Before he closed the rear door of the Stork, the hauptmann called out to Zurngibl.

"Sergeant!" he said.

Zurngibl turned awkwardly in his seat to look at the hauptmann.

"Heil Hitler!" said the hauptmann with a stiff-armed salute.

Zurngibl was surprised by the hauptmann's words. He'd expected something like "Good luck!" or "See you soon!" but no, he'd chosen to say "Heil Hitler!" No wonder he was on this mission.

"Heil Hitler," Zurngibl said softly.

The hauptmann closed the door, gathered up his supplies and ran off the field.

There was enough room for a takeoff, so Zurngibl throttled up the areoplane's tiny engine, until it whined. Moments after it began rolling, the wheels of the Stork hit a bump and the entire aeroplane vaulted into the air. Zurngibl nearly clipped the tops of the trees at the end of the field, turned east and stayed close to the ground all the way to the coast.

When he was over the North Sea he breathed a sigh of relief.

But along with the relief he also felt a pang of regret.

For some reason, he had the feeling that he had just delivered a man to his death.

CHAPTER TWELVE
Tuesday, August 6, 1940

1

Flight Lieutenant Ballard was waiting for Air Commodore Trask when the air commodore arrived at his office just after seven in the morning.

"Ah, Flight Lieutenant Ballard," said Trask. "I heard you were back."

"Just last night, sir."

"Good, good. Come into my office, then."

Ballard followed the commodore into his office and took the same chair he'd sat in on his previous visit.

"Now," said Trask. "What have you learned?"

Ballard hadn't expected to be asked to give his report so quickly without any small talk or chatter about the war. He had been gathering up his confidence so that when he was called upon to lie to the commodore he would be able to do it convincingly with few, if any, stumbles. But here he was, asked to speak to the man without so much as a cup of tea to settle his nerves.

Ballard had decided late the night before that he would not tell the commodore the whole truth. He knew the risk he was taking, but concluded that it was the only way to get the dragon safely back to wherever it came from. After all, he'd seen and spoken with the dragon and still had trouble believing it existed. What would a fifty-year-old stick-in-the-mud like Air Commodore Trask say to Ballard's request that he be allowed to go looking for a wizard?

Ballard licked his lips and swallowed in an attempt to moisten his suddenly parched throat. "There is something in the area around Derby," he said. "The number of eyewitness accounts can't be easily dismissed. I've also found some evidence . . . footprints and the like, on some of the farms I visited, but there have been no new sightings reported in the past twenty-four hours."

Trask nodded, no doubt already aware of the same information.

"So what's your opinion?"

"Well, sir . . ." He paused, realizing he had been given the opportunity to outline the ideal situation for the dragon. "I think our boys really tore it up that last go-round, a probable kill, I'd say. The thing's likely floating face down somewhere out in the North Sea by now."

Trask seemed unconvinced. "What if it wasn't killed?" he asked.

"From the reports I've read, I'd say it's gone from the sky for good."

"I'd like proof of that," said Trask. "And what if there's more than one of them?"

Ballard couldn't tell the air commodore there was just a single dragon because "The wizard only sent *one* of the beasts a thousand years into the future." No, he would have to come up with something logical that explained everything to the commodore's satisfaction. "If the Germans had a second dragon, they would have sent the pair of them out hunting together. Obviously, this dragon was a secret weapon, perhaps even a prototype that was being tested operationally in the skies over England."

Trask was silent, as if considering the possibility.

Ballard was rather pleased with himself. The story was so plausible that he almost believed it himself.

"That just may be," said Trask with a slow nod.

Ballard breathed easily. "Then may I consider my official investigation into the matter closed? I'd like to spend the next little while—"

"No, you may not consider your investigation closed."

"Sir?"

"If that dragon came down on British soil we've got to intensify our efforts in locating it. I told you before, I want proof!"

Ballard let out his breath slowly.

"Just imagine the technological advances we could glean from it in terms of aerodynamics, armor and armament."

"I'm sure it would be a boost to our war effort, sir," said Ballard unenthusiastically.

"Right!" said Trask. "Now, because this dragon seemed to be most active around Derby, RAF Intelligence thinks that perhaps it's holed up in the caves there. Regular troops are being armed and mobilized to help in the search. They should arrive there in the next few days. If the dragon came down on British soil, we'll find it."

"Yes, sir," said Ballard, thinking that the Intelligence branch had been aptly named.

"I want you to go back up to Derby right away and help coordinate the search effort. You might even be able to help them from the air."

Ballard was silent. He had entered the commodore's office in the hopes of giving Tibalt the time he needed to heal, and Lavena the time she needed to find the wizard Asvald. But instead of more time, they now had less.

"Something wrong, Flight Lieutenant?"

"Sir, request permission to remain in the Intelligence Office today to look through the records."

"What are you looking for?"

Ballard found himself in the same awkward position as before. He could either tell the truth and say, "The wizard who sent the dragon forward in time to 1940," and be relieved of his commission in the RAF, or he could tell a half-truth as he'd done previously, and make the situation worse than it already was.

He decided on the half-truth, since things weren't likely to get any worse than they already were. "I'm looking for a man who is an expert on such things as dragons and . . ." He hesitated, realizing he'd just described everyone from a young child to a school mistress. "And special weapons."

The commodore nodded. "Yes, of course," he said. "Feel free to use all the resources the RAF has to offer."

"Thank you, sir!" he said, both surprised and relieved that this part had at least gone according to his wishes.

Air Commodore Trask nodded, then busied himself with some paperwork on his desk.

Ballard was free to go. He got up from his chair and hurried out of the office.

Hopefully, Lavena hadn't had enough time to make herself too conspicuous in the halls of Bentley Priory.

After looking through half the offices of Fighter Command without any luck, Ballard found Lavena in the hallway outside the main Ops Room. She was standing by a water fountain, turning the tap on and off and delighting in the spurt of water that came up from the spigot.

Several WAAFs walked by at that moment, curious about what Lavena was doing, but too polite to interrupt her.

"It's a water fountain," said Ballard. "For drinking."

Lavena took a drink and smiled. "Can we start looking for Asvald now?"

"Yes," said Ballard, taking Lavena by the arm and leading her down the hall. "Right away."

"What is the hurry?"

"Tibalt is in danger," answered Ballard. "If we don't find Asvald soon, as in sometime today, Tibalt might not live till the end of the week."

2

After carefully hiding the bulk of his supplies, Von Hesse traveled west for most of the night, hoping to reach the outskirts of Derby by morning. If he had any chance of fitting in, it would be closer to the city where one might expect the odd familiar face to be passing through on a fairly regular basis.

Shortly after he'd landed, he had slipped into the dark-blue coveralls of the Post Office Engineers. It was the perfect cover, since it allowed him to wander the countryside in search of downed telephone and telex lines. The disguise also proved to be rather utilitarian because of the oversized toolbox he was required to tote around with him. He also carried yards and yards of fuse cord, wound up to look like telephone wire. And the bag over his shoulder that was supposed to carry his government-issue gas mask was the perfect pouch for his Luger. Gas masks were an interesting precaution on the part of the British, but he knew they were an unnecessary one. Still, it didn't hurt to have the civilian population living in fear.

As he strode along the dirt roads of Derbyshire, Von Hesse scanned the countryside for any evidence of a dragon. He didn't know what he was looking for, but he felt that he would recognize it when he found it. Several times along the way, people passing, on bicycles or in cars, waved hello. Von Hesse smiled and nodded, wishing he could answer their friendliness with a round from his Luger.

After several hours on his feet, Von Hesse felt comfortable enough in his new role to approach people in the area and enquire about the dragon. It was a poor starting point, he knew, but it was the only real starting point he had.

As he came upon a crossroads, he recognized the intersecting road as the highway leading into Derby, after diligently studying a road map of the area produced by British Petroleum in 1938.

Through the intersection and down the road several hundred yards was a small cottage. Von Hesse headed toward it. As he neared, he saw that it was bordered in front by a stone wall and in back by a white picket fence. It was a bungalow with perhaps a loft in the attic. There were no children's toys about, no heavy tools either. The gardens surrounding the house suggested a definite green thumb, and the flowers in bloom a woman's touch.

He stopped at the gate in front of the house and looked it over one last time. He'd thought that an elderly person lived here just by the look of the house, but the cane resting against the wall by the front door confirmed it.

"Hello there," he said in perfect English, with hardly any hint of an accent. "I say, anyone home?"

There was no response for a few moments, so he repeated his call. He was about to move on when a faint voice could be heard coming from inside. "Hold on," said the voice. "I'll be out in a minute."

The door opened a few seconds later and an elderly woman wrapped in a shawl—despite the warm summer day—picked up the cane by the door and came down the walk to meet him.

"Good day, mum," said Von Hesse. "Had some reports of lines being down in the area. Your phone working, then?"

She looked at him strangely. "I haven't got a telephone."

Von Hesse realized he'd made a mistake, but carried on as if there were nothing odd about what he'd said. "Then you haven't got a problem then, have you?" He forced a laugh.

"No, and I don't know anyone else who has one either," she said.

"Well, I've been told to check out the lines," said Von Hesse. "Said one of them's been pulled down by a dragon. Can you believe that?" He'd decided to mention the dragon, thinking it would either get the woman talking, or convince her he was crazy.

"I sure can," she said. "I've seen the dragon in my backyard eating my flowers."

"You're joking me, right?"

"I am most certainly not. Anyone who knows me will tell you, Edna Abernathy is no joker."

Von Hesse smiled.

"I saw it there, munching away. I ran after it with my broom, but it flew away."

"Where did it go?" In his haste to ask the question, Von Hesse had pronounced the 'Wh' in *Where* as a 'V' allowing a bit of a German accent to slip in behind his words.

She looked at him suspiciously. "Where are you from?"

"Birmingham," he said.

"You're not from Birmingham," she said. "No one from there pronounces it Bir-ming-ham, it's Birmingum."

"That's where I serve with the Post Office . . ."

"Then where's your little yellow Post Office badge, supposed to go over the tools on your left chest . . ."

Von Hesse knew that the British Ministry of Information had circulated a pamphlet called, "If the Invader Comes," which basically instructed British citizens to trust no one. He'd had the opportunity to read one of the pamphlets in Berlin and remembered that it had said things like—*Most of you know your policemen and your ARP Wardens by sight, you can trust them. If you keep your heads, you can also tell whether a military officer is really British or only pretending to be so. If in doubt ask the policeman or the ARP Warden. Use your common sense.* The pamphlet had seemed silly to Von Hesse when he'd read it, but here he was, an SS officer, Hauptmann Hermann Von Hesse being foiled by Mrs. England. It was almost laughable.

". . . My nephew is a Post Office Engineer and he has a little yellow Post Office badge on his chest. You haven't got one."

"Because," said Von Hesse, allowing his thick German accent to shine through. "I forgot it . . . in Berlin."

Von Hesse found the look of surprise on the old woman's face thrilling. But it was nowhere near as satisfying as the look of sheer terror in her eyes, as he raised the knife over his head . . .

And drove it straight down into her heart.

3

Where to begin?

Of the millions of people in England, where were they to find a wizard named Asvald—if that was even the name he went by in 1940?

"He would be a respected man, working at a job that discovered new knowledge," Lavena said when Ballard asked her to tell him a little something about the man.

"A man of science, eh?"

She looked at him strangely, and shrugged.

It occurred to him that in her time the word science had likely not been in common usage. Nevertheless, scientists were probably as good a starting point as any since every bit of technology Lavena had come across had fascinated her as if it were magic. It might be logical then that as technology advanced a wizard would have a keen interest in the sciences that developed those technologies.

And so they started with the roles of British doctors in the fields of chemistry, physics, electricity and a half dozen other disciplines. They spent an hour looking for people with the surname Asvald, then searched for it listed as a first name. No luck.

"Perhaps he would want to help people with his powers. Maybe he became a healer."

That seemed a more logical assumption to Ballard and he spent the next hour looking over the lists of the various British medical associations. Again they widened the search, this time for any name that even resembled Asvald, but the closest they were able to come was a pharmacist named Osbaldason. At first the discovery excited Ballard, but the feeling quickly waned when he discovered that Inga Osbaldason had recently come to England from Sweden. Again, no luck.

On and on they went, checking lists in all the professions, from solicitors to dentists, diplomats to engineers, but all of their efforts came up empty.

Ballard even tried an amateur magician he knew in London, asking him if he's every heard of anyone by the name of Asvald. "No, Italian and Chinese names are in style now, although there isn't much call for magicians these days anyway, on account of the war," said the man.

That information wasn't much help since Asvald was free to use a stage name like everyone else. Ballard handed over the telephone to Lavena so she could describe him to the man, but the description failed to ring any bells.

Ballard thanked his friend, arranged to have him entertain his squadron in the next couple of weeks, and hung up the phone. "Do you think this Asvald might be in the army?"

Lavena thought about it. "He was never a fighter," she said. "Even when the dragon came to Dervon, he wanted to avoid fighting it at all cost."

"Not everyone in the army carries a weapon."

"No?"

"There are medics and radio operators, lorry drivers and cooks . . ."

"If he were in the army he would use his powers to help people."

"A medic, then," said Ballard. "That's someone who tends to soldiers who are wounded in battle."

"Yes," nodded Lavena. "If he were in the army, he would be a medic."

And so, they began checking the thousands of soldiers currently stationed in England. It was a daunting task, and Ballard managed to utilize the help of several WAAFs in the Intelligence Office to help.

But this new lead, one that had held so much promise, soon suddenly turned cold, literally, when they found an ambulance driver by the name of Sergeant William Oswald. Unfortunately he had died a month earlier in the final days of the Battle of France.

They soon turned to the lists of Home Guardsmen, Air Raid Wardens and members of various brigades, but with no luck.

"I'm sorry, Lavena," said Ballard, late in the day. "I don't know where else to look."

"He is here in these lists somewhere," she said confidently. "We just haven't found him yet."

Ballard admired her fighting spirit. She simply refused to give up the search.

And so they tried again.

4

Von Hesse had buried the troublesome old woman in the garden behind her house. There had been a lot of blood, but he'd been able to hide the stains on the walk by covering the path with dirt. More blood had spattered on his coveralls, but luckily the dark-blue color of the material had turned the blood black, making it look like grease from a recent repair.

Before the woman had begun to suspect him, she had said

the dragon had flown off. She had pointed in a general direction as she spoke and Von Hesse decided it was as good a direction as any.

But as he walked along the roads, he recalled the geography of the area he had studied the night before leaving France. The area of Derbyshire was home to some of the largest underground caverns in all England. Perhaps it was possible that work on the new British secret weapon was being developed in underground facilities.

This was a definite possibility.

After all, there were plans to construct concrete pens on the French coast that would make the German U-boats almost invulnerable to attack. And wasn't secret German rocket testing and development currently being conducted in underground installations in the Bavarian Alps?

If the Fatherland performed secret research underground, then why not the British as well?

Von Hesse stopped at the side of the road and checked his BP map of the area. One of the openings to the caves was clearly marked as a point of interest to tourists. He took a look around at the roads and made a rough guess as to his location based on visible landmarks and his memory.

Satisfied he knew where he was, he folded up his map and headed north.

Toward the caves.

5

"You still looking for that bloke named Asvald?" asked a middle-aged WAAF with slightly greying hair. Ballard recognized her from the RAF Protocol Office which processed medals and commendations.

Ballard looked up from a book listing citizens of the City of Manchester and rubbed his tired eyes. "Yes, we're still looking," he said. "Why do you ask?"

"Well, I was going over the last DCM list from the Battle of France and there's a name on it that sort of fits with the name of the man you're looking for."

Ballard immediately perked up. He got up from his chair and went to the woman's side.

"His name's not exactly Asvald, but—"

"What is his name?" asked Ballard abruptly.

"Private Alexander Seldon Vald."

Ballard was silent a moment, then said, "A.S. Vald."

"Asvald," said Lavena.

"He served as a medic and driver with the British Expeditionary Force in France. He has an exemplary service record."

"What did he do to earn the DCM?" asked Ballard.

"Apparently, he took a van into enemy territory and rescued a downed flier."

Ballard nodded. Whoever this A.S. Vald was, he was certainly brave, but that didn't exactly make him a wizard.

"The amazing thing about the rescue is that the pilot swears he was shot in the leg and shoulder before he bailed out, but by the time Private Vald got him to Dunkirk he was fit for duty and was back flying the next day."

"That's Asvald," said Lavena, a bright smile across her face.

Ballard was ready to concede to Lavena that they'd found her wizard, but he was curious to know more about the man. "How old is he?"

"You know," said the WAAF. "It's funny that you ask because I pulled his card and the numbers that are supposed to list his age are quite smudged. He could be eighteen, could be seventy-eight."

Ballard nodded. "That must be him, then."

"Really?"

"Yes," said Ballard. "Thanks love, you're a lifesaver."

"Me and this Asvald, eh?" she said, smiling.

Ballard turned to Lavena. "All right then. We're off to see the wizard."

CHAPTER THIRTEEN

1

After the fall of France and the evacuation of Dunkirk, Private Alexander Seldon Vald's unit had been assigned to Anti-Aircraft Command, a branch of the British army that was placed loosely under the direction of Air Chief Marshal Dowding at Fighter Command.

Vald's unit had been positioned on the banks of the Thames estuary where they were kept busy firing their AA guns at the Luftwaffe fighters and bombers that flew over London on the way to their targets.

Ballard and Lavena reached the gun site just after tea time and came across a scraggly group of men happily eating biscuits and drinking tea from an assortment of tin cups and plates. Many of the men had eyes for Lavena, giving her a wink and a whistle. Ballard glanced over at her and was surprised to see that she didn't seem to mind the attention at all.

"Cup of tea?" the sergeant said, offering both Ballard and Lavena a grimy, dented metal cup.

"What?" asked Ballard. He turned to see the teacup before him. "Uh, no, thank you," said Ballard.

"Suit yourself."

"I'm looking for someone in your unit."

"Who's that?"

"Private Alexander Seldon Vald, do you know him?"

The sergeant laughed. "The old man? Sure I know him,

everyone knows him. Hard to miss a character like that."

Ballard craned his neck and looked over the group of men. None of them seemed to match the description Lavena had given of the wizard.

"You'll be looking all day, sir," said the sergeant, taking a sip of tea. "He's not here."

"Why not?" asked Ballard fearing the worst.

"He won't fire a gun. Absolutely refuses to do it, so I put him on barrage balloons."

"Where is he, then?"

"Should be sending up a blimp a few miles up river right about now."

"Thank you," said Ballard. He turned to Lavena. She was smiling at several of the men. "Let's go," he said.

They headed back to the staff car.

Whistles could be heard behind them all the way.

2

Ballard could see the barrage balloon slowly rising up over the horizon long before he reached the site. As he neared, he spotted the balloon crew's attendant wagon and trailer filled with hydrogen cylinders, and drove toward it.

"Stay in the car," Ballard told Lavena, remembering the reaction she'd gotten from the men back at the AA gun site.

"All right," she said, her eyes fixed on the large balloon as it floated serenely into the air.

Satisfied she wouldn't be going anywhere for the next little while, Ballard got out of the car and headed for the ragged collection of men on the ground.

"Excuse me," he said to one of the men.

"Sir."

"I'm looking for Private Alexander Seldon Vald. Is he with this group?"

The man took out a handkerchief and wiped his brow. "You mean the old man? What's he done now?"

"Nothing," said Ballard. "I'd just like to speak with him."

"Baldie!" the man called.

"What is it?" a voice said.

"A big noise is here to see you."

Ballard knew that *big noise* meant *important person* in RAF slang, but he couldn't be sure if the term was being used ironically or not. However, there was no time to dwell on the matter because a few moments later he was standing face-to-face with Private Alexander Seldon Vald.

A.S. Vald.

Asvald.

He had a head of pure white hair, a thick white mustache under his nose and a bit of white growth around his cheeks and neck. He looked old, but watching him approach, Ballard thought him to have the fluid body movements of a twenty-year-old. The lines around his eyes reminded Ballard of his grandfather, but the light in his eyes reminded him of his kid brother. The WAAF back at Bentley Priory had been right—he could be twenty-eight, he could be seventy-eight.

"Private Vald?"

"Yes, sir," he answered softly.

"I'd like to have a word with you."

"If you like."

This could be him, thought Ballard, looking at Private Vald more closely. He certainly seemed different enough from the rest. But then again, what was a wizard supposed to look like? "You did quite well over in France," said Ballard.

"Thank you, sir. I did my part."

"You amassed an excellent record. According to what I've read about you, no wounded soldier ever died while under your care."

Private Vald shrugged. "That's just lucky, I guess."

"I've been told you've been recommended for a DCM."

"That so?" he answered. "Well, well."

"Yes, and I must say I find it rather curious that an airman could be wounded in his aeroplane, but delivered back to his squadron as good as new on the very same day. I'm curious to know how you did that, considering we can't even mend pranged Hurricanes and Spitfires that quickly?"

"It's nothing, really," he said. "I guess I know a few tricks that maybe some other fellas don't."

"Indeed," said Ballard.

Private Vald simply shrugged.

"A.S. Vald," said Ballard, deciding on a different tack.

"That's me."

"Do you sometimes go by the name Asvald?"

His eyes moved up and down Ballard's body, as if sizing him up. "Used to, years ago."

Ballard was only partially convinced that this man was the wizard Lavena had spoken about. He could continue to ask questions about who he was, but somehow Ballard got the feeling that the wizard would have vague answers to every one of his questions no matter how direct they were. And so he decided to cut out the silly posturing and simply ask for the wizard's help. Ballard cleared his throat and said, "I need your help . . . to save a dragon."

The playfully innocent look on Asvald's face disappeared, but he still didn't seem quite ready to admit his identity. "There's no such thing as dragons," he said.

Behind Asvald, the other members of the balloon crew burst into raucous laughter.

"You tell him, Baldie!" one of them quipped.

"At least we've got *our* feet on the ground," said another.

It was then that Ballard realized that Asvald had known the

other men were listening to their conversation, which was amazing since his back was to them.

"Let's start walking," said Ballard.

"Lead the way."

Ballard turned and began walking away from the balloon crew. After they'd traveled a few dozen yards, he stopped and faced Asvald again. But instead of speaking, this time Ballard reached inside his jacket and pulled out one of the dragon scales that Tibalt had given to him back in the cave.

When Asvald caught sight of the dragon scale his face changed slightly from being that of a youngish man to that of a wizened, battle-hardened old-timer. Looking at him now, Ballard had no trouble at all believing he was Lavena's wizard.

"The dragon . . . Tibalt, gave this to me," said Ballard.

Asvald unbuttoned his sweat-stained tan shirt to reveal a dragon scale hanging from his neck by a leather thong. It was old and faded, but it was almost identical to the one Ballard held in his hand.

"Where is it now?" asked Asvald.

"In a cave, just northeast of Derby."

"Is it alive?"

"Barely."

Asvald nodded.

"Can you help?"

"Do you have any idea how long I've been waiting for this dragon to appear?"

"Good," said Ballard, feeling as if an incredible weight had begun to be lifted from his shoulders.

"The dragon's giving you a bit of trouble, eh?" said Asvald with a wry smile.

"Both the dragon and the girl."

"The girl?" Asvald said hopefully.

"Oh, yes," said Ballard. "There's something else I need to tell you."

3

It was growing late in the day and Von Hesse was no closer to finding the cave—any cave—than when he'd started. He began thinking about finding a place to spend the night since it was unlikely he'd be able to find anything in the dark and he would be drawing even more attention to himself traveling alone at night.

If there were telephone wires that needed to be repaired at night, they would likely be worked on by a crew of engineers equipped with a lorry and a set of high-powered lights. A single engineer would be a curiosity to be sure.

There were farms all around, which was part of the problem. All of the land looked so similar that he had trouble distinguishing one farmyard from another. Many of the farms had shacks or barns in their yards, but most of them were close to farmhouses, which meant people. He needed to find someplace comfortable and isolated.

As he crested a hill, he saw a barn standing at the edge of a field. It looked solid enough, and best of all, there wasn't another barn or building anywhere to be seen. He headed for it quickly, doing his best to ensure that no one saw him dash across the field toward it.

Inside, there was a single dairy cow. An added bonus, he thought. Some fresh milk would certainly go well with his rations. He stored his wires and toolbox up in the hay-covered loft, then went back down to the stall housing the black-and-white cow.

The animal seemed skittish when he neared, moving away from him when he tried to place the pail beneath its udders. When he finally had everything in place and put his hands on the cow's teats, the animal let out an irritated sort of *moo.*

"Now, now," said Von Hesse. "I only want a little bit."

Moo! the cow said, this time a little louder.

He pulled on two of the cow's teats, but his efforts failed to yield any milk since he wasn't quite sure of what he was doing. He tried again, pulling harder.

The cow let out an even louder *moo,* and tried to move away from him, but only managed to bang its hindquarter against the side of the barn.

The cow continued making noise and moving about, forcing Von Hesse to give up on the milk or risk someone hearing the cow thrashing about.

"Stupid British cow," he said at last, climbing the ladder up to the loft.

The cow let out a long, satisfied, *moo.*

Von Hesse ate in silence, struggling to get his bone-dry rations down his throat.

4

The staff car was parked just down the riverbank. Ballard said nothing more to Asvald as they approached it, and the wizard seemed content to walk in silence.

When they were a few dozen yards away, Ballard saw Lavena's head moving up and down, and from side to side, as she tried to get a better look at the approaching Asvald. He could also see that she was smiling brightly, confirming for Ballard that he had indeed found *the* Asvald she and the dragon had spoken about.

When they were several yards away, Lavena opened the door of the staff car and stepped out.

Asvald stopped in his tracks.

She posed for him, showing off her uniform, then waved.

The wizard's mouth moved, but he seemed unable to say a word.

She started walking toward him.

"Lavena?" he said at last.

"Asvald?" she said.

Asvald moved forward to meet her.

They ended up running toward each other, coming together in an embrace.

"Thank god you're alive," they said in unison.

They laughed at that, ending their embrace and holding each other at arm's length.

"You're even younger and more beautiful than I remember," said Asvald.

Hearing that, Ballard felt a pang of jealousy course through his body. Even though Asvald was old enough to be Lavena's father (forefather, in fact), there was a bond between them that Ballard knew he could never match. He could only hope that their relationship was one of friendship and mutual respect.

"And you haven't aged a day," said Lavena.

"I might not look it, but I've aged many a day. Too many, if truth be told." He laughed in a way that a grandfather might. "But enough about me. What of the dragon?"

"I'm afraid Tibalt has not fared well in this place . . ."

Lavena began telling Asvald about the dragon, and slowly the two of them began walking along the bank of the river.

Ballard followed closely behind, allowing the two friends the chance to be brought up to date about each other's lives and the current situation.

CHAPTER FOURTEEN
Wednesday, August 7, 1940

1

Von Hesse was up before the sun. As he walked along the roadway he heard the roosters in the distance, marking the dawn of a new day.

After walking several miles in a northwesterly direction, Von Hesse noticed the sun had become a burnished gold disk floating over the eastern horizon. Its warmth felt good on his coveralls after the chilly night spent in the drafty loft.

He stopped at a crossroads and looked out over the countryside. The land here was less flat than what he had seen elsewhere and could now be described as rolling. Fields crested and dipped like ocean waves and at the bottom of one of the dips, he knew, was a cave where secret British weapons were being tested and developed.

As he turned to look to his left, he saw something curious.

Rising up over a serene green field was a line of smoke, or perhaps even steam, curling toward the sky. At first he thought it was a natural phenomenon, but as he looked at more of the surrounding countryside, he realized that there were no other signs of rising smoke or steam anywhere to be seen.

It must have some significance, thought Von Hesse.

Perhaps it was smoke from a smokestack, or the exhaust port of a facility buried deep under the ground.

It seemed fantastic, but no more so than some of the other experiments conducted by the British. In July they had studied ways to alight the sea and beaches most likely to be used in the event of a German invasion. They had managed to set the sea on fire by pouring oil onto the waters of the Channel coast. The oil was then lighted and the fires were fed by perforated fuel pipes beneath the water's surface.

Ambitious, but utterly impractical.

However, if they were capable of such grand plans, then anything was possible.

Von Hesse set off across the field to investigate the rising smoke.

2

Flight Lieutenant Ballard spent the morning arranging Asvald's special leave from barrage-balloon duty so that he could assist him in his investigation into the dragon.

"A private?" asked the major in charge of issuing leaves and transfers to all ground crew under RAF's command.

"In the army, Alexander Seldon Vald might be just a private, but in the civilian world he's one of the world's leading authorities on dragons."

"I wasn't aware that anyone kept track of that sort of thing."

"Oh, yes sir. There are at least five others, but Private Asvald is the only one in the British army."

"Fine," the major said. "But a private? How long could he have been studying dragons in order to become a world expert?"

That was a good question. Ballard thought about it and didn't have an answer. Privates were usually teenagers or men in their early twenties. Asvald was neither. "All his life, I suspect, sir."

The major was silent a moment, considering the request. "All right," he said at last. "You can have him assist you in your investigation. How long will you need him for?"

"Indefinitely."

The major looked annoyed. "Twenty-four, forty-eight or

seventy-two hours?"

"Seventy-two hours."

"Fine," the major said, stamping a slip of paper, then signing his name over the stamp. "Now, what about that WAAF out in the hall. Is she on leave assisting the investigation too?"

Ballard felt his heart leap up into his throat. He'd been so busy looking for Asvald he'd forgotten all about her situation. Basically, she didn't exist. Not as a WAAF, and not as a British citizen. But how could he explain that to the major?

"She is assisting me, yes," Ballard lied, realizing that a small lie wasn't about to do here. If he was going to get away with it, he was going to have to lie big. "She's on special assignment to the Intelligence Branch by order of Air Chief Marshal Dowding himself."

What a whopper, thought Ballard, feeling himself growing warm inside the confines of his uniform. He had gambled that the major would not question an order that came from somewhere as high as Dowding's office. And if he did call the Intelligence Branch or Fighter Command to confirm Lavena's status, he risked wasting their valuable time as well as looking rather foolish.

"She's a good-looking girl," the major said with a wink. "You take care of her, now."

"Yes, sir," said Ballard, breathing a very deep sigh of relief.

3

The smoke Von Hesse had thought held so much promise had turned out to be nothing more than mist steaming up from a small pond nestled between two hills. The discovery had made Von Hesse feel somewhat foolish, but he consoled himself with the knowledge that there was no such thing as being too careful, and no harm in leaving no stone unturned.

Besides that, the water was cool and clean, and helped to

soothe his dry throat and mouth.

After allowing himself a good chuckle, he drank his fill and continued on with his search.

After about an hour's walk he came upon a small village consisting of several buildings on either side of the road and a large stone church standing watch over the village from the north end. On the road in the middle of the village were two groups of boys at play.

In one group the boys were running around in circles with their arms stretched out like aeroplanes. They made roaring noises with their mouths and every so often one of them would yell "ah-ah-ah-ah-ah." Then another of the boys would make an exploding sort of noise, fold in one of their arms and begin spinning toward the ground.

"Another Hun won't be home for supper," exclaimed the victorious boy.

Von Hesse had seen the game played out before in Germany. The only difference was that in Germany it was Tommy who would be missing his evening meal.

Nothing out of the ordinary there.

The other group was doing something quite extraordinary. They were playing with some curiously shaped objects, throwing them to each other by spinning them in the air like barn shingles. But, from the way they sliced through the air, they were heavier than barn shingles, and stronger too, since they didn't break up when they smacked against the road.

"What'cha got there, boys?" said Von Hesse, with all the British good cheer he could muster.

"It's a dragon scale," said a wide-faced young boy of five or six. "It came from the belly of a dragon."

"No it didn't," said one of the older boys, quite possibly the leader of the group. "It's a piece of armor plating from a British tank what got blown off by a German mortar shell in France."

"That so?" Von Hesse raised his eyebrows to let them know he was impressed. "Mind if I take a look?"

The older boy proudly handed one of the pieces to Von Hesse. He looked at it carefully. It was indeed diamond-shaped like the scales of a large fish or snake. It was light, very light, and strong too. Von Hesse took it in his hand and tried to bend it, but could not. He tapped it with his knuckles.

"This one's got a bullet mark on it," said another one of the older boys, holding up a second scale in his hand.

"Let me see that one," said Von Hesse.

The boy handed it to him and there was indeed a mark on it consistent with what might be made by a bullet strike. There was a deep scratchy gouge in the center of the scale, and then an etched line toward the edge of it, as if the shot had hit and been deflected away. He turned the scale over and was surprised to find that the other side bore no scars or scratches. The impact of the bullet had been absorbed by the outside of the shell, leaving the inside intact.

It was a revolutionary new material, and evidence of a new and dangerous British weapon.

"Wow, that sure is a wonder. My boy would be thrilled if I could bring him home something like this," said Von Hesse. "Mind if I keep it?"

"It's mine," said the boy who'd given him the scale.

"How about just for one night. I'll be back through here tomorrow. I'll give it back to you then."

"No, I don't think so."

"It'll only be for a night."

"He said no," said the oldest boy, stepping to the front of the group that had gathered round. "Now give it back to him, mister."

Von Hesse fingered the flap of the bag that was supposed to carry his gas mask, knowing that his Luger was mere inches from his fingertips. He could have the flap open and several rounds fired off before the gun was even clear of the canvas bag. He'd have the scale then, proof of the weapon's existence, but he'd also be a hunted man, with little hope of making it back to the Fatherland. He closed the latch on the bag.

"Why don't you just get your own?" said the boy.

"My own?"

"Sure." He gestured over his shoulder with a jerk of his head. "There are all kinds of them lying around the opening to the cave."

"Cave?" said Von Hesse. "Where is it?"

Several of the boys pointed north across a field. "About a mile that way," said the oldest.

Von Hesse looked in the direction they were pointing, but couldn't discern any cavelike features. "Maybe you can take me there?"

The oldest shook his head. "Sorry, we already caught hell for going there once. Our mums don't want us going anywhere near there. If a bomb falls anywhere nearby the whole thing could collapse down on top of you."

"You've got a wise lot of mothers, you have." He patted the youngest one on the head. "Maybe you can just show me where it is, you know . . . so I can get one of those things for my son."

"Sure, mister," said the oldest. "Come on."

Von Hesse had to hurry to keep from being left behind.

4

Lavena and Ballard picked up Asvald at the AA gun site on the Thames estuary before ten in the morning. It had been Ballard's plan to drive straight back to Bentley Priory and then fly to Digby by noon, but Asvald said he couldn't do it.

"I have to go home and pick up a few things first," he said, as he made himself comfortable in the front passenger's seat next to Ballard.

"All right, then," said Ballard, putting the car in gear. "Where do you live?"

"Well, I have several homes throughout England, even some overseas, but I think most of what I need is in Luton."

"Luton?" asked Ballard. It was a small city northwest of London.

"Yes, I have a townhouse there with a shop in the basement."

"A workshop?"

"I prefer to think of it as my magic shop."

Getting to Luton was going to take some time. There was an airport there, but if they flew to Luton they'd need a staff car on the ground. That meant Ballard would have to put in a request, which would result in more questions being asked, and more lies on his part. It would take longer, but it was likely best for all concerned, including Tibalt, if they just drove out to Luton. They could be back at Bentley Priory by early afternoon, and then fly up to Digby in time for tea. If they were lucky, they'd be able to check in with Tibalt before dark.

"All right," said Ballard. "Luton, it is."

The ride up to Luton was full of chatter. Lavena was especially interested in hearing what had happened to the people in Dervon after she'd been snatched up by the dragon and was overwhelmed by the news that she had been made a hero for saving the entire village.

"They erected a statue of you in the village square," said Asvald. "A very good likeness, I might add."

"I would have liked to see that."

"Many people are interested in hearing what effect their passing has on the lives of the people around them," said Asvald. "Just be glad that you're alive to hear of it."

"What about you, Asvald?" said Ballard. "What was it like for you in France?"

Asvald's expression turned grave. "The German army is very strong, very powerful. They've caused much misery to a great many people."

"It was terrible what they did in Poland."

Asvald shook his head. "The war is only a small part of it. I fear there will be worse crimes committed against humanity before it's over and done with."

Ballard wasn't sure what the wizard meant, but he knew that it had been tough going over in France and that the romantic notion of combat that had lasted all the way into the Great War had finally been pushed aside by the realities of modern warfare.

"You must have been a big help to the boys over there," said Ballard. "I imagine your talents came in handy more than a few times."

"No!" said Asvald. "I am not a practitioner of the black arts. I cannot use my powers to kill, or even lure people to their death. I can only work to save people's lives."

"So you were a medic."

"Yes, I thought it the best way to save the lives of men who were too young to die."

"And the barrage balloons?"

"Helping to protect the people of London from death from above."

Ballard continued driving in silence, thinking that Asvald seemed not only a wise man, but a noble one as well.

5

"Come on, Edna," said Rose Whitworth as she stood at the gate leading up to Edna's tiny cottage. "We're late enough as it is."

They were on their way to the parish hall to sit in on the knitting circle and knit wool socks for the RAF. They'd been doing it for the past nine months, and Edna had never been late once. In fact, she'd always been waiting for Rose at her front gate, chiding her for taking her own sweet time.

It was then that Rose noticed the blood on the stones of the walkway. "Edna," she said weakly.

Rose looked at the trail of blood and saw that it ran around the back of the house. Perhaps Edna's cut herself pruning her bushes, she thought.

"Oh, I hope she's all right," she whispered under her breath. Rose stepped through the gate and walked around the side of the house.

"Edna?" she called. "Edna."

There was no answer.

Rose turned the corner and saw a fresh mound of earth had been piled up in the middle of the garden. Someone had been working here recently.

And then she saw it.

The hand, Edna's pale dead hand, sticking out from beneath the pile of dirt.

Rose felt faint, but remained on her feet. She closed her eyes, brought a hand to her mouth, and took several moments to catch her breath.

And then she ran all the way to the parish hall without stopping once.

6

Asvald's home was an unremarkable townhouse in the middle of a row in one of the poorer neighborhoods in Luton. There were similar rows of houses along each street and if you didn't know your way around you could get lost quite easily. It was also, thought Ballard, an interesting place for a wizard to create his base of operations.

"Have you lived here long?" asked Ballard.

"Not for twenty years or so," answered Asvald, producing a large ring that absolutely bristled with brass and silver keys. He began searching through the keys, trying each one in turn. "Some thousand years have passed since I lived outside of Dervon. Just imagine the curiosity people would have for an elderly man living in one place for fifty years or more, never growing older, not holding a job, and with little information about him on the public roles. I could only live in one place for ten years or so, before people became suspicious. Ten years here, ten years there . . . Eventually I acquired a number of homes throughout England and lived in them all in rotation. Some were kept up by housekeepers, or rented out to students and the like."

He tried another key in the door. This one turned, and the lock snicked open. "After you," he said.

Ballard stepped aside to allow Lavena to go first. He followed her in, with Asvald behind him.

The first thing that struck Ballard was how utterly ordinary the inside of the house was. If Asvald's intention had been to be inconspicuous while he lived here, he had succeeded brilliantly. There was aged furniture about, framed watercolors on the walls and lace curtains over the windows. From all appearances it looked as if Mr. and Mrs. England lived here.

"Doesn't look much like a wizard's den," said Ballard.

"No it doesn't, does it?" said Asvald. "I'm quite proud of that. This way, please."

He led them to a small door tucked into the wall beneath the stairs. It was only about four feet high and likely led into the basement where coal and bits of junk were stored.

The lock on the door was ordinary, like everything else in the house. But when Asvald took the key for the lock out of his pocket, it was absolutely extraordinary. It seemed to be made of gold, shining under the dim overhead light like a piece of crystal.

It looked too big for the lock, but somehow it slid in easily and silently released that latch.

"This," he said, raising his arms to indicate his surroundings, "is my home. And this," he opened the small door and gestured inside, "is my den. My magic shop. My inner sanctum." He smiled. "Follow me."

Again Ballard let Lavena go before him, then he ducked his head and slipped through the doorway and down the stairs.

"Oh my," gasped Lavena, a hand over her heart.

"Indeed," thought Ballard.

The basement was cavernous, with more square footage than the basic dimensions of the house.

"If you're wondering, I had a few of the houses on the row converted to oil heating, freeing up their basements for my purposes. Over the years I've done some remodeling and renovating, nothing fancy mind you."

That was an understatement, thought Ballard. Much of the basement was laid out like the research department of an international chemical concern, with beakers and tubes and Bunsen burners stretched out across several tables. Another corner looked like the pantry of some mad witch or warlock. The shelves were lined with large glass jars filled with colored liquid that preserved their contents—everything from the feet of pigs to the hearts of animals unknown, from modern packaged industrial chemicals to a leather sack labeled *Ground Bones, Black Cat*, from dusty leather-bound books to pre-war paper-jackets. There was also a large assortment of dragon scales, their shape and color suggesting they had been taken from different areas on Tibalt's body. Perhaps even from the hides of other dragons.

It was truly an impressive sight. For the first time in days, Ballard felt truly confident that the dragon problem would soon be resolved to everyone's satisfaction.

"Feel free to look around," said Asvald, placing a large duffel bag onto one of the empty tables. "I'll only be a few minutes." He began looking through his books, some of their spines cracking loudly as they were opened, testament to the fact that they hadn't been touched for centuries.

"Tell me something, Asvald," said Ballard as he ran a finger down the embossed spine of a leatherbound book of magic.

"Yes," answered the wizard, continuing with his work.

"Why did you send the dragon into the future?"

"To save its life." The answer came without hesitation.

"But you nearly got it killed."

"Nearly getting it killed isn't exactly the same as making it dead, now is it?"

"But how could you possibly hope to save its life by putting it into the middle of the Battle of Britain?"

"I am a wizard, not a scientist," said Asvald abruptly. "I merely intended to show the dragon that if it continued to kill men, they would continue to kill dragons, eventually growing strong enough to wipe the dragons completely from the face of the Earth."

"But 1940?"

"In casting the spell I mentioned that there would come a time in which men would learn to fly and take full control of the air. I had thought that the dragon might appear sometime in 1918, but looking back on it, a dragon could have easily torn up the Fokkers, Spads and Sopwiths of the Great War. It really wasn't until this year that modern aeroplanes, their armament, the men that fly them, and the tactics they use, were able to dominate the sky. That's what the current battle is all about, domination of the skies over England."

Asvald resumed packing his bag.

Ballard thought about what the wizard had said. Put into those terms, it seemed only logical that the dragon reappeared in 1940. It also made it seem silly for Ballard to think that the dragon could join forces with the RAF. Tibalt had been successful in his initial attacks due to the element of surprise, but a concerted effort by either side to shoot him out the sky would invariably succeed. That much had already been proven.

It was almost like the appearance of the British Boulton Paul Defiant fighter aeroplane over France. At first it scored success because it looked like a Spitfire but had a rearward firing turret. Once the enemy realized what the aeroplane was, German pilots shot the Defiant out of the sky with ease.

Ballard was silent for several minutes watching the wizard pack his bag, and Lavena inspected the shelves surrounding the room. Finally, he asked him, "Are you sure you can send the dragon back?"

Asvald nodded and leaned heavily on a long, gnarled—and obviously quite ancient—walking stick. "As sure as any wizard can be about such things, I suppose."

Ballard wondered if that meant yes, or no.

CHAPTER FIFTEEN

1

When they were done in Luton, Ballard drove back to Bentley Priory, hoping to catch Air Commodore Trask in his office so he could inform him of his plans to return to Derbyshire.

The commodore's office was empty, which was just as well, since Ballard was more than happy to fly up to Derbyshire without letting the commodore know his business. He left a note with one of the WAAFs in the outer office and headed back to Asvald and Lavena waiting for him in the staff car parked on the grounds.

He was almost out the large front foyer of the main building when he was stopped by a familiar voice.

"Flight Lieutenant Ballard!"

It was Air Commodore Trask.

"I'm glad I've caught you," said Trask.

Ballard turned around and saluted. "I was just in to see you, sir," he said.

"Oh."

"I wanted to let you know that I'll be flying up to Digby this afternoon. I've found my dragon expert and I'm quite confident that we'll find the dragon within the next day or two."

"It'll have to be sooner than that, Flight Lieutenant."

"Sir?"

"The army is already moving into the area. Tanks from the 23rd Army Tank Brigade, and a few regiments from the First

Canadian Infantry Division."

"But sir—"

Trask shook his head. "I'm confident that you've been conducting a thorough investigation, Flight Lieutenant, but there have been some strange happenings up there of late and we need to find out what's going on."

"Strange happenings?"

"There was a Post Office Engineer roaming around up there, but when someone checked with the office in London they were told there haven't been any engineers posted anywhere but London and the surrounding airfields for weeks."

Ballard said nothing.

"And an elderly woman named Edna Abernathy was found dead and buried in her own garden, stabbed to death with a knife."

Edna Abernathy, thought Ballard. The name seemed to ring a bell. Edna Abernathy. He'd been on his way to question her. She'd been one of the people who had reported seeing the dragon . . . Ballard felt the blood drain from his face.

Trask looked at him curiously. "Are you all right, Flight Lieutenant?"

Ballard took a moment to compose himself. "Fine, sir. If you'll excuse me, I think I'll be on my way."

"Take care, Flight Lieutenant," said Trask. "I expect to hear from you tomorrow with a report."

Ballard didn't answer. He was already out of the building and hurrying across the grounds toward the staff car.

"What is it?" said Lavena when he reached the car. "What's wrong?"

Ballard got in and quickly started the car.

"The army has moved in."

"That's not good," said Asvald.

Ballard put the car in gear. "And that's not all. An elderly

211

woman in the area has been found murdered in her own garden."

"Tibalt couldn't have done that," said Lavena.

"No, not now," said Ballard. "But before, maybe."

"What do you think it means?" asked Lavena.

"It means," said Asvald, "that the army will be shooting to kill."

When they reached Northolt, they were made to wait for permission to take off. The squadron had been scrambled an hour before to intercept a flight of German bombers attacking shipping on the coast and they were due back at the airfield any minute.

Ballard parked the staff car next to the Lysander and all three of them began loading Asvald's supplies into the rear of the aeroplane since the ground crews that were usually around to help with pre-flight preparations were all getting ready for the return of the squadron. On the other side of the field there were fire-fighting trucks, ambulances and tractors stationed around the airfield in a scene that was all too familiar to Ballard. He hoped none of the emergency vehicles would be needed.

"I was a flier in the Great War," said Asvald, as they waited for the fighters to return. "Observer."

Ballard looked at Asvald in surprise.

"I thought it would be the best way to find the dragon when he appeared in the skies over France. But of course he didn't appear, and my pilot and I made it through three years of war without a scratch."

"That's a miracle," said Ballard. Pilots' life spans in the Great War had been measured in days. To last for so long in an observation aeroplane—a slow, obsolete aeroplane with no defensive armament or parachutes—was a truly remarkable feat.

"Not really," said Asvald. "We were hit many times, wounded too, just never fatally so."

Lucky, thought Ballard.

The first of the Hurricanes began landing a few minutes later—not a scratch on them. Another flight of three returned a few minutes after that, also without damage. Then the airfield was cleared for a lone Hurricane trailing smoke from its left-side exhaust. The cockpit canopy was open and there was some smoke coming out of the cockpit. The pilot must have been too low to bail out and decided to try and make it back to base.

The aeroplane's landing gear was up, which would allow it to stop more quickly, giving the pilot a better chance of getting out before the aircraft became engulfed in flames.

Ballard felt for the pilot in this horrible situation, but could do nothing but watch and hope that it was the man's lucky day. He looked over at Lavena who seemed fascinated by the smoking aeroplane, but perhaps didn't understand the drama going on inside the cockpit. Asvald, on the other hand, looked as if he knew exactly what was at stake.

"Think he'll make it?" said Ballard.

Asvald nodded. "Yes, he'll live." He said the words confidently, as if he knew.

The Hurricane touched down in the middle of the airfield, throwing up a wall of dirt before bouncing into the air once more. Fire started coming from the engine cowling and the cockpit looked to be in flames. On the second bounce the Hurricane veered left toward the very spot where Asvald, Ballard and Lavena stood next to their Lysander. The Hurricane came toward them, streaking flames down both sides of the fuselage.

Ballard turned to run, but Asvald remained where he stood. Seeing this, Ballard stayed put as well, waiting for the Hurricane to come to a stop.

It ground to a halt not ten yards in front of where they stood.

The Hurricane was shrouded in flame and with the firefighters racing across the airfield it looked as if the pilot would be dead long before they could arrive and put out the fire.

But then Asvald did an incredible thing.

He ran to the plane, walked into the inferno—through the flames—and lifted the pilot from the cockpit. The wizard seemed to have the strength of ten men as he carried the man easily away from the burning fighter and put him onto the ground some distance away. From the way the pilot's limbs hung limply at his sides, it was obvious to Ballard that he was dead, or at least knocking on death's door. But as Asvald put the man onto the ground, he placed his hands on the man's head and chest, then on his stomach and limbs. Ballard ran toward them, and as he did the pilot stirred. He began to cough, then sat up looking around himself as if to ask, *Where am I?*

"Billy!" called the firemen as they neared.

"Are you all right?" asked one of the other pilots who had leaped from his Hurricane.

The pilot looked shaken, but otherwise all right. In fact, although parts of his trousers were burnt away, there wasn't a mark on him. "I don't know what happened," he said. "There was smoke, then fire, and then . . . And then I was here on the grass." He looked at his Hurricane burning to the ground. "Sorry about the kite," he said to one of the officers in the crowd around him.

"Don't worry, Billy," said the intelligence officer. "We can always get another Hurricane, but there's only one Billy in 504."

Ballard searched the crowd for Asvald, but he was nowhere to be seen. Then there was a tapping on his shoulder. He turned to look behind him and saw Asvald standing there.

"Best be on our way," said the wizard. "I think we can be cleared for takeoff now."

Ballard simply nodded, realizing that luck had had nothing to do with Asvald making it through the Great War, or otherwise living for as long as he had.

They climbed into the Lysander and were on their way to Digby a few minutes later.

2

When Von Hesse reached the mouth of the cave, he took a long look around. Incredibly, the surrounding countryside looked familiar to him.

Very familiar.

As he studied the landscape further, it became apparent to him that he was quite near to the spot in which he had landed two nights before. That was both good and bad. It was good because it meant that his supplies were safely hidden very close to the cave. It was bad because it meant that he had wasted nearly two days walking around in circles. In his line of work, the longer he spent behind enemy lines, the less chance he had of survival. Those two days might very well have cost him his life.

Nothing to be done about it now, he thought.

Von Hesse stepped into the cave and stopped when he was surrounded by darkness. He waited there until his eyes had adjusted to the shadows, then pressed on.

The further he went, the stranger it seemed to him that such an important secret weapon was not guarded by soldiers or armed guards. Perhaps the facility was too well hidden and the presence of soldiers would only attract unwanted attention from the surrounding civilian population. It was also possible that this cave was merely a decoy, a diversion to draw attention away from the true entrance to the facility that was perhaps some miles away.

Von Hesse laughed under his breath at the thought. The British had not been preparing for war long enough to have worked out such elaborate defenses for their research facilities. Only a month before there had been reports that the offices of RAF Fighter Command were being defended by a battery of just four anti-aircraft guns.

Von Hesse moved further into the cave, tempted to switch on a light, but not daring to do so. He stopped a moment to look behind him and gauge how far he was below the surface. The light shining down from the cave opening had shrunk to about the size of an apple. Perhaps he'd come fifty yards or more.

He turned to continue his descent and slipped on something loose under his feet. He reached down to feel the rocky floor beneath him. There was something thin and hard there. He picked it up. In the dim light of the cave he was unable to make out much detail, but it felt just like one of the scales the boys in the village had been playing with.

Perhaps they were fragments of some new sort of lightweight armor. He had to take a better look at it. He reached into his toolbox and took out a small penlight. Then he huddled behind a large rocky outcropping, flicked on the light and shone it on the object. It glittered and sparkled as if it were woven with threads of steel. It changed color slightly across its width, from blue around the outer edges to green in its center.

No wonder the weapon had been referred to as a dragon. The square of armor plating looked very much like a dragon's scale and a geodesic pattern of such scales on an aeroplane would indeed cause it to bear a striking resemblance to a dragon.

Von Hesse hefted the scale in his hand. It was incredibly light. With such material soldiers could go into battle wearing suits of armor that weighed no more than a wool sweater or leather pants. Key areas on fighter planes could be armored and protected from attack without sacrificing speed or maneuverability. Bombers could be covered with armor plates and become virtually invulnerable to attack. Tanks could be . . .

The possibilities were endless. Obviously the British had been conducting tests on armored fighters—dragons—and were using this cave system as a base of operations.

The Reichsmarshall had been right to send him here. If the British were allowed to fully develop this magnificent innovation, it would delay Germany's conquest of England for several months. He searched the rocky floor around him for more scales and was easily able to find fragments of several more strewn about. If nothing else, he could return to Germany with these samples for the Reich's top scientists to examine.

Von Hesse raised his light slightly in search of further scales and heard a sound emanate from deep within the cave. It was a strange sound. A wheezing, snorting sort of sound, like an old man asleep with a cold.

He switched off his light and moved deeper into the cave. The further he went the louder the sound became. Also, the cave seemed to grow warmer, as if there was a heat source somewhere in its depths.

At last the cave began to open up into a large cavern. Here was room enough for any number of operations from research and development, to testing and manufacture. But while the sound was louder now and seemed to echo off the walls of the cavern, Von Hesse was unable to find its source.

It was obvious that the cavern was empty of people and it occurred to him that this might be the outer area of a facility buried deeper within the rock. He decided to risk shining his light.

After taking a deep breath, he switched the light on and shone it across the expanse of the cavern. The tiny beam of light seemed to be swallowed up by the shadows of the rough and jagged surface of the cavern walls and for a moment Von Hesse thought that he might have taken a wrong turn somewhere.

But as he moved the light around the cavern, the beam glinted against something shiny. He focused the light on the spot and saw more glinting and sparkling—the same sort of reflection he had seen with the scale. This however, was something that was made up of hundreds—perhaps even thousands—of scales, all symmetrically placed to form a wall.

He switched off the light and made his way across the cavern toward the wall of scales. Minutes later he was standing in front of the wall. It seemed to stand three meters high and six or seven meters wide. He switched on his penlight again and examined the scales. They were the same as he'd seen on the cavern floor, but these seemed to slide against one another like movable armor plates, with the pattern interrupted at intervals by horny defensive spikes.

He moved along the wall, tracing a line along its length with his penlight. Soon the defensive spikes became more numerous, eventually overtaking the scales in number and size.

Suddenly the tiny beam of light shone onto something different. Not scales, not spikes, but . . .

An eye.

Von Hesse quickly switched off the light and held his breath. Luckily the eye had been closed and his light had not disturbed the creature's sleep.

The creature? thought Von Hesse.

He moved away slowly, realizing that the dragon he was looking for was indeed a dragon.

A fire-breathing dragon.

No wonder their fighters had been knocked out of the sky with such ease. A huge armored beast able to breathe fire was an incredible weapon—even against Messerschmitts.

Von Hesse drew his knife from its sheath and approached the scale wall which he now realized was likely the dragon's side or belly.

He raised the knife, positioned its tip between two scales, and hesitated . . .

It was madness to try and kill a dragon with a knife. At the very least he would need a sword to slay it. The best he could do with his knife was wound the beast, likely making it angry and of a mind to kill him. No, he needed something big that would destroy this dragon and any other dragons that might be lurking in the shadows.

He needed high explosives.

He had none with him at the moment, but he knew where to get the materials in order to do the job right.

He would be back.

He switched off the penlight and quietly headed back the way he came, out of the cave.

3

The late afternoon sky was clear as Ballard guided the Lysander over central England. Below them was the town of Coventry, halfway between the airfields of Northolt and Digby. The land beneath them was green and lush and for a moment, Ballard imagined that there was no war on, that he was out for a nice pleasant flight on an afternoon that would end with a picnic in the company of a beautiful young woman.

He looked over his shoulder at Lavena and she smiled at him. Next to her, Asvald sat hunched over one of his dusty old books, reading a passage in a mumbling sort of voice as if he were glancing over the words simply to refresh his memory.

At one point Asvald looked up and saw Ballard looking at him. "Are we there yet?" said the wizard.

"Almost," said Ballard. "A few more minutes and we'll be in radio contact with the airfield at Digby."

"Good, good," said Asvald, nodding.

"What are you reading?" asked Ballard.

"Something that might help me send the dragon back to its own time."

"A spell?"

"You might say that."

Ballard was silent a moment, checking the terrain below for the familiar landmarks leading toward Digby.

"Tell me, Asvald," said Ballard, after he was satisfied they were on course. "What are you going to need to send the dragon back?"

"Most of what I need is in here," he said, tapping a finger against the side of his head.

"Okay, but other than your knowledge?"

Asvald said nothing as he thought about the question. "Well, we'll need to be in an open field, so we'll have to get Tibalt out of the cave. For that reason it's important that the dragon be co-operative. Tibalt must wish to return to his own time and must want to help us accomplish that."

"You won't have to worry about that," said Ballard, turning back around to check the sky around him, and the ground beneath. "Tibalt wants no part of 1940 anymore."

"Yes," said Lavena. "Tibalt has learned his lesson. I assure you, it will be a much humbler and wiser dragon that returns to Dervon."

Asvald's gaze shifted from Ballard to Lavena, his brow knitting together in a show of concern. He stared at Lavena, as if looking beyond her outer layer and seeing the thoughts and feelings that lay just below the surface of her mind, her heart, her soul. Lavena felt the wizard's penetrating gaze like a cold chill cutting right to the bone.

"What about you?" asked Asvald with a slight nod of his head.

"What?" said Lavena, trying to make her voice sound sweet

and innocent.

"Do you wish to stay, or go back with the dragon?"

Ballard turned around again at that point, no doubt curious to know her answer. Lavena was curious to know the answer herself. She had thought about it often, wondering if she might stay in this place, discovering more of its wonders and . . . falling in love.

After a long moment of silence she cleared her throat and said, "I thought I might stay."

Asvald nodded pensively, as if he had suspected as much.

Ballard smiled, gave her a wink, and turned back around to resume flying the aeroplane.

Yes, she thought.

Staying in this place would be a good thing.

Chapter Sixteen

1

As he neared the mouth of the cave, Von Hesse felt the earth begin to shake around him. There was a loud rumbling noise inside the cave, as if . . .

He rushed up to the entrance, slowing as he reached daylight. He cautiously stepped forward, being careful to remain hidden in the shadows. There was movement all around, soldiers and vehicles and a few ridiculously antiquated tanks. But despite the decrepit condition of their weapons, the presence of the British army still posed a few problems for Von Hesse.

First of all, he could not use this exit to leave the cave. If he did he'd be apprehended, questioned and executed as a spy, or perhaps he'd simply be shot by an anxious soldier as he tried to leave. Second, the army's presence meant that any fleeting plans he might have had for studying the secret weapon or obtaining more information about it would have to be forgotten. Clearly, his only task now was to destroy the cave and the dragon within it.

Easier said than done.

It all depended on whether there was another entrance to the cave that was some distance away from the concentration of army personnel. If there was, he might have a chance to exit the cave, retrieve his stash of explosives and return to the cave in order to set up the charges inside it.

But finding another entrance meant he would have to go

back into the cave and sneak past the dragon itself. What was waiting for him further into the cave? There was at least one dragon, maybe more, and there could easily be soldiers, guards, or any number of other hazards lying in wait as well.

In a word, he was *stuck,* with the British army in front of him and a dragon behind him.

He weighed the odds and decided that he'd rather risk the cave and the dragon than attempt to sneak through the ranks of the British.

Without another moment's hesitation Von Hesse turned around, and headed back into the cave.

2

When they arrived at the manor house, the grounds were a scene of confusion. There were military vehicles parked all over the lawn and soldiers moving back and forth carrying equipment and supplies. Along the far edge of the grounds there were two rows of tents with soldiers lingering about, eating rations and smoking cigarettes.

It was as if a garrison had been stationed at the manor house in order to quell some local uprising. It didn't bode well for the dragon.

As they exited the staff car, Ballard saw Mrs. Norris at the front door of the house looking as if she had been anxiously awaiting his return for days.

"What is happening?" said Ballard.

"I was hoping you would be able to tell me," said Mrs. Norris. "They just appeared this afternoon, lorries full of soldiers, and told me they'd be using the grounds for the next few days. I don't mind hosting a few officers, but—"

Ballard raised a hand. "Calm yourself, Mrs. Norris. They'll be gone by tomorrow night. Friday morning at the latest."

That seemed to comfort her.

"All right," she said. "I suppose I can put up with them for a few days."

"That's the spirit, Mrs. Norris."

She looked past Ballard at Lavena and Asvald. "How are you, dear?" she said, sliding past Ballard and giving Lavena a loving hug. "Did you enjoy your trip?"

Lavena smiled. "Oh, yes."

"And who's your friend?"

"Mrs. Norris," said Lavena. "This is Asvald. He's a—"

"Helping me with my investigation," interrupted Ballard. He couldn't be sure what Lavena had been about to say, but he couldn't risk her saying, "He's a wizard."

"Pleased to meet you." Mrs. Norris looked impressed by Asvald, and perhaps just a little intrigued. "I haven't seen many men in the service your age."

"I doubt there are any my age in the service anywhere," Asvald said with a gracious smile.

"Well, then I'm honored to be your host."

"No," said Asvald. "The honor is all mine." He took her hand and gave it a kiss.

"Ooh, I like him."

"Uh, we'd like to get settled in," said Ballard.

"I'll show these two to their rooms," said Mrs. Norris. "But there's someone waiting to see you in the dining room."

"Who?"

"A Major Reaves. I think he's in charge of the army."

"Right," said Ballard. He turned to Asvald and Lavena. "You two go with Mrs. Norris. I'll be by in a few minutes."

Major Reaves was sitting alone at the dining-room table looking over a map of the area. From where he stood in the doorway, Ballard could see that it was one of the surface maps of the area that showed only the largest entrance to the cave.

"You wanted to see me, sir?" said Ballard.

The army major looked up. "Flight Lieutenant Ballard, I presume. Come in."

Ballard entered the dining room and took a chair opposite Reaves. The man had a hard face, long dark mustache and his mouth seemed to be turned down in a grim frown. Ballard felt uncomfortable sitting across the table from him.

"I understand you've been conducting an investigation into the dragon sightings in the area."

"That's right, I have," said Ballard, not wanting to tell his opposite number in the army anything more than absolutely necessary.

"And what have you come up with?"

"Well, since the dragon hasn't been sighted in the past few days, I'm inclined to believe that it was shot down by the RAF."

Reaves's face darkened and Ballard realized that he'd made a mistake in so easily crediting the RAF with the kill.

"Do you have any proof of that?"

"Not exactly. No."

"Then it's quite possible it could have been damaged and is simply hiding somewhere nearby, effecting repairs and preparing for another attack on you . . . *glamour boys.*"

Ballard bristled at the use of the sometimes-derogatory term for fighter pilots. "I happen to know that the dragon you're looking for won't be causing any more trouble."

Reaves looked at him. "Oh, and how do you know that?"

Ballard wanted to say, "Because it's been wounded and is waiting for a wizard to send it back in time a thousand years, you stupid clod," but he managed to hold his tongue. "I'm not at liberty to tell you."

"That so?" Reaves had a look on his face that suggested he didn't know whether to believe Ballard or not.

"Yes, that's so."

Reaves looked Ballard over, then said, "Just remember this. I've been told to station my men in around the caves north of Derby and my orders are to shoot anything that comes out of the ground. If this dragon's been shot down by the RAF, fine. But if it hasn't, the army will be finishing the job the RAF couldn't."

Ballard rose from his chair and left the dining room without saying a word.

He hurried upstairs to the bedrooms where Asvald and Lavena were getting settled in for the night. When he got to the second floor, Asvald's door was open and he could see Lavena helping him unpack his duffel bag.

"What's wrong now?" said Lavena.

Ballard looked at her, wondering if there might be some sort of spiritual connection between them. As much as Ballard tried to keep a stiff upper lip, she always seemed to know when there was a problem.

"The army's moved in," said Ballard. "And the commanding officer appears intent on killing whatever comes out of the cave."

"Meaning?" asked Lavena.

Ballard opened his mouth to speak, but Asvald spoke first.

"It means," said the wizard, "that it will be even more difficult getting Tibalt safely out of the cave."

"But can't you just tell the officer that Tibalt no longer means anyone any harm."

Ballard shook his head. "No. I'm afraid he's as stubborn as the dragon once was."

"We'll just have to be even more careful," said Asvald.

"Right," said Ballard. "Now I imagine you have preparations to make. Lavena, you help Asvald. I'm going to the cave to check on Tibalt and to let him know that we're here and that he'll be going back tomorrow. I'll be downstairs waiting for you at the break of dawn. Be ready." He turned to leave.

"Ballard," said Lavena.

"Be careful," she said, kissing him lightly on the cheek.

"No need to worry about me," he said. "I've pranged up my kite a couple of times, always came out without a scratch." He smiled at Lavena and the wizard and gave them each a wink.

"Do be careful," said Asvald, his expression grim.

Ballard nodded, and felt a chill run down his spine.

3

Two Canadian infantrymen, Privates Sellers and Hutchison, sat with their backs against a pair of trees. In the twilight they gazed out over the field looking for some movement in the growing darkness.

"You know what we're supposed to be looking at?" said Sellers.

"Months of boredom," quipped Hutchison.

"No, I mean in this field?"

"Not sure. I've heard talk of dragons."

"Dragons? What kind of codename is that?"

"It's not a codename," said Hutchison. "It's what I heard we're looking for. Dragons."

After a moment of silence, both men snickered.

"Well, I don't know about you," said Sellers, poking himself in the chest with a proudly outthrust thumb, "but I'm looking to shoot me a big pink bunny rabbit with huge floppy ears and a great fluffy puff of a tail."

The sound of their laughter carried a long, long way in the still night air.

4

When Ballard reached the area of the main entrance to the cave, he found it quite well guarded, just as Major Reaves had been ordered. There seemed to be a large number of soldiers milling about and Ballard only hoped that it was because Major Reaves was unaware of the alternate entrances to the cave and as a result had concentrated his forces in just this one place.

Ballard wasn't too keen on entering the cave via one of the smaller entrances to the north, because it would add to his travel time to and from the cave and he'd wanted to get at least a few hours' rest before morning. But, looking around at the well-armed soldiers—some armed with mortars—it didn't seem likely that they would be letting him step into the cave without a fight.

Reluctantly, he turned north.

5

Von Hesse returned to the cave.

The dragon had moved slightly, but was still asleep and snoring away with the same regular rhythm as before.

Von Hesse took a deep breath and switched on his penlight. The dragon continued sleeping, undisturbed by the light.

Methodically, he shone the light around the cave, starting from one end and moving it left to right in a series of long up-and-down motions, as if he were writing a continuous "W" of light.

The first wall he examined in this way showed no evidence of any tunnels leading to the surface. The wall there was just as rough and scraggly as the rest of the cave. He skipped over the area of wall blocked by the sleeping dragon and tried the wall to the right of it.

There he had a bit more luck.

The tiny beam of light peeked into a few small dark holes that might have led to the surface, but were much too small for a man to travel through.

And then he saw it.

The hole in the wall was roughly as high as he was tall and the tunnel behind it seemed to keep its general size and shape. There looked to be a few tight spots, but it seemed fairly passable. Best of all, when he was standing at the entrance to the tunnel, he could see the moon shining through at the other end. This one led to the surface, and was probably far enough away from the main entrance not to attract the attention of the soldiers above ground.

Von Hesse switched off his penlight and headed toward the silver disc of the moon.

Ballard looked into the sky and checked the position of the moon. It seemed to be in the right position to help to illuminate the tunnel he'd be taking into the cave.

With any luck, he'd be in and out of the cave, and on his way back to the manor house within the hour.

The tunnel proved to be easier going for Von Hesse despite its sometimes-narrower passages. The angle of the tunnel was easier to climb and it was generally taller, allowing him to walk standing up for most of the way.

He kept his eyes focused on the moon, continuing to move closer to it.

And then the moon disappeared.

Von Hesse stopped where he stood and held his breath.

The moon reappeared for a moment, and then was blocked out again.

Obviously there was somebody up there, somebody entering the cave.

Von Hesse reached into his pocket with his left hand and took out his penlight. Then he curled the fingers of his right hand around his knife handle and removed the long blade from its sheath.

Whoever was entering the cave was doing so very casually, as if he'd been in the cave before. Von Hesse wondered if this person might be an ally of the dragon, a friend who could control it or otherwise instruct it what to do.

In a few more moments, he would find out.

Von Hesse placed himself flat against the wall of the cave and waited for the person to descend into the tunnel.

Patiently he counted off their steps.

Three more steps . . .

Two more . . .

One . . .

Von Hesse moved into the middle of the tunnel, and switched on his penlight.

"What the—"

An RAF officer.

Without a moment's hesitation Von Hesse drove his knife into the man's throat, cutting off his words.

He twisted the knife several times before pulling it out and allowing the man to fall to the tunnel floor.

Dead.

CHAPTER SEVENTEEN
Thursday, August 8, 1940

1

Lavena was up well before the sun. She had waited for Ballard to return, anxious to hear the sounds of his footsteps in the hallway outside her door, but she had heard nothing.

She knew that he was a busy man and there were many things he had to attend to. It was quite possible that he had returned to the manor house after she had eventually fallen asleep, or perhaps he'd been unable to get any rest at all during the night and had remained awake, working on something or other throughout the hours of darkness until morning.

She hoped that that was the reason she had not heard from him. Any other possibility frightened her.

After rising from bed, she quickly dressed in her blue uniform. She had taken great care to make sure it would not become creased or wrinkled in the night and when she put it on she was pleased that it still looked as if it were new. It was a smart outfit made with the smallest and neatest of stitches, some of them almost invisible to the eye. But best of all, it showed off her young woman's figure better than anything she'd ever worn before. She had noticed the way Flight Lieutenant Ballard had looked at her and she didn't mind admitting that she'd like the attention. He had looked at her, not only as a woman, but also as a fellow soldier, or dare she say it—an equal. She had felt herself falling in love with the man from the first moment they'd met and with each day that passed that feeling had grown stronger. She could only hope that he felt the same way she did.

After getting dressed she went down the hall to Asvald's room. She knocked gently on the door and was answered by the wizard's soft voice.

"Come in," he said.

Lavena had expected to see him still under the covers, but to her surprise he was sitting on the edge of the bed already dressed with his boots on and his steel helmet on his head. His duffel bag was packed and seemed all ready to go. From the looks of it, he might have been ready for hours.

"Did you hear Ballard return last night?" Asvald asked before she had a chance to ask the same question herself.

"No, I was hoping that you had."

Asvald shook his head.

"He could have been busy," offered Lavena. "He might have had soldier's work to attend to."

"Let us hope," nodded Asvald. He picked up his duffel bag and together they left the room.

As they hurried down the stairs, Lavena hoped to find Ballard waiting for them there as he said he would. But the landing was empty.

Lavena craned her neck to look around the corner and down the hall for any sign of Ballard.

"Perhaps Tibalt needed Ballard's help, and he had to spend the night in the cave with the dragon."

Lavena nodded agreement. It was a reasonable explanation.

They could hear Mrs. Norris preparing breakfast in the kitchen and they looked at each other expectantly.

"Hungry?" asked Asvald.

"No," said Lavena. "I couldn't eat a thing."

"Nor could I."

"Then let's go."

Together, they crept out of the manor house as quietly as a pair of mice.

As they neared the main entrance to the cave, the sun was just beginning to peek over the eastern horizon. It looked as if it was going to be a beautiful day.

Lavena hoped it was a good omen.

The morning sun also helped illuminate a problem. The main entrance to the cave was surrounded by soldiers, making it virtually impassable.

"Well," said Asvald. "So much for that idea."

"No!" said Lavena. "There's another entrance to the north."

There was relief in Asvald's smile. "Lead the way."

By the time they had made their way north around the groups of camped soldiers the sun was high in the sky and beginning to lift the morning dew off the surrounding fields and pastures.

At the mouth of the alternate entrance to the cave, they stopped for a look around. Asvald seemed particularly interested in the ground at the very mouth of the entrance.

"The grass," he said, pointing at the ground. "It's matted and worn down, as if there had been some traffic in the area of late."

Lavena wasn't sure what Asvald had meant by traffic, but it did look as if someone had been going in and out of the cave through the night.

"Age before beauty," said Asvald, suggesting he should go first.

Lavena did not want him entering the cave before she did. He possessed the ability to return the dragon to its proper time, so it was obvious that he must be protected from harm. If there were new dangers inside the cave, she should be the one to take the risk. "No," she said abruptly. "After me."

"Very well, then," said Asvald, looking surprised by the conviction in her voice. "Ladies first." He made an exaggerated gesture with his arm.

"Thank you," Lavena smiled, and gave a slight nod. She'd never been called a lady before.

She took a step into the cave, but stopped as she noticed something incredible happening to Asvald.

The wizard's hair suddenly began to grow. His beard also grew rapidly, quickly framing his mouth with a full white beard.

The change was both startling and dramatic. He didn't look quite the same as he had back in Dervon—his hair and beard were both not nearly as long as they had been—but he certainly looked more wizard-like than before.

Lavena stared at him curiously.

"Sorry, I guess I should have warned you," he said. "I thought it might help if I look a little more like the Asvald Tibalt remembers."

"Yes, of course," said Lavena, her eyes lingering on the transformed Asvald. Finally, she turned to enter the tunnel and began the descent into the cave. She put her hands out to the sides to steady herself and realized that the walls were quite damp with moisture. She pulled her right hand away and rubbed her fingers together to test the texture of the liquid.

"It's just water," said Asvald behind her. "The sun is up and warm, but the rocks are still quite cool, causing condensation to form on their surface. The same thing is going on underfoot, so be careful where you—"

Asvald's words were suddenly cut off by a gasp.

Lavena turned around in time to see Asvald's feet slip out from under him, sending him down onto his bottom. His steel helmet flew off his head and clanged noisily against the rocky tunnel floor. It bounced several times, ringing like a church bell before Lavena could grab hold of it when it came to rest at her feet.

"—step," said Asvald, completing his thought.

"Are you all right?"

"My bum is sore, and I feel a little stupid, but other than that, I'll survive."

She handed him his helmet, and helped him to his feet.

"Thank you," he said. "Shall we continue?"

Lavena turned and resumed the descent.

2

Tibalt dreamed.

He was falling through the air tail over head.

Falling . . .

Falling . . .

Falling . . .

All around him steel dragons spit hot steel at him. He was being hit all over as he fell.

His wings had been shredded.

His legs mangled.

Arms broken.

Steel sprayed against his belly like rain.

And the spinning wings on the noses of the steel dragons cut deeply into his flesh, sending blood and scales flying in all directions.

Falling . . .

Falling . . .

The ground was growing closer.

He tried to flap his wings.

They were heavy and would not move.

He tried again.

But his wings remained at his side, useless.

Falling . . .

The ground was close now.

He could make out paths and trees.

The steel dragons would not leave him alone. They continued to pelt him with angry bits of steel.

But then Tibalt smiled.

It would all be over in a moment.

The ground was so close now, he could almos—

Tibalt jolted awake, not so much awakened by his dream, but by the loud metallic crash that echoed through the cave.

Someone was here.

Someone had come for him.

He hoped they were friendly.

3

Von Hesse had spent much of the night traveling across the English countryside. He'd been lucky enough to remember the general area in which he'd landed, but he had done such a good job at hiding the explosives that he himself had some trouble finding them again.

After a couple of aborted attempts, he found the explosives where he'd buried them. He'd moved the large log away from the mound and dug up the wooden boxes lying just beneath the surface.

He was back in the cave two hours after he'd left, and had spent the rest of the night stringing wires. He'd begun at the main entrance so he would be able to close off the opening if British soldiers began entering it before he had completed his task. That done, he ran wire and explosives through the cavern and around the sleeping dragon, always careful not to awaken it.

Now he was at the bottom of the alternate entrance with only the alternate entrance left to be set with explosive charges. He could have it rigged in another twenty minutes, leaving him the rest of the day to reach the coast and contact the U-boat waiting for him in the North Sea some ten miles offshore. With any luck he would be dining at the right hand of the *Fuhrer* tomorrow evening.

The thought made him happy, but his smile didn't last for long.

Voices.

Von Hesse stopped wiring explosives for a moment and listened carefully to the sound.

The faint voices of people entering the tunnel.

Then a loud crash, like the clanging of a bell, ringing just a few times before stopping.

Silence.

Von Hesse put down the rest of the explosives, realizing that whatever charges he had already set would have to do. He set the timer on the explosives for fifteen minutes, and flipped the switch that began the countdown. Then he pulled his Luger from its holster and headed up the tunnel to investigate.

4

Lavena moved forward, both hands placed against the tunnel walls to steady herself, her feet firmly planted before each new step was taken.

She glanced over her shoulder once to see how Asvald was doing. He seemed to be even more cautious than she was, relying heavily on his walking stick for balance and moving his feet as if he were stepping through a swampy bog.

She turned back around and kept moving forward. She'd hoped that the noise Asvald's helmet had made rattling against the tunnel floor would have been enough to bring Ballard up into the tunnel to welcome them to the cave, but that hadn't happened. In fact, there had been no sign of Ballard anywhere since they'd left the manor house.

Just then, Lavena's foot came up against something on the floor beneath her where the dim light from the cave opening didn't reach. Rather than being a jutting rock or stone formation as one might have expected, this thing was somewhat softer.

Asvald came up behind her. "What is it?"

"I don't know. There's something at my feet."

Asvald moved beside her and raised his walking stick. The thick end of the stick began to glow, bathing the tunnel in a faint, dim light.

He lowered the light.

"No!" cried Lavena, her breath escaping her as if she'd been hit in the stomach with a mailed fist.

Asvald let out a moan.

In the dim light, the body of Flight Lieutenant Sheridan Ballard lay flat on its back, eyes wide in surprise, mouth agape in terror. There was a jagged hole in his neck and his uniform had been turned black by his own blood. The blood ran down the tunnel in a scarlet river, trailing past the reach of the light from Asvald's walking stick and into the darkness beyond.

"No," Lavena cried, falling to her knees next to Ballard's body, just as she had done with Warrick not so long ago. "No, no, no . . ."

Asvald put an arm on her shoulder.

"Do something," she sobbed. "Heal him, make him better!"

"I . . . I can't," muttered Asvald.

"Please."

"You know I can't bring back the dead, only save the living."

"But you're a wizard . . . Surely, you must be able to do something for him!"

Asvald was silent a moment, then said, "There might be a chance."

"How? What is it?"

"We have to save the dragon first."

"All right," she said. "Let's do that."

Asvald pulled Lavena to her feet, then put his arms around her, holding her tight.

"Can you go on?" he asked.

"Yes," she said. "I think so."

"Then let's go."

Lavena nodded, but as she turned away from Asvald she felt the press of something cold and hard against the side of her head.

"You're not going anywhere," said a voice.

CHAPTER EIGHTEEN

1

"Please leave us alone," said Lavena. "We have no weapons. We mean you no harm."

"You are a soldier!" He pointed at her with the barrel of his gun.

Lavena looked down at her uniform. "No," she said, shaking her head. "I'm only dressed like one—"

"Silence," said the man, poking her in the shoulder with his gun. He turned to Asvald. "And what about you?"

"I'm a medic, British Second Army."

Just as Asvald finished speaking the man raised his hand and struck Asvald heavily on the side of the head with the butt of his heavy steel weapon. The blow knocked Asvald's helmet from his head and split open the corner of his mouth. Blood began to trickle down Asvald's chin.

"What kind of a fool do you think I am?" said the man. "The British army is in shambles, but even such a feeble force would never have anyone as old as you on its front line. At your age, old man, you could only be one of the scientists who created the dragon weapon at the bottom of the cave."

"What dragon weapon?" asked Asvald, his words slurred slightly by the blow to his head.

Again, the man raised his weapon, bringing it crashing down on Asvald's head. Asvald let out a grunt and the force of the blow sent him heavily to his knees.

"Asvald!" cried Lavena, moving quickly to the wizard's side to keep him from falling face first onto the rocky floor.

"Leave him alone," said the man, striking Lavena this time.

It felt as if she'd been hit by a club. There was a sharp stab of pain behind her eyes and for a moment she swore that she could see stars in the darkness of the cave.

"Now, let me say this again," said the man, towering over them with his weapon trained upon them. "What role did you have in the development of the dragon?"

"None," said Asvald, rubbing his sore head. "I told you I am a medic."

"In what war, old man?" The man turned to face Lavena. "And you, WAAF? What do you do?"

Lavena thought about it a moment. What did she do? She had helped bring the dragon to this place, had helped Ballard find Asvald and prepare for the dragon to be sent back to its own time, but what would she do after that? "Nothing," she said. "I don't do anything."

"She's just joined up," said Asvald. "She hasn't been assigned anything yet."

"And I am the Kaiser," said the man, clearly growing more annoyed with their answers. He moved the gun closer, and spoke slowly and softly. "Now, let me tell you how this appears to me. An old man and a young woman sneaking into an underground cave where a secret weapon is housed. Lovers?" He shook his head. "Father and daughter? I don't think so. The only reasonable explanation for your presence is that you have arrived to begin your day's work."

Asvald said nothing.

Lavena followed his lead.

"And since the dragon is much too big to bring back with me to Germany, I will do the next best thing."

"What's that?" asked Asvald.

He held up a small box in his left hand. "Explosives like this are strung up throughout the cave. I've already engaged the timer and your dragon has"—he glanced at his wristwatch—"less than fifteen minutes to live."

"No," said Lavena, moving toward the man, only to be held back by Asvald's strong right arm.

"Oh, yes," said the man, smiling. "The British dragon is as good as dead. But while I can't take this dragon back to the *Fuhrer,* I can take you two. Together you can design and build a new dragon that will help to affirm the Luftwaffe's mastery of the skies."

"Never," said Asvald.

Lavena looked at Asvald, then at the man. "Never."

"You really have no choice in the matter. You either come with me, or die here in the cave."

"I'll take my chances in the cave," said Asvald.

"As will I," said Lavena.

"Very well, then. For you two the war is over."

He raised the gun to Asvald's head . . .

And was slammed against the side of the tunnel by a blast of flame.

Lavena and Asvald scrambled back for cover as flames filled the tunnel from below.

The man turned to look behind him for the source of the flames and was hit again by a much longer and more intense gout of flame. His clothes instantly caught fire, shrouding his entire body in flame. He twisted in agony, trying to escape the fire as his flesh began melting away from his bones, but his efforts only sent him crashing into the rock walls on either side of him.

Lavena could hear the man's skin sizzle and pop. She covered her ears and cowered behind a rock in an attempt to escape the searing heat that blasted up through the tunnel.

The man screamed a long, keening wail. It was a terrible sound and Lavena was glad that she had already covered her ears to prevent herself from fully hearing the sound of the man's horrific cries.

And then the man's screams died out.

He had fallen against a wall, his body bent in an unnatural position and still burning.

Through the pall of smoke and flame, Lavena saw the head of Tibalt looking back at her.

"Tibalt!" she cried. "You're feeling better."

"Just," answered the dragon.

"Thanks for saving us," said Asvald. "Although you might have done it a bit sooner."

Tibalt craned his neck in search of Asvald. "This from a wizard who saves my life by almost getting me killed."

"You are alive, aren't you?"

"As alive as you are."

"Why didn't you stop him yourself?" Lavena asked Asvald.

"Yes," said Tibalt. "Powerful wizard that you are."

"I was going to try," said Asvald. "But the blow to my head . . . muddled my thoughts."

The expression on Tibalt's face changed from surly and arrogant to anxious and worried, as he perhaps realized that his own fate was tied to that of the wizard. "Will you be able to help me?"

"Yes, yes . . ." Asvald nodded, rubbing his head. "I'm feeling much, much better now that the man's dead."

"Speaking of this man," said Lavena, gesturing to the burnt husk that smoldered before them. "He said something about ex-blow-sifs, and Tibalt having a short time to live."

"That's right," said Asvald. "We must get out of here right away. All of us."

Lavena turned around to head back up the tunnel.

"No," said Asvald. "This entrance is too narrow for Tibalt to pass. We'll have to go out the main entrance."

"But what of the soldiers?"

Asvald sighed. "I'm afraid we'll just have to risk it."

2

Private Sellers looked curiously across the open field at a tiny stream of black smoke rising up out of the ground. He placed a hand on the shoulder of Private Hutchison to his left and shook the man awake.

"What?" grumbled Hutchison. "What is it?"

"Look there," Sellers said, pointing. "See the smoke?"

Hutchison rubbed the sleep from his eyes and squinted in the direction Sellers was pointing. "Smoke," he said.

"What do you think it is?"

"Don't know."

"Think there's a dragon in there?" Sellers said with a smile.

"No," answered Hutchison, the older and wiser of the two. "But I do think we should get the major."

"Right."

3

They followed Tibalt down into the large cavern.

Despite his heroics in the tunnel, Tibalt was still plagued by his wounds. He moved slowly, and every so often he cried out in pain as his movements stretched one of his barely healed wounds and reopened it.

"You're in no shape to fly," said Asvald, when they were settled onto the large and expansive cavern floor.

Tibalt looked at Asvald, the last of his anger fading from his face. "Can you heal me, wizard?"

Asvald nodded. "It will take a few minutes, and I'm not sure we have any time to spare."

"What good would it be if we escape the cave in time but I am unable to fly? The soldiers you spoke of will likely kill me anyway."

"That is true," said Asvald.

"Then heal me."

"Very well. Stand up straight and spread your wings."

Tibalt did as he was told.

Asvald began mumbling a string of words under his breath and approached the hulking shape of the dragon. He raised his walking stick and began touching the glowing end of it to the larger wounds on Tibalt's body. Immediately upon contact the wounds healed, leaving patches of fresh, reddish-grey flesh behind. Obviously Asvald had sufficiently recovered from the severe blows he'd suffered to his head.

While Asvald worked, Tibalt's face took on an expression of relief. Each wound that was healed by the wizard was one less source of pain and discomfort for the dragon.

Asvald had finished the underside of the left wing and had now begun working on the underside of the right. When he had closed up the largest of the holes, he started around back of the dragon, but Tibalt stopped him. "The wounds near the wing-roots," said Tibalt.

"Right," said Asvald, moving close to Tibalt's body and healing the battered flesh connecting his wings to his body. When he was done, he mended a few spots in the belly area.

"That will do, wizard," said Tibalt.

Asvald nodded and the light at the end of his walking stick slowly dimmed.

"It will take us a few minutes to get to the entrance."

"No it won't," said Tibalt. "Climb onto my back."

Tibalt lowered his head and shoulder to allow Lavena and Asvald to climb onto his back.

At first Lavena was stunned by the gesture. It was almost inconceivable to her that a dragon would bow down to allow human riders upon its back. Obviously Tibalt's outlook had been significantly altered by his journey to 1940.

"Come on," said Asvald, hurrying past her toward the dragon. "We have no time to lose."

She climbed up onto Tibalt's back, using his defensive spikes and armor as convenient handholds and footholds to lift herself into place. They took a moment to get comfortable and secure, then Asvald said, "We're ready."

Without a word, Tibalt bolted toward the large tunnel that led to the cave's main entrance.

The rock walls were streaming by at a fantastic rate . . .

And then everything stopped.

"What's wrong?" said Asvald.

"I need to see where the soldiers are."

"But they're all around."

"Perhaps, but I want to put myself between the two of you and the bulk of the soldiers."

"Oh, well," said Asvald. "Never mind me, then. Carry on."

Tibalt slowly lifted his body so that he could see out of the cave. His head turned in almost a complete circle as Tibalt looked out over the surrounding countryside.

Asvald glanced at the timepiece on his wrist. He seemed worried that they were running out of time.

There was a loud pop from outside the cave and Tibalt's head suddenly pulled back.

"Are you all right?" asked Asvald.

"The soldiers are coming closer. We have to leave now!"

Tibalt's legs and arms tensed in a crouch. Beneath her, Lavena could feel the muscles along the dragon's back tensing in preparation for a powerful leap into the air.

"Hang on!" Tibalt warned.

And then they were up and away.

CHAPTER NINETEEN

1

Tibalt leapt straight up.

The air rushed past.

All around them were sharp *cracks* and *pops* as the soldiers fired upon them. Lavena heard the steel spits thudding heavily against Tibalt's body, or else whizzing past their heads like deadly bees.

Tibalt grunted several times as the steel spits hit him, but he continued to flap his wings, each flap bringing them higher in the air and farther away from the guns.

Asvald was busily using the glowing end of his walking stick to repair some of the new damage to Tibalt's body. He reached out to bring his healing touch to the leading edge of the dragon's right wing and lost his hold on the dragon's back. Lavena reached out with her hand and grabbed Asvald's collar, keeping him from falling to the ground.

Suddenly there was a larger *pop* on the ground. It was a booming sound that hurt Lavena's ears. She searched the ground for the source of the sound and saw one of the larger weapons was surrounded by a cloud of smoke.

"Get down!" shouted Asvald.

Lavena clung to Tibalt's back, but kept her eyes open to see what was going on. A large steel spit was screaming up from the ground. Asvald slashed at the air with his walking stick and the steel spit turned to the left, whistling loudly as it passed them on the right.

"That was close," said Asvald.

They continued rising, each powerful flap of Tibalt's wings lifting them a few more feet off the ground. The dragon seemed to be growing tired of trying to rise straight up from the earth. Either that, or the new wounds on its body were beginning to have an effect on its ability to fly.

"Just a little further," said Asvald, touching his walking stick to a large hole on the dragon's tail.

"I will not fail you, wiz—"

Lavena felt hot blood spray against her face. At first she thought she had been hit by one of the steel spits, but when she opened her eyes she realized that a large hole had been punched into the dragon's left wing.

Tibalt was falling.

Asvald reached as far as he could and managed to touch his walking stick to the flap of skin fluttering loosely in the wind.

The wound healed over.

Tibalt regained his balance, thrust out his wings and swooped down low over the soldiers.

Many of them ran for cover.

The speed of Tibalt's fall made it easier for him to fly. There was wind beneath his wings now and he was able to rise more easily.

In seconds that were away from the soldiers, safely out of the range of their weapons.

"We made it!" Lavena said.

"Not quite," said Asvald, tending to the smaller of the dragon's wounds within his reach. "Now we need to find an open field. Preferably one that isn't crawling with soldiers."

2

Private Sellers had been the first to see the thing's head appear in the hole. It was big and green and covered with horns and spikes.

"There it is!" he said.

He couldn't be sure if it was a dragon or not, but he didn't have to be sure about its identity. His orders had been to shoot anything that came out of the hole, and from the looks of it, the thing—whatever it was—was coming out of the hole.

"What is it?" asked Private Hutchison.

But Sellers didn't answer. He was too busy firing his rifle.

The dragon had risen out of the hole, quickly at first, but its speed soon slowed. It looked as if it were having a hard time getting off the ground.

Which made it an easy target for Sellers and Hutchison.

They fired their guns as quickly as they could.

Soon, others were joining in.

Even the big AA guns took a crack at it.

One of them even hit it.

The thing was falling, looking as if it had bought it. But the damage to its wing suddenly repaired itself and the thing was flying toward them like it was coming in on a strafing run.

Sellers and Hutchison jumped for cover and the dragon swooped over top of them, blowing their helmets clean off their heads.

They got up to fire at it again, but it was too far away.

"Come on," said Sellers. "Let's check out the cave."

"What do you want to go in there for? The thing's gone now."

"It was a dragon, wasn't it?"

"That's what it looked like."

"Aren't dragons supposed to have treasures in their lairs? You know, gold and silver and stuff."

"I think you might have something there."

They headed across the field to the entrance to the cave.

When they got there, Sellers was the first to peer into the darkness. "Looks okay."

"Then go ahead," said Hutchison.

"You first."

"It was your idea. You go first."

"All right."

Sellers stepped into the cave.

Hutchison followed.

They were about a dozen yards inside when they heard an explosion go off deep inside the cave.

It was quickly followed by another explosion, and another, each one closer than the last.

"Let's get out of here!" shouted Hutchison, turning around and hurrying back to the entrance.

Sellers was behind him, pushing at his back.

The explosions were getting closer.

They were outside and running across the field.

"Get back!" shouted Sellers. "Get ba—"

An explosion at the cave entrance knocked them headlong onto the grass. They were pelted by falling rock and debris.

When the air had cleared and there was silence all around, Hutchison raised his head and looked over at Sellers. "Treasure, my arse."

3

Calls began coming in from Observer Corps stations from all over the middle of England. Most stations along the coast identified what they saw as a dragon, while those observers manning the stations further inland—not used to identifying many aeroplanes—reported seeing everything from German Stuka dive bombers to British Bristol Blenheim twin-engine fighters.

The group captain in charge of the morning's shift in the Ops Room at Bentley Priory had been well briefed on the dragon situation. And although the dragon had not been a problem over the past few days, there were still specific instructions about what to do should it reappear over British skies.

The group captain considered all the reports and discarded those that were inconsistent with the eyewitness accounts of the infantrymen that had been stationed around Derby. They had reported seeing the dragon leap out of the cave and fly in a northeasterly direction. That meant it was likely being sighted by observation stations around Digby, Kirton-in-Lindsay, perhaps even Hull.

A quick check of the reports confirmed it.

"What have we got in the air at the moment?" the group captain asked the WAAF at his side.

She made a check of the war map. "222 Spitfire Squadron from Kirton-in-Lindsay and 611 from Digby have been scrambled to intercept a formation of enemy aircraft approaching from the Low Countries in the southeast."

"How many enemy aircraft?"

"No more than twelve, sir."

Twelve, he thought. He had already scrambled nearly twenty aircraft, half of which would be enough to beat back the hun. In a recent issue of the magazine *Punch* the cartoonist named Pont had best summed up the confidence of the British pilots in their battles with the enemy. In the cartoon, a fighter pilot reports to the squadron intelligence officer and says, "But you must remember that I outnumbered them by one to three."

"Divert 611 inland to Derby and send up 229 from Wittering in their place."

"Yes sir," said the WAAF, picking up the phone.

4

Hauptmann Waldemar Leuders led his *staffel* of Messerschmitt Me-110s in a daylight raid against British radar installations along the east coast of England. Leuders was flying in a slightly northwestern direction at ten thousand feet. The eleven fighters behind him all carried forward-firing cannons that would provide effective fire against the radar towers that dotted the British landscape in groups of three and four.

Easy enough targets, but reaching them was a problem.

For days the Luftwaffe's senior officers had boasted about how the RAF would be brought to its knees within a few short weeks. That was not in line with the impression men like Hauptmann Leuders—men who had been flying into the mouth of the lion for days—had been getting from their flights over England. The RAF was growing stronger, and developing better tactics every day.

The joke among Luftwaffe pilots each time they saw an enemy aeroplane went something like this—"Ah, here it comes, the last British fighter."

Leuders was skeptical of the Luftwaffe's chances of defeating England by itself without help from the army and navy. They could harass them for many, many months, but defeating them outright seemed unlikely. Nevertheless, Hauptmann Leuders' orders had been to destroy enemy radar installations, and they would be destroyed. If they did run into British fighters, then it would be up to the Messerschmitt Me-109 fighters about three minutes behind them to keep them off the 110s' tails.

But before they even reached the coast, the call came over the radio.

"*Achtung,* Spitfire!"

Leuders searched the sky around him, but saw nothing.

"There, below our left wing," said Heinz Kempf, Leuders' observer and rear gunner.

"I see them now."

Leuders wanted to take evasive action immediately, but under the circumstances he would be severely reprimanded by his superiors. First of all, the sun was behind them, and second, they had a distinct height advantage. They could at least dive toward the enemy fighters, make a single pass and then continue diving toward the British mainland and their target. After that the 109s would be on the scene to keep the Tommies busy.

Leuders gave the order to attack the approaching Spitfires, then put his Me-110 into a dive and gave the cry of the hunter, *"Horrido!"*

The twin-engined fighter streaked toward the enemy. When he was several hundred yards away he picked one of the aeroplanes on the edge of the formation and opened fire. The Messerschmitt's nose-mounted cannon and four machines guns tore into the Spitfire. Almost immediately after he opened fire, the enemy squadron broke formation.

But instead of doing the same, Leuders' adversary turned toward him, firing the Spitfire's eight wing-mounted machine guns.

Surprised by the maneuver and growing nervous at the combined approach speed of the two aeroplanes—somewhere near seven hundred miles per hour—he pushed the nose down into an even steeper dive and broke off the attack.

The Spitfire seemed to graze the top of the canopy, causing Leuders' Messerschmitt to shudder as it roared past.

"He hit our tail," cried Kempf as he fired at the departing Spitfire.

Leuders looked over his shoulder. One of the Me-110's twin tail fins was missing, shorn off by the Spitfire's propeller.

Before he could turn back around and check his instrument panel, the Me-110 rolled onto its back and began spinning toward the Earth.

5

"Are you all right, Tibalt?" shouted Asvald so he could be heard over the sound of rushing wind.

"I've been hit," said the dragon, his voice loud and clear. "I can carry on for a short while, but I must land soon. There is a wound in my belly that needs your attention."

Lavena looked behind her and saw a thin line of blood trailing off the dragon's tail.

Asvald moved higher up on Tibalt's back so he could peer over the leading edge of one of his wings. The windstream here was strong and he firmed up his grip on the wingroot. "Is there anything nearby?"

Tibalt shook his head. "There are many suitable fields, but they are all spotted with soldiers."

"Hang on, then," said Asvald. "There should be some empty fields over that ridge to the north."

6

"All right, boys," said Flying Officer Peter Higgins over the radio. "I've spotted the dragon. We're going to attack."

The dragon loomed large in the distance. Its wings were fully extended and it seemed to glide easily through the air, a stark contrast to the incredible destructive power the thing had been reported to possess.

This looked like a real piece of cake.

Higgins pushed the throttle of his Spitfire forward and peeled off slightly to the right. He would lead the squadron in on the attack, make his pass and then get out of the way so that the next one in line could have a crack at the dragon.

After that he'd circle around and if the thing was still flying after the tail-end Charlies had their go, then he'd be in position and ready to give it another try.

"Going in!" he said, and screamed in on the target.

7

"They're coming!" cried Lavena.

"Who's coming?" said Asvald.

"The steel dragons . . . I mean, aeroplanes." She pointed at the incoming planes.

"I see them," said Asvald. Then to Tibalt, "Can you get out of their way?"

Tibalt shook his head. "I can barely stay in the air," said the dragon. "You must protect me, wizard."

"I can put up a protective spell, but the machine-gun bullets are too small, too fast, and too many for me to stop them all."

"You must try, wizard."

Asvald grabbed hold of his walking stick by its middle with one hand and held it out before him in a horizontal line. Then he raised the stick over his head, and drew it down over his body, as if he were pulling down a window shade.

The aeroplanes began shooting, one after another.

Asvald's spell stopped many of the steel spits, but some managed to get through. They hit Tibalt in the wings and back, causing him to cry out in pain. Some even came very close to hitting Asvald and Lavena.

While Asvald began healing Tibalt's newest wounds, Lavena decided she must do something to help the situation. She had no idea what she could do, but after a moment's thought she had an idea.

The men inside the aeroplanes were soldiers like Ballard. When Ballard learned the true nature of the dragon, he tried to help it. Perhaps if these soldiers realized that the dragon was carrying a young woman and an old man upon its back, then maybe they would stop trying to kill it.

It was worth a try.

She slipped off her uniform jacket and began waving it over her head like a flag.

The aeroplanes kept shooting.

8

Flying Officer Higgins had come around for another pass.

Whatever fighting abilities the dragon had demonstrated previously, an uncanny ability to take a beating could be added to the list.

Six Spitfires had had a go at the thing and it was still gliding along its merry way.

Higgins decided to come in very close behind it this time so there would be no mistake.

He kept his finger off the firing button, patiently waiting for his fighter to close the gap.

As he neared, he gently rubbed his thumb against the button . . .

He was just about to push it when something caught his eye.

It looked like a woman.

He was overtaking the dragon too quickly and throttled back to match its speed.

It was a woman . . . and an old man.

The woman was dressed in the blue uniform of a WAAF.

And the strangest thing of all was . . . she was waving at him.

"Break off the attack," cried Higgins over the radio. "Break off the attack."

The Spitfire in line behind him zoomed past on his right.

"What in bloody hell is going on?" shouted its pilot.

"There are two people on the dragon's back," said Higgins. "One of them's a WAAF."

"You've got to be joking," said someone.

"No I'm not," said Higgins. "Whatever this thing is, it's one of ours."

9

The aeroplanes stopped shooting.

"It's a miracle," said Asvald.

"No miracle," said Lavena. "They are Ballard's friends."

The aeroplanes lined up on Tibalt's right and flew alongside him, each one moving in closer for a better look.

"I see a clearing," said Tibalt.

Asvald peered over Tibalt's wing. There was a clearing below, but it was strewn with lines of old cars and cement blocks. There wasn't much in the way of landing area, but it would have to do.

"Take us down, then," said Asvald.

The dragon slowly descended.

The aeroplanes remained in the sky above them.

CHAPTER TWENTY

1

Tibalt struggled to ease himself to the ground. Lavena knew little about dragon's landings, but it seemed to her that they were going much too fast.

"Hang on!" said Asvald. "I think it's going to be a rough landing."

Lavena grabbed on to Tibalt, wrapping both arms around the wingroot of its left wing. She could feel the dragon's wing twisting and adjusting against the force of the wind as it tried to ease them to the ground, but it still seemed to be coming up too fast.

And then Tibalt's hind feet hit the ground.

For a moment, it seemed that the dragon's powerful hind legs would absorb the force of the impact, but Tibalt lurched forward, his hands going out to stop himself.

But even that wasn't enough.

The dragon's head and neck snapped down against the ground and there was a jarring bump as everything screeched to a shuddering halt.

Asvald and Lavena were thrown forward over Tibalt's head. Lavena landed with a heavy jolt, the air knocked from her lungs. When she looked up, she saw Asvald, gliding gently to the ground, landing squarely on both feet.

"Sorry about that," he said.

Lavena said nothing. She was checking her body to see if she was injured. She was bruised in a dozen places, but at least nothing seemed to be broken. She rose to her feet and slipped into her uniform jacket.

Asvald was already attending to Tibalt, healing the larger wounds on his underside and belly.

The battle had taken its toll on Tibalt. His body was a mass of scars, and more area on his body seemed to be healed over than was not. If not for the healing touch of Asvald, the dragon would have been dead long ago.

There was a sound of aeroplanes circling overhead. Lavena looked up, but could not see them. Perhaps they were further away, or hidden by some of the light clouds in the distance.

"Hurry, wizard," said Tibalt, his voice both anxious and weary. "I want no more of men and their steel dragons."

2

Hauptmann Leuders wrestled with the controls of his Me-110 for several minutes. His first priority had been to pull the fighter out of its spin, a task that was made all the more difficult by the loss of one of its tail fins.

When he finally did get the aeroplane level, he'd lost several thousand feet and—from the looks of the landscape below—had traveled several miles inland.

Leuders took several minutes to re-trim the aeroplane, adjusting the trim tabs on the ailerons, elevators and one remaining rudder to compensate for the loss of much of his directional stability.

All the while, Leuders and Heinz Kempf, his observer, were busily searching the sky for enemy fighters. But as so often happened in engagements between fighters, the sky was full of aeroplanes one moment, completely empty the next. Lucky for Leuders, since his partially disabled aeroplane would have been an easy target for a British fighter.

He checked his fuel gauges and saw that they still had enough fuel for a few more minutes over England. If a target presented itself, they could attack it before heading for home.

"What is that?" said Kempf.

"What? Where?"

"On the ground, on your left."

Leuders looked out the cockpit at the ground below. In an open field, some sort of aircraft was parked. It had broad green-blue wings, a long thin fuselage and an equally long thin nose. "What kind of aeroplane is that?"

"A Blenheim fighter?" said Kempf.

"No, it's too big."

"A Wellington bomber, then."

"But its wings are moving," said Leuders. "Like an animal's."

"Perhaps it is one of the new dragons we've heard the others talk about."

Leuders looked again. "I think you're right."

"Then let's get it."

Leuders didn't answer. Instead he turned the plane slightly to the left, and put it into a shallow dive.

As the Me-110 began rushing toward the Earth and the dragon began to grow larger in his Revi gunsight, all Leuders could think of was how good a Knight's Cross might look hanging from his neck.

3

Asvald stopped his efforts to heal the dragon's wound, but said nothing in response to the dragon's words about men and steel dragons. He was already busy preparing for the spell that would send Tibalt back to his own time.

At one point Asvald stopped what he was doing, to rub the spot on his head where the man had struck him. He seemed to be in some pain, but after a moment, resumed his work.

"I'm waiting, wizard," said Tibalt.

The sound of aeroplanes flying overhead grew louder.

"Right," said Asvald, looking up at the dragon. "Ready, then?"

Tibalt stood up straight, thrusting out his chest and doing all he could to recapture some of the pride and self-confidence he'd lost in the few short days he'd spent in this place. He looked very eager to be going home.

Home.

It was the first time Lavena had thought about it in that way. Dervon was her home, wasn't it?

Asvald stepped forward, moving closer to Tibalt. He pointed the thick end of his walking stick at the dragon and began moving it in tight little circles, slowly at first then faster and in progressively larger circles.

The noise from the aeroplanes was even louder now.

Lavena looked to the east and saw it . . .

A large, two-motor aeroplane sweeping down over the trees.

4

"It must have come down in this field," said Hauptmann Leuders. "There are ground crew repairing it."

"We will make sure it never flies again!" said Kempf.

Leuders skimmed the tops of the trees that edged the field, waiting until the very last moment before opening fire with the 110's nose-mounted cannon and four machine guns.

5

The aeroplane approached at a terrific speed, flying just a few feet over the ground, looking very much like a bird of prey.

As it passed over the trees at the end of the field, its nose lit up with flickers of firelight.

Steel spits began slamming into the ground all around them.

Lavena ran from the line of fire.

Tibalt tried to move as well, but was not fast enough to get out of the way. His body was hit by several steel spits, some of them larger than the ones he'd been hit with before.

Asvald, however, did not move.

As the steel spits slammed into the ground all around him, he remained standing where he was.

Once again he was in his own little world, uttering strings of mysterious words and syllables.

In front of him, bits of earth begin spouting upwards like dirty geysers.

One steel spit threw up the ground between Asvald's legs.

And still, he did not move.

6

"Is that an Me-110 down there?" came the chatter over the radio.

"What would it be doing here?"

"Why don't you radio the pilot and ask him?"

"Shut up, the lot of you!" cried Flying Officer Higgins.

The radio was silent.

"It looks like a 110, all right," he said calmly. "Why don't we go and give him a proper welcome."

7

"Did we destroy it?" asked Hauptmann Leuders, pulling up and putting the Me-110 into a tight turn.

"I don't think so," said Heinz, looking out behind the aeroplane. "I see no explosions."

"Nor I," said Leuders, looking back over his left wing.

"Can we make another pass?"

Leuders didn't want to remain so deep over England for

longer than he had to. His aeroplane was damaged and he was reaching his limit on fuel, but catching the British dragon on the ground was such a stroke of luck that he simply had to make the most of the opportunity.

He quickly searched the sky for enemy fighters, but couldn't see any in the clouds.

"One more time," said Leuders.

8

The aeroplane was gone.

For the moment, the field was quiet.

Asvald continued casting his spell. The end of his walking stick glowed more brightly than before. In the sky above them, the light fluffy clouds that had floated so peacefully over the Earth began to spread apart.

Then the clouds slowly began to churn into a funnel shape and soon part of the horizon was also bending as it was pulled into the swirling mass of earth, air, space and time.

The wind began to pick up.

Tibalt slowly slid backward toward the funnel.

Something to the east caught Lavena's eye. It was the two-motor aeroplane—the same one as before. It had come back for another pass.

"Look out!" she cried. "It's coming back!"

But neither Tibalt nor Asvald could move. They were too engrossed in what was happening to them to stop now.

Tibalt couldn't survive another attack like the last one, Lavena knew. If he were hit again, he'd likely be dead upon arrival in Dervon. For all its wonders, this place, she realized, was far more barbaric than the one she'd left behind.

She looked to the east again. The two-motor aeroplane was almost upon them.

But this time Lavena did not run.

She remained by Asvald's side, aeroplane be damned.

The air was filled with the *rat-tat-tat* sound of steel spits being fired.

Lavena took one last look.

The two-motor aeroplane was burning.

It was turning to the left and losing height, smoke trailing behind it in a long curve.

It cut through the line of trees at the south end of the field, then crashed into the pasture behind the trees, sending the cows there running for their lives.

As the aeroplane burned, Lavena turned back around, just in time to see a pair of Spitfires zoom overhead.

Asvald had almost completed his spell now. The mouth of the long funnel was creeping in closer to the dragon. Soon, it would swallow Tibalt up and send him down the timeline back to his rightful place in time.

Dervon.

Asvald paused a moment and turned to Lavena. There was a strange look upon his face. His thick white eyebrows were raised expectantly and one side of his mouth was turned up in a smile.

"Well?"

He had only said one word, but Lavena knew exactly what he was asking. Did she wish to stay in this place, or did she wish to return to Dervon—her home?

It was a difficult decision to make.

This place was filled with wonders. Each time she turned around there was something new to thrill and delight her.

There was also so much she didn't understand.

She had fallen in love with Flight Lieutenant Sheridan Ballard, only to see him die in the attempt to help her save the dragon. And now that the dragon would be sent back to its own time there was a chance that Ballard might live again.

But only a chance.

What if she stayed here in this place and he did not live again? What then? She would be a thousand years from home in the middle of one of the most brutal and deadly wars she had ever seen—that mankind had ever seen.

The dragon was going home to his rightful place and time. Perhaps she should as well.

She looked at Asvald. "I don't belong here either, do I?"

Asvald shook his head. "No, you don't." He gestured toward Tibalt with a movement of his head. "He'll be needing a friend back in Dervon."

That was true.

When he returned to Dervon, everything about Tibalt would be changed. He would no longer be an enemy of man, and he might even go as far as to have some respect for mankind. While that would help the people of Dervon, it might also estrange some of his own kind, none of which would understand the sudden transformation within him.

Tibalt would be needing someone to talk to about his experiences in this place . . .

And so would she.

Maybe if they worked together, they could even bring about a lasting peace between man and dragonkind.

"And what about Flight Lieutenant Ballard?" she asked Asvald. "Will he live again?"

"His chances are better if you go back with Tibalt."

Then it was settled. She couldn't possibly remain in this place now. "I'll miss you," she said to Asvald, kissing him on the cheek.

"No you won't," he said. "I'll be there when you arrive."

She looked at him curiously, then suddenly understood.

"Good-bye," she said.

"No," said Asvald. "See you soon."

She ran toward Tibalt.

The dragon took her securely in his arms and held on tight.

Asvald finished the spell, stepping forward to strike the dragon with his walking stick and send it on his way.

He gave Tibalt a push.

The two of them moved slowly at first, but were quickly pulled into the funnel. They lingered just inside the mouth of it for several seconds . . .

There was a bright flash of blue-white light.

. . . And then they were gone.

9

Asvald threw an arm across his face to shield his eyes from the blinding light.

When he removed his arm and opened his eyes, the dragon and Lavena were gone.

The sun was shining.

And the aeroplanes slowly faded away, disappearing into a large bank of clouds overhead.

Epilogue

1

Asvald caught his breath, collected the scales that were scattered about the ground, and slowly got up from his knees.

The dragon and Lavena had only just disappeared, but he expected them to be back at any moment.

Just then the sky began to roil as it did before. The funnel appeared in the clouds and began working its way down toward the Earth, picking up the horizon line and bending it up to join it with the sky.

"Stand back!" Asvald cried warning to the people who had joined him on the plain.

The crowd ran for cover.

Moments later the mouth of the funnel burst apart, vanishing in an explosion of fragmented cloud, air, space and time.

Out of it all came the dragon and Lavena.

They fell through the air, turning slowly until Tibalt could spread his wings and steady himself. Moments later, they were gently gliding toward the Earth.

Tibalt came in for a somewhat rough landing a dozen yards from where Asvald stood.

Behind him the villagers were silent, obviously stunned by the dragon's condition.

Tibalt had been severely wounded. His body was covered with scars and open wounds, while individual scales were missing all over his belly, back and tail. In some spots whole patches

AUTHOR'S AFTERWORD

Although *Battle Dragon* takes place over the course of a few days in August 1940 during World War II's famous Battle of Britain, it is obviously more a work of fantasy than one of history. Nevertheless, I have done my best to make it as historically accurate as possible.

I am indebted to Keith Scott—a writer and Canadian World War II veteran who flew Hurricanes on patrol of Canada's east coast and Spitfires over Europe from D-Day until the end of the war—for reading an early draft of the novel shortly before his death in 1999, helping to make sure I got the flying bits right. "I flew my first Spitfire off the grass at Digby with 416 Squadron," he said upon finishing the manuscript. "I didn't see any dragons . . ."

If *Battle Dragon* has piqued your interest in the true story of the Battle of Britain and the brave men and women who fought it, here is a list of books (and one video) that might be worth a look.

BIBLIOGRAPHY

Bader, Douglas. *Fight for the Sky.* Sidgwick and Jackson Ltd., 1973.

Barker, Ralph, and the editors of Time-Life Books. *The RAF at War.* Time-Life Books, 1981.

Constable, Trevor J., and Raymond F. Toliver. *Horrido! Fighter*

Aces of the Luftwaffe. Ballantine Books, 1968.

Deighton, Len. *Battle of Britain.* Clarke, Irwin & Company Limited, 1980.

Deighton, Len. *Fighter: The True Story of the Battle of Britain.* Jonathan Cape, 1977.

Forrester, Larry. *Fly For Your Life.* Panther Books, 1959.

Galland, Adolph. *The First and the Last.* Ballantine Books, 1957.

Haining, Peter. *Spitfire Summer: The People's Eye–View of the Battle of Britain.* W.H. Allen & Co., 1990.

Haining, Peter, ed. *The Spitfire Log.* Souvenir Press Ltd., 1985.

McKee, Alexander. *Strike from the Sky: The Story of the Battle of Britain.* Grafton, 1990.

Mosley, Leonard, and the editors of Time-Life Books. *The Battle of Britain.* Time-Life Books, 1977.

Price, Alfred. *Spitfire.* The Promotional Reprint Company, 1991. (Omnibus of *Spitfire at War,* 1974, and *Spitfire at War 2,* 1985, both originally published by Ian Allen Limited.)

Townsend, Peter. *Duel of Eagles.* Simon and Schuster, 1971.

Wood, Derek, and Derek Dempster. *A Summer for Heroes.* Specialty Press, 1990. (Based on the book, *The Narrow Margin.*)

VIDEOGRAPHY

Battle of Britain. Directed by Guy Hamilton. Screenplay by James Kennaway and Wilfred Greatorex. Produced by Harry Saltzman and S. Benjamin Fisz. MGM/US Home Video, 1969.

ABOUT THE AUTHOR

Bram Stoker and Aurora Award–winner **Edo van Belkom** is the author and editor of more than 30 books, including the novels *Teeth, Martyrs, Scream Queen* and *Blood Road.* His more than two hundred short stories of horror, science fiction, fantasy, and mystery have appeared in a wide variety of publications including *Arrowdreams, Alternate Tyrants, Conspiracy Files, Star Colonies, Northern Frights* and *Year's Best Horror,* with the best tales gathered into the collections *Death Drives a Semi* and *Six-Inch Spikes.* He's also won the prestigious Silver Birch Award from the Ontario Library Association for his series of young-adult novels, which includes the books *Wolf Pack, Lone Wolf, Cry Wolf* and *Wolf Man.* Born in Toronto in 1962, Edo graduated from York University with an honors degree in creative writing. In addition to being a writer, he's held a wide variety of jobs, from school-bus driver to security guard, from political speech writer to prisoner escort officer. He has appeared on countless television and radio shows and was the first ever movie host on SCREAM, Canada's all-horror television channel. Edo lives in Brampton, Ontario, with his wife Roberta and son Luke. His Web page is located at www.vanbelkom.com.